ROBBERS
AND
COPS

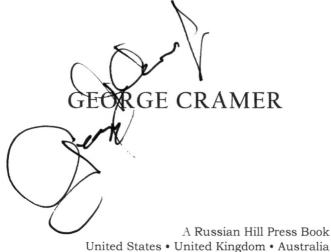

GEORGE CRAMER

A Russian Hill Press Book
United States • United Kingdom • Australia

℞ Russian Hill Press

The publisher is not responsible for websites or their content that are not owned by the publisher.

ISBN: 9781737824664 (softcover)
ISBN: 9781737824671 (eBook)

Library of Congress Control Number: 2022914344

Bank robbery is an initiative of amateurs.

~ Bertolt Brecht

ROBBERS

AND

COPS

1

JAMES TUCKER WAS BORN April 17, 1912, into a family of Georgia sharecroppers. Jim's earliest memories of home were of what had once been a one-room shed. The shack now had three rooms where he, his parents, brothers, and sisters ate, slept, and grew old long before their time. The rooms included a bedroom for his father and mother, and another held two straw-filled mattresses shared by the younger children—one for the girls and one for the boys. The third room contained a civil war relic—a Victor Range wood stove—an icebox, and an eight-foot rough-hewn table the older boys and their father built. Jim and his younger brother, Ben, slept on the table and benches they helped build.

The Tucker family had occupied their home ever since sharecropping replaced slavery. The walls were old planks so cracked and decayed they no longer kept out the weather. It was left to Jim's father to wage a constant battle with the elements to keep the place habitable. The two older boys and their father nailed scrap lumber and applied tar paper and tin sheets to the walls. All efforts failed to keep the wind or rain at bay.

There were no closets in the home. His parents had a decades-old armoire of unknown origin that held their meager belongings. The children each had an old wooden fruit crate acquired at birth—slept in for the first months of their lives—holding all their possessions.

With life in such a small house, affording so little privacy, there was only one place where any peace could be found—the privy behind the chicken coop. Still, they considered themselves lucky. Theirs was one of the few families in the area with running water.

The Tucker children attended a one-room schoolhouse until age twelve. The schoolhouse was the only new structure in the area, and the county had built it. "They know their numbers and can read and write a little. That's all they need," said Mr. Tucker.

Mrs. Tucker was proud of it. Built less than a mile from her shack, she had campaigned successfully for the school. Wanting it safe for her children, she insisted the county build it of asbestos siding and shingles. "We want our children safe from fire."

Ben learned to play cribbage with his father, the one form of recreation they'd shared. The father-son competition became a passion for Ben. Adding and playing the combinations came effortlessly to him. "Fifteen two, fifteen four, and a run of four for eight." Counting their scores aloud was a nightly ritual for the man and his son. All the Tucker boys knew how to play. It was mandatory, but Ben was the only one who shared his father's passion for the game.

It didn't take long before Ben was as proficient as his father. Though Jim never shared his brother's love for the game, he played well enough to help while away the few hours they had when not working.

As the Great Depression's grip tightened on the country, the elder Tucker died on Jim's eighteenth birthday. Mr. Tucker succumbed to consumption at the age of forty. And like many of his generation, he left a wife and six children. While the average American family earned $750 in an entire year, the Tuckers survived on less than $400 the year their father died.

The Tuckers still grew cotton even though its demand had dried up. Besides working their farm, Mr. Tucker and Jim had hired out two or three days a week to neighboring farmers. There was no time left for Jim to continue hiring out with his father gone. "Ma, somebody gotta work the farm. Ben and I can't do it alone."

"Well, son, we'll have to tighten our belts. You're a good shot. Use Pa's old twenty-two and bring in some rabbit or raccoon."

"Yeah, Ma. And every other farmer's son in the county."

As predicted, game was scarce, and the family struggled to survive. With no man in the house, there was no longer any credit. Ma and the older boys ate one small meal a day. It wasn't enough; Daisy, the youngest, died. The doctor said, "Malnutrition. Not enough of the right foods."

"Not enough of the right foods, hell, Ma," Jim said.

"Watch your language, young man."

"Sorry, Ma, but we all know she starved to death. If we don't do something, more of the little ones are gonna die."

Nine months after Mr. Tucker died, their mother married a widower with four children. With a dozen mouths to feed, Jim knew it would be easier on the family if he left.

"Ma, we have way too many mouths to feed. It'd be best if I left."

"But son, we need you here, working the fields with your stepdad."

"There are twelve of us. At least half are old enough to help with the crops."

"If you go, I'm going too," said Ben.

"No," Jim said, pointing his finger at his brother. "You're too young, and besides, Ma needs you here with the kids."

"Look, big brother, take me with you, or I'll take off alone."

Jim gave in to his younger brother after arguing back and forth, and Ben went with him. They stole a car, their first step on what was to become a life of crime.

The following week, broke, hungry, and nowhere to sleep, they held up a gas station. Unsophisticated and without street smarts, they were caught within hours.

There was no trial. The deputy sheriff who arrested them told the boys, "It'll go better for you if you plead guilty and get it over with." Without money for an attorney, they had little choice but to take the man's harmful advice.

The judge who presided over the boys' arraignment didn't bother asking them if they wanted a lawyer. Instead, he'd said, "The deputy tells me you want to plead guilty. That true?"

"I guess," Jim answered.

"Did you steal the car?"

"Yes, sir."

"Did you hold up the gas station?

"I guess so." After mulling it over, Jim added, "Yes, sir, we did."

"Then it would seem you all are guilty. James Tucker, how do you plead?

"Guilty."

"Benjamin Tucker. How do you plead?"

"Guilty, sir."

"I have no choice but to send you to prison. But because of your young age, I sentence you to only three years in state prison, the shortest time required by law.

Years away from becoming a National Wildlife Refuge, the Okefenokee Swamp covered over 400,000 acres of Northern Florida and Southern Georgia. This shallow peat-filled marsh, home to more than 400 species of animals, including alligators, venomous snakes, and panthers, is where the Tuckers served their three-year sentences. Assigned to a chain gang laying down a roadway for what was to become Georgia State Route 94, the prisoners cleared a swath of land wide enough to accommodate a two-lane road into the heart of the swamp. Suffering from the sweltering heat, oppressive humidity, and relentless swarms of insects, the inmates had no protection from the harsh elements other than rotting and mildewed tents, which the warden and guards referred to as inmate shelter. In truth, the guards fared little better in the shacks the inmates tore down and re-erected whenever the roadway inched another five miles into the merciless swamp.

Along with the other convicts, the boys worked shifts of twelve hours on and twelve off, except Sundays when they worked four hours. The work and shelter conditions were rudimentary. Using picks and shovels, the prisoners, shackled at their ankles, cleared a wide path through the swamp and turned it into a dirt roadway. They broke large rocks into gravel with sledgehammers.

During the workday, the guards spent much of their time sitting under umbrellas, talking, or playing cards. The convicts often heard their keepers complaining about their lives with comments like, "If I have to put up with this shit, dem fuckers will suffer even more."

"What's that about?" Jim asked another convict when he heard a truck pulling up to the guard shack about a month after the brothers started their sentence on the chain gang. Trucks weren't uncommon—this one was. A half dozen scantily dressed women scrambled from the bed of the ancient Ford pickup.

After the other man uttered a few choice curse words, he said, "Once or twice a month, prostitutes come out to the shacks to spend a night or two with the guards. A treat we'll never see." The convict explained that visits were the only time the guards enjoyed the pleasure of female company. "We convicts don't getta enjoy the carnal delights, but there is an upside to the visits."

Jim asked, "What's that?"

"The girls refuse to eat the slop the guards serve up, so they bringin' their own food. And they always treat us to the leftovers. It ain't much, but sho better'n our slop."

"Do the girls ever hump a convict?" Jim mused.

"Nope. We get to listen. That be it."

After the guards and girls finished their dinner and went off, the convicts had their dinner—whatever the women had brought.

"Damn, they sure are loud," Ben exclaimed to the sound of men grunting and women urging them on. "You hear that one, sounds like a pig going to slaughter."

While the guards relished the sex, these visits negatively affected the prisoners. After each visit, the tension and desire for sexual release escalated sharply within the convict population.

The only entertainment the prisoners

enjoyed was one Sunday a month when they were required to listen to preachers praising God's grace for three hours. Ben, not a believer, told one of the guards, "I'm not interested in hearing some pious hypocrite tell me about the path to salvation."

The guard laughed and said, "Boy, that can be arranged."

"How's that?"

"You work all the while the preacher talks. After they leave, you get a couple of lashes."

"I guess I'll go see what the man has to say," Ben said.

"I figured you might."

Convicts who fell asleep were subject to the Whip Man's strap the next day, usually three lashes but more if the sleeper was a repeat offender.

When the preacher arrived, he was accompanied by two of the homeliest women Ben had ever seen. They sat beside the makeshift altar with their heads down the entire time. He asked another convict what the reason the two girls were there was.

"I don't know for sure, but the story is that if'n a convict was to marry one of 'em, he could get a parole to live with the preacher and dem two, his daughters."

Ben asked, "Anyone ever give it a try?"

"They say, ain't nothin' but a rumor that

back a few years, one fella tried it."

"What happened?"

"Heard tell he came back a month later and asked to finish his prison sentence."

The warden, who oversaw all the gangs in the county, lived in Fargo. A small community near the Suwannee River, the gateway to the Okefenokee Swamp. He and his wife lived in a small gable-front house painted red. It was rented from the Sessoms Timber and Turpentine Company for three dollars a month. One prisoner served as a janitor for Sessoms and a housekeeper for the warden, who inspected the prison camp once a month. His stays included verifying that the reported convict numbers were correct. He was required to review the records of new, released, and deceased inmates. If an inmate died, his remains were buried in a shallow, unmarked grave; the only record was a brief note in the daily logbook.

On the warden's second visit after the arrival of the Tuckers and the mundane records updated, he turned to the figures that interested him most, those dealing with camp discipline. "Captain, how often did you find it necessary to have the Whipping Man apply the strap?'

"We had a few more than usual. We even

had one arsehole disciplined twice."

The warden's curiosity was piqued. "I bet it was a new arrival."

"Yes, sir. Inmate Ben Tucker."

"Well, don't stand there, Captain. Tell me about it."

"The man was caught gambling, not once, but twice."

"Why was he disciplined? That don't happen often for gambling."

"Well, sir, he didn't see the need to share his good fortune with the guards. He refused, even when I explained how it works."

"Three and six lashes?"

"Yes, sir. He got the message and now pays what's owed."

"Poker?"

"Nope. Cribbage."

Prisoners were allowed to have playing cards, and even though gambling was forbidden, it flourished. Ben wasn't a poker player, but he liked to gamble.

Ben carved a far-from-perfect cribbage board on a stave from an old water barrel. Still, it worked reasonably well. Wooden matchsticks served as pegs. Jim played when Ben couldn't find anyone else, which wasn't often.

Although some of the prisoners were skilled players, Ben far outclassed his opponents but was smart enough to let others win often enough to keep them coming back. His prowess kept the brothers in prison currency—tobacco.

Once the roadway progressed enough into the swamp, the guards thought they no longer needed to spend nights close to the inmate camp. "Look, why should we spend our time standing around the camp? These fuckers got nowhere to run," said the guard captain.

"Captain," one guard spoke up. "The warden, what if he catches us? He'll be downright poxed."

"Nah, he doesn't give a fuck as long as his numbers look good."

So, the captain clamped down on any dissent. Instead of remaining with the convicts, two guards parked a truck a mile from the camp at nightfall and kept watch. Armed with shotguns and revolvers, they took turns. One slept while the other watched the roadbed leading to the prison camp, and the others stayed at their encampment of hastily erected shacks. They were as happy as hogs in slop and were still paid to have four guards in the inmate's camp.

When the warden came for his next visit, announced a week in advance, the guard's camp was in place near the convict's encampment.

"Everything looks like you have it under control. You see any need for me to spend the night?" asked the warden.

"No, sir, the convict count is the same as your last visit. And, I can report that there have been no escape attempts," said the captain.

The warden thanked the captain and was on his way home a mere two hours after his arrival.

Even without the required number of guards, there was little chance of escape. The roadway back to civilization was blocked by the guards in the truck and again at the shacks. An escapee could run in three other directions, all of which led into the swamp, not an option anyone bent on escape would consider. Those who'd tried hadn't lived to enjoy their freedom.

The lack of guards meant nights were filled with the sounds of four-legged predators, their victims' screams, and those of two-legged beasts. Men could be heard fighting. Mornings found victims nursing black eyes, busted lips, and the occasional stab wound.

A few days after the guards withdrew from the inmates' camp, the brothers finished their meal and were relaxing when Jim pulled his sack of Bull Durham for a smoke when a half dozen convicts approached.

"Howdy, boys. I'm Pete Doyle. Me and my friends are here to welcome you to our little slice of heaven." Doyle, a bull of a man, was doing life for the rape and murder of a young mother and her infant daughter. A vicious degenerate, Doyle was the prisoners' acknowledged leader. A true sadistic, he took pleasure in beating and raping weaker men— a position held by brute force.

"I'm Jim Tucker. What can we do for you?" He kept his tone casual. It wouldn't do to show weakness in the face of this predator.

Doyle spat a large, especially wet wad of tobacco at Jim's feet. "Why, thanks for asking. It's your brother I'm here to see. Today is his first day as my special friend." As Pete spoke, his followers spread out, surrounding the Tuckers.

The brothers were on their feet in an instant. "What do you mean, your special friend?"

"It means you and I will get to know each other. I want a piece of ass, and you're the one that's gonna be my bitch," Pete answered with a smirk.

"Over my dead body," Ben yelled, his chest out and fists clenched.

"Same here," Jim shouted.

"Little shit on my dick, little blood on my

knife, makes no difference to me." Pete laughed before urging his companions to attack.

Jim was as strong as an ox but slow, while Ben, not as hard-hitting, was fast on his feet. They got in a few licks before three men pinned Jim long enough for Pete to kick the helpless man unconscious. Ben, beaten senseless by the other men, was powerless to stop what happened next.

With Jim out cold, Pete and his pals dragged the younger Tucker to Pete's tent, the only one intact in the camp. Inside, the men stripped Ben naked and left him alone with Pete. "Like I said, punk, shit on my dick or a bloody knife. Tonight, it'll be on my dick." Pete rolled the semi-conscious Ben onto his stomach, propped him up, and savagely assaulted him. Ben's muffled screams only added to Pete's pleasure. Satisfying his animal lust, he dragged Ben outside and flung his victim's clothes out. When Pete joined his friends around the campfire for a cigarette, he joked, "Nothing like a smoke after a little fun."

Ben managed to pull himself up, get his clothes on, and go to Jim, where he found him still unconscious. Ben was subject to Pete Doyle's brutality from then on.

During one of Ben's early encounters with Pete Doyle, Doyle branded him with a

"P" carved into his back after knocking him out. When Ben regained consciousness, Jim was tending him. "Pete wants everyone to think he owns you. The arsehole carved his initial into your back."

Three months into their sentence and a few weeks into Doyle's attacks, Jim settled down to sleep when Ben spoke. "Jim, I'll kill myself if we don't do something."

Jim was instantly awake and alerted by his brother's words. "I know Ben," he whispered.

"I mean it. I can't take it no more." The brothers talked late into the night. They agreed escape was impossible. Even if they escaped the camp, survival was chancy at best. They would likely be captured and brought back if somehow they managed to endure the swamp.

"What if we kill Pete?"

Jim, always the thinker, said, "If we kill him and get caught, they'll execute us. If we do this, it has to be in a way no one'll be able to prove it was us." He paused, then, "Still, we gotta make sure the rest of the prisoners understand we're responsible, so they'll be afraid of us." As the days came and went, they came up with one idea after another, only to reject each as too risky.

When they settled on what they thought was the most feasible plan, the one with the highest likelihood for success, they weren't sure who'd come up with it but embraced it before they focused on executing it.

Ben, not yet eighteen, the youngest on the chain gang, was the water boy. Shuffling up and down the line, he lugged a pair of canvas buckets that hung from a yoke and handed out water. A tin cup was attached to the yoke by a cord the prisoners used to dip into the dirt-clouded water. They were allowed a drink twice each hour. Pete reveled in his domination of Ben by forcing him to dip the cup and hand it to him; this act would prove to be the bully's downfall.

"We grind glass into a fine powder and put it in his cup. It'll cut his innards to pieces," Ben suggested.

"It'll cut you, and the guards will see your bloody hands."

"No, Jim, I'll carry it in something and slip it in before I get to him."

"I like the idea, but not glass—too many risks. If you get caught, what'll you say?"

The chain gang was on a particularly tough project, clearing brush and bamboo. Hardly a week passed that someone didn't get snake bit. Everyone was on edge, even the guards.

As one of the prisoners said, "Yah had-ta peek where you were cutting every time you swung your machete. Otherwise, you might come across a snake." Many men cut long bamboo shafts to poke the vegetation, allowing the poisonous serpents time to move away. Even the guards carried these poles.

Ben had read in a murder mystery set in the orient that bamboo shaved into fine, unseen slivers killed slowly and painfully punctured the stomach and intestines— scant evidence remained. On the chain gang, convicts buried bodies alongside the roadway, and any evidence of wrongdoing went into the swamp along with them.

"Let's try the bamboo." *God willin' and the creek don't rise, it'll work, and we'll be rid a the bastard.* Ben shrugged. "What's the worst that could happen?"

"Nothing. Except the fat bastard keeps attacking you if it doesn't do the job," Jim responded.

"If that's the case, we'll try something else."

The next day Jim cut a few inches from his bamboo pole. That night, working with a jailhouse knife fashioned from a piece of tin, he shaved shards off the shaft that were so fine they were invisible to the naked eye. Careless and in a hurry, a sliver got stuck in his finger. Jim felt the pain but couldn't find the offending shard. "Damn, this hurts."

Ben said, "Be careful it doesn't get

infected." After a pause, he took Jim's hand and said, "I can't see it either."

Jim pulled his hand away, "Now, how we gonna test it?" A pack of feral dogs hung around the camp, surviving on scraps of what they could beg or steal from the prisoners and guards. "I'll try it on one of those mutts."

"How can you do that?" asked Ben.

"Easy. I'll save my meat Saturday and mix in the bamboo."

Upset, Ben retorted, "I mean, kill a dog?"

"Easy if it'll help get rid of Pete."

Ben slumped, held his head in his hands, and whispered, "Oh, God." After a moment, he looked up. "Okay."

Two days later, it was Saturday, the one night a week, they got meat—if you could call the ground up hog, beef entrails, and chicken scraps meat. Ben slipped one of the dogs a handful of the bamboo-laced concoction.

Sunday was supposed to be a four-hour day, but the warden reprimanded the guards for not making enough progress on the road's right-of-way. So, they forced the prisoners to work an extra two hours. Ben and Jim watched the mongrel. They saw no change in the animal's behavior on the first day. On the second day, the dog started to whimper and crawl around in visible pain. On the third day, it passed blood from its rectum and coughed up more. On the fourth day, it died.

Their trial run was a success. Ben slipped Pete Doyle a water and bamboo cocktail. Based on their experience with the dog, they expected some signs on the second day, but Pete seemed as normal as the sadistic bastard could be. Ben thought about another dose of bamboo for Pete. Jim vetoed the idea as too risky.

Later in the day, Ben asked Pete, "How's the water?"

"What da hell you saying?"

Ben smiled, making sure Pete's crew overheard the exchange. On the third day, Pete complained of stomach pain. With a wide grin, Ben not quite sang, "Hey Pete, you want another cup of water? I fixed it real special for you." Pete declined, but by then, it was too late. On the fourth day, Pete was shitting and puking blood, unable to walk. Even the guards knew the man was dying. Ben offered to bring him water.

"What the fuck are you up to?" Pete demanded. Ben's only reply was to laugh.

It took Pete five days to die—no autopsy, no investigation, a quick burial in a shallow unmarked grave on the swamp's edge.

The captain of the guards wrote in the daily log: *Convict Pete Doyle died today of unknown cause.*

The prisoners knew, and the guards

suspected, Ben killed Pete—just not how.

The Tucker's abandoned their ragged tent and moved into Doyle's. No one objected—neither guards nor prisoners. Not only was it much more agreeable, but they also discovered the tent held a treasure—$400.00 in coins and bills.

Life on the chain gang remained hard, but Ben was never attacked again.

2

As familiar a gesture as taking a sip of coffee, two men slipped on ski masks. Had anyone been close enough, they might have heard a whispered, "Let's go." The men entered the bank through the double glass doors after a final glance around for danger. Each man drew a Colt .45 Model 1911 pistol. The shorter of the two bellowed, "This is a holdup. Everyone, down on the ground, now!" Not an announcement—a command. Every person in the bank dropped to the floor.

Jennifer, a new accounts clerk, recalled her training and put her left hand on the manager's desktop, on the right side under the edge. She knelt beside the desk, found the alarm button, pushed it, and fell to the floor. Jennifer's heroics for the day finished, the terrified woman's bladder voided. The pungent odor of urine filled the stale air.

It was over in less than ninety seconds, and the robbers were gone. Minutes later, Mountain View Police officers arrived at the scene, summoned by the silent alarm. The first used his radio to broadcast "Units 4 and 7 at Bank of America." Both officers held shotguns pointed in the direction of the bank's doors as they leaned across the hoods of their police cars.

"Units 4 and 7, be advised the desk officer's calling the bank manager," was broadcast by the police dispatcher.

"Copy," Unit 4 acknowledged as the patrol sergeant and two other units skidded to a stop in front of the bank.

The dispatcher came back on the air. "The bank manager advised the suspects left via the side entrance a minute ago, the direction of flight unknown. He'll come out the front with his hands in the air." The front door opened, and out came a middle-aged man in a dark business suit wearing a purple paisley necktie, his arms in the air.

His hands trembled, and his voice quivered, "Don't shoot. I'm the manager."

The sergeant spoke over the loudspeaker attached to the roof of his car. "Stop at the curb," he ordered. The banker did as directed. "Keep your hands in the air and turn around. That's it, keep turning." Once the man completed a 360-degree turn, an officer approached and patted the banker down.

"What's your name?"

The officer had already asked the radio dispatcher to check the emergency card for the contact information. The names matched, and he relaxed. "Is everything okay inside?"

"Yes. The robbers left a minute before you got here. Everyone's okay."

Holding up a hand, the sergeant said, "Slowly take your wallet out of your pocket and show me your ID."

"Here's my driver's license."

"He's the manager, and he says they're gone and no one's injured. I'll stay here and take his statement," the officer said.

The sergeant told the second officer, "Come with me." They cautiously entered the building. A minute later, the sergeant came out and used his portable radio. "It's all clear."

Detective Al Smith had been on his way to the police station when the call came over the air. *Damn, as if I didn't have enough open cases already.* Arriving moments after the uniformed officers had secured the scene, he pulled to a stop and took a deep breath. It happened every time he arrived at a bank robbery call. Although Smith tried, he couldn't stop the vivid memory as it flashed in all its clarity—the memory of his first bank robbery—the day his life changed forever.

He had been a happy-go-lucky ten-year-old with his mother. "Mom, please let's eat somewhere besides Chef Chus."

"You know Chinese food is your father's favorite, and he only gets to eat it when we all go out to lunch together. Now hush up and mind your manners."

"But Mom, every week?"

"Shush. No buts."

Al pushed against the single glass door he and his mother used whenever they visited his dad at the bank. "It's stuck, hard to open."

"I'll remind your dad. He promised he'd get it fixed."

Inside the bank Mr. Smith managed, he wasn't in his glassed-in office. A new poster was on one of the walls about opening a new account and saving money. Young Al Smith chatted with the guard while his mother visited with the new accounts clerk. That's when it happened. Two men walked in with flour sacks over their heads. Al still remembered the three black holes, one for each eye and one for the mouth. But that wasn't what stood out. It was the guns that each held. They looked huge to his young eyes—the barrels massive. His memory held only the description of the masks and the guns.

"This is a holdup! Nobody move."

The man that said it waved his gun around. Al's father stepped out from behind the teller cages, where ladies transacted business through their wickets. Al thought wicket was a funny word for the openings in the glass.

The robber turned and fired. The sound shattered the silence and hurt young Al's ears. Mr. Smith dropped to the floor, and a pool of blood formed beneath him.

Al's mother shrieked—a long and loud wail of sorrow—almost a siren. The robbers fled.

"Mom, Mom, Dad's hurt." Al remembered his mother holding his dad's head in her lap. Kneeling in his father's blood, unable to catch his breath, the young man took his father's hand. His father squeezed Al's hand once—and died. Al's hand was red with his father's blood.

Al didn't cry then. It was later that the tears came—and they came, over and over. At his father's funeral, as young Al watched his father's casket lowered into the ground, he vowed he would be a police officer and catch bank robbers.

The memory remained as vivid as the day Al lost his dad. Smith shook it off and walked toward the sergeant, who held a portable radio to his ear.

A call blasted over the sergeant's car speaker. "The FBI has been notified, ETA thirty minutes. The detectives should be there already." The sergeant looked around and saw Detective Smith in his ever-present trench coat, a gray fedora covered his head, and his right hand raised in a half-assed salute.

Two officers returned to their units. Both carried Remington 870 pump shotguns—*The same weapon that killed his father.*

"Hey, Sarge, it's still your scene. What can I do to help?"

"Yeah, right, and I'm turning it over to you, Detective Smith. I'm out of here before our friends from the FBI show up. What do you need?"

Smith said, "I know you're shorthanded, but besides the beat officer taking the report, could you leave one or two long enough to help me out?"

"Yeah, you got 'em." Turning to the uniformed officers, "You stay with the detective until he cuts you loose."

One officer said, "Jeez, Sarge. Do we have to do all Al's work? Again?" The officers, the detective, and the sergeant shared a quiet laugh.

The sergeant introduced Smith to the manager. "Sir, this is Detective Smith. He'll be handling the investigation."

"Hello, Detective. What do you need from me?"

"Thanks. We'll need you to lock all the outer doors. Then we'll have to separate everyone who was inside during the robbery."

"I can do that."

As they walked to the door, Smith spoke to an officer. "Go with him. Make sure the doors are locked, and the witnesses are quiet and kept separated." Before the two had taken more than a step, he added in a raised voice, "And, don't forget to get someone to make a closed sign for each door."

"You got it, Detective Smith."

Before the sergeant managed to get away, a man approached him and claimed to be a witness. "I was at the diner across the street when I saw two men run from the bank with guns in their hands. One of them carried a beat-up old bag, reminded me of a doctor's black bag."

Smith heard the sergeant tell the man, "We need you to wait around until Detective Smith can talk to you."

Once inside the bank, Smith told the tellers, "Ladies, I'm Detective Smith. I have to interview each of you alone. You've had a scary time, so I'll be as quick as possible. Once the FBI arrives, they'll want to question you as well. I want you to think hard. Is there anything you remember about the robbers?

Please don't talk to each other until after we've spoken." The four tellers nodded in agreement. "Now, which of you was the first teller they robbed?"

"It was me." A fortyish woman raised her hand.

"Okay, please come with me. Is there a conference room or somewhere we can talk in private?"

"Let's go back by the safety deposit boxes."

Detective Smith saw the semi-private area contained six individual stations, each dark and gloomy, with a small shelf, side-walls, and one chair, all a deep mahogany. "I've seen better places to talk, but it'll do. Please sit here," followed once they were seated by, "I know you've had a tough time. Do you feel okay enough to talk for a few minutes?"

"I do. I want to tell you what I remember."

"Okay, let's get started. Please tell me what you were doing before the robbery."

The teller didn't hesitate. "I knew it was a holdup the second the first one came through the doors."

"How'd you know?"

"When a man wearing a mask and holding a large pistol comes through the door, he's not here to make a deposit." She paused and shook her head left to right before adding, "After that, it was pretty much a blur." Within minutes, they had covered what she had done before and during the robbery. *Getting anything out of her is going to be more challenging than I thought. I'll have to take her through this one step at a time.* It took another fifteen minutes before Smith had all he could hope to get from her.

"Let's talk about the one who yelled first. You said all you got was a glance, but you might have seen something that could help us."

"He stood by the marks on the side of the door. The top of his head was above the six-foot mark."

"Good. Now, could you tell his race?"

"No, but there was a picture of a Black man on the front of a T-shirt."

"Were his arms exposed so you could see the color of his skin?"

"Sorry, detective, he had a black long-sleeved shirt under the T-shirt."

Smith did not get any helpful information about Suspect #1.

"Okay, let's talk about the man who came to your window."

"My guess, the man was taller than my husband. I would say at least six-two and thin. Yes, skinny with a large pistol in his left hand, he pushed a beat-up old leather bag across the counter with his right. It looked like a doctor's black bag."

"Did he say anything, anything at all?"

"Yes."

After a long silence, Smith prompted her, "Can you tell me what he said?"

"Oh, I'm sorry, yes. Yes, I can. The robber said, 'Don't put the dye pack in the bag.' That's all."

"Anything else you remember?"

"He had one of those wool pullover things covering his face. I don't know what you call them. Yes, they both wore masks, but his eyes were blue, and his hands were white."

"Thank you. If I have any more questions, where's the best place to reach you?"

"Here at the bank, I work five days a week, Monday to Friday."

He said, "Thanks again," as he turned to walk away.

"Wait, Mr. Smith. There's something else, but I'm not sure if it means anything."

"What's that?"

"The man with the bag walked funny. It wasn't a limp."

"Can you describe how he walked?"

"No, I'm sorry. The man's walk struck me as odd, different. I can't tell you why." She hesitated and then said, "There is something else. It might make me look foolish."

"You never know what will help. Please go on."

"Well, it might seem odd, it does to me,

but I had the strangest sensation. It was as if I knew the robber who came to my cage wouldn't hurt me, even if I refused to do what he said." The calm teller stopped and shook her head again. "It was his eyes. I swear the man smiled through the darn mask when I handed him all the cash."

The other employees and customers all remembered three things, the mask, a large pistol, and a "Free Huey" T-shirt.

It was another forty minutes before Smith got to the witness who was still waiting outside. The man was anxious to leave. Smith asked, "What can you tell us about the men?"

"One was White. I couldn't tell you about the other one. The men ran like they were older, at least fifty. They had ski masks and got into a new green Ford with the new style blue license plate on the back. I got a quick look, 2-4-1-A, or something like that."

"Did they see you?"

"I doubt it. The one in front glanced left and right when the men came out, and both ran straight to the car. They never looked back."

Once the FBI agents arrived, the employees and witnesses were reinterviewed. The robber who approached the tellers was described as a male between thirty-five and forty-five. All were positive he was White. His right hand was wrapped around the biggest handgun any of the tellers had ever seen. Asked to estimate the gun's size, all but the first teller put their hands together in a circle three inches in diameter. "It looked that big." He was portrayed as a husky man over six feet tall with clear speech—direct—polite—commanding—and may have spoken with a southern accent. They all agreed the robber wasn't a man to be disobeyed, particularly while pointing a pistol with an enormous barrel at one's chest.

The two young FBI agents did not comprehend the significance of the "Free Huey" T-shirt nor why it might suggest the wearer was a Black man. Smith found it necessary to explain. "Huey Newton's a violent Black Panther. In sixty-seven, Newton killed an Oakland Police Officer in cold blood. How long have you been with the Bureau?"

Smith failed to conceal his disbelief when the older of the two replied, "This is our first field assignment."

In a kind tone, Smith downplayed their ignorance with, "Oh, that explains it." *What are they sending us? These guys are still so green, they're almost useless.* "I don't think the incident made the national news." Smith knew everyone was new at one time and deserved to be treated with respect, even dumber-than-dumb rookie FBI agents. "The

T-shirt was likely an attempt to confuse the witnesses."

The FBI agents and Smith agreed—two-man robbery teams were not unusual—Black and White teams were uncommon. Before Detective Smith left, he overhead the agents joking about his old man's style of dress.

"Did you catch that hat? It reminded me of an old gangster movie."

"Yeah. And that trench coat. I swear if Detective Smith was a hundred pounds lighter, he could pass for that old TV show I watched as a kid. You know that Joe Friday guy on *Dragnet.*"

The agents gathered witness statements and went back to their office. They filed their reports and moved on to more promising cases.

Smith's appearance belied what he was. With two decades on the job, fifteen in the detective bureau, he could remain a detective as long as he wished. When his mentor became the chief of police, they talked. "Al, you've been in the detective bureau longer than any other officer."

"Yes, sir. I want to stay."

"You can stay as long as I'm chief or until you step on your dick so bad, I can't save you. Understand?"

"Yes, sir."

"I'm talking about the booze as much as anything."

"I've got it under control."

Smith attacked every case that came his way, be it theft, a murder, or in this case, a bank robbery. For the most part, Detective Smith worked alone and refused to allow anything like quitting time to interfere with his pursuit of bad guys. The consummate investigator, his high clearance rate was a tribute to the devotion and manner in which he worked.

Suspect #1 was James "Jim" Tucker. When he announced the robbery in a loud and gruff voice, everyone in the bank turned toward him. Jim's hands were not covered. Had anyone taken the time, they would have seen white hands. No one took the chance as they hurried to get prone on the floor. All described Jim, except the witness outside, as a Black man of unknown age who stood at least six feet tall.

Suspect #2 was Benjamin "Ben" Tucker, born in 1915, who was fifty-five, stood five-ten, thin with blue eyes, and was taller than Jim. He did not limp but walked with an unusual gait, resulting from a bayonet wound to his right leg delivered by a Japanese soldier during World War II.

Jim Tucker was quiet and not one to act without careful planning and preparation. His habit was to surveil target banks for weeks, longer if necessary. It was essential to know the bank employees' routines and the businesses within the target block. Dressed in nondescript garb, Jim walked the area throughout the day. He did not attempt to hide his features other than dark glasses and a faded John Deere ball cap. To the casual observer, the man might well have been a retiree out for a stroll. Jim did not avoid people, instigate conversation, or show any visible interest in the target.

Jim learned patience decades ago on the Georgia chain gang. He often told his crime partner, Ben, "It's all in the details. Learn the details, and you won't get caught." Then laugh and add, "At least not as often."

By the time he brought Ben to see a target, Jim knew the goal and how best to reduce the odds of capture. Jim never picked a bank within a quarter-mile of a donut shop. He told Ben, "You never know when a cop will show up for coffee and donuts."

3

DETECTIVE AL SMITH ARRIVED at the bank driving a Dodge Polara Brougham two-door with a 440 V-8 power block; only a few hundred were built that year. His coupe could outrun anything made in America except a Corvette. An experienced and diligent investigator, Smith was a nineteen-year veteran of the Mountain View Police Department. At six-four, two hundred forty pounds, Smith was an imposing figure. Closer examination revealed a man around fifty years old with sundried wrinkled skin and a bulbous red nose from his many years of heavy drinking. Smith had a distinct limp visible after he climbed from the Dodge, stepped on a piece of debris, and stumbled. A jolt of pain stabbed his right ankle as the tiny piece of shrapnel embedded there scraped bone. The flashbacks always started this way.

Smith carried visible scars from wounds received in combat, as well as those he could only feel, picked up during the Korean War. The politicians refused to admit it was a war, instead calling it a police action. Smith had been a young Marine Corps lieutenant in command of a platoon of experienced World War II veterans when he arrived in Korea. He still suffered flashbacks of his time at the frozen Chosin Reservoir. The battle had begun in November 1950. For Smith, it ended the day the man who was to become his best friend, Staff Sergeant Robert Kennemore, lost his legs saving the lives of Smith and several other Marines in a snow-filled shell hole.

Their platoon had suffered many casualties earlier that fateful day as the unit retreated under heavy and constant attacks by Chinese regulars. Ten days earlier, when the battalion arrived in Korea, Smith commanded a full-strength platoon of fifty-five combat-ready Marines. Now thirty remained—if he was lucky.

Sergeant Kennemore had been carrying a .30 caliber machine gun when he spotted a series of linked craters. One was large enough to hold the platoon's remaining Marines and machine gun. Lieutenant Smith carried enough ammo for two men. The ammo carrier had been killed in a bayonet attack several hours earlier.

Kennemore considered the young lieutenant a good Marine, a decent officer. *He's a damn good platoon commander.* Finding all three in a young officer wasn't something one lucked into every day.

Kennemore scrambled into the shell hole while yelling to the one corporal still alive, "Get this setup and firing now." Lieutenant Smith climbed in behind Kennemore and shucked the load of ammunition he carried. "Lieutenant, we've got men down. We can't leave them. Get this gun operational while I go back for them."

Smith said to his sergeant, "Bob, these guys need you more than me. I'll go." Smith turned and ran down the slope and into the enemy fire. It was reckless, but he knew his men had a better chance of survival with Sergeant Kennemore than a still-green lieutenant. Reaching the first Marine, Smith experienced pain and a burning sensation in his left calf. It didn't stop him. "How bad you hit?"

"I can crawl," the wounded man replied. He struggled up the slope. It was a miracle the Marine made it to the crater without being hit.

Smith continued past the next two Marines, both dead, to one who had lost a leg. A Navy Corpsman had put a tourniquet above the deep wound, keeping the young fighter from bleeding out.

"How are you doing, Marine?"

"I'll make it, sir." The wounded man pointed at the dead corpsman, saying, "He died saving my life. Please take him back."

"I will, as soon as we get you and everyone else still alive up the hill." Smith picked up the young Marine and carried him back to the shell crater.

Smith braved heavy enemy fire to rescue his wounded Marines. Neither Smith nor his Marines could recall how many trips the young lieutenant made for his fallen comrades. But they knew bullets had smashed into his left arm and both legs, and shrapnel from an exploding artillery shell had torn into Smith's legs. His fourth wound of the day knocked him out. Coming to as the first of two Chinese grenades landed a few feet away, all Smith managed to say before Kennemore stepped on the explosive and drove it down in the snow was "Grenade!" Seconds before the projectile exploded, another one landed next to Kennemore. He stepped on the second grenade and drove it down next to the first. Both devices detonated with snow-muffled booms. Muffled or not, the explosions were enough to throw Sergeant Kennemore up and clear of the shell hole. Blood and parts of Kennemore legs splattered every man in that hole. He wasn't killed but lost the lower half of both legs.

Sergeant Robert Kennemore and Lieutenant Al Smith ended their Marine careers in that filthy snow-filled shell hole in North Korea on that miserable and cold November day in 1950. They survived their physical wounds, and like so many other warriors—neither survived the emotional scars.

Sergeant Kennemore received the Medal of Honor, the military's highest combat decoration. Smith wrote the recommendation for the sergeant's medal—he was still in awe of the man. The two Marines were returned to the United States in December 1950. They were hospitalized at the U.S. Naval Hospital, Oakland, California. Lieutenant Smith for a few weeks, Kennemore for nearly a year.

Smith was present at the White House when President Harry S. Truman presented U. S. Marine Corps Staff Sergeant Robert Sidney Kennemore (Retired) with the Medal of Honor on November 24, 1952.

Al Smith's commanding officer recommended him for the Navy Cross, the second-highest military decoration. The Awards Board reduced the award to the Silver Star. Smith didn't believe he deserved a medal for doing what all Marines considered their duty. Smith knew Bob Kennemore felt the same about the award he'd received as Al did about his.

The memories contributed to his demons,

often flashing through his head in seconds. Closing his eyes and running his fingers through his hair, Smith willed them away so he could do his job. *I need a drink.*

4

A MONTH OR SO before the brothers' time on the chain gang was up, Jim Tucker received a letter from his youngest sister. The only letter either of the brothers received the entire time they were imprisoned. "Must be bad news," he said. Ben agreed, and true to their expectations, it was.

"Mother had another child, a boy. He and our oldest sister both died of something the doctor said was cancer."

The brothers had discussed returning to life as sharecroppers with their mother and stepfather until the letter arrived. Their mother had died, and the rest of the kids had been farmed off to relatives, except the next to oldest girl, who got pregnant by their stepfather and married him. With their mother dead and their siblings scattered, all thoughts of returning to their old life vanished. The problem they faced was what they would do when released.

Eating their meager lunch a week before their release, the brothers were sitting in the shade of the guard's truck, getting some respite from the 102 heat, when one of the lifers plopped down by Jim. "You guys got plans when you leave this resort of ours?"

Wary of being approached by a convict who had never spoken three words to him, Jim said, "Why?"

"You're smart, and your kid brother showed balls getting rid of Pete."

"Whatcha, mean?"

"Don't play me for a fool. The kid killed him. More power to him. If you're interested, my brother runs a crew out on the West Coast, Marshfield, a small town in Oregon."

Jim talked it over with his brother. They knew "crew" meant a group of criminals. With little to lose and wanting to get as far away from Georgia as possible, the two decided to go to Oregon. *We're going where there ain't no depression.* When their sentences were complete, they were paroled to Savannah. Instead, they hitched a ride to Montgomery, Alabama.

The choice sealed their fate—for life.

Walking along the tracks through Montgomery, the Tuckers found a lively uptown bar and grill. They knew it was for them when they heard a loud Jimmie Rodgers song. Sliding in, they saw the sounds were from a music machine. Inside, they were right at home in a crowd of men and women whooping it up. The long wooden bar top didn't look like it had gone unused since prohibition had begun over a decade ago. After a few drinks, Ben asked the bartender, "We're looking for a clean whorehouse and a place to spend a few nights without worrying we'll get robbed. Any suggestions?"

The bartender said, "Miss Flora's. She got both women and beds, even breakfast. The house's been around since the Civil War. Wait a minute." He returned with a slip of paper. "Here's the address. Tell Miss Flora I sent you."

The brothel was located on the outskirts of Montgomery. They were surprised at the building's appearance, an antebellum mansion in excellent condition, painted light pink. The yards were cared for and would have made the most discriminating horticulturist proud.

A Black man dressed in a tuxedo answered their knock at the door. "May I help you, gentlemen?"

Jim and Ben had never seen a tuxedo. Jim stuttered, "Uh, we were looking for a sporting house. Are we at the right place?"

With a smile and an almost imperceptible bow, the man answered. "Yes, your pleasure is our business. I'm Earl. Please come in and meet Miss Flora." They followed Earl to a sitting room with walls covered with expensive maroon patterned wallpaper and furniture fit for a plantation manor house.

Within minutes, Earl returned with an obese Black woman dressed in a yellow gown that looked dark against her light chocolate skin. Wearing a blonde wig and lips glossed with bright red lipstick, she carried herself with poise and dignity. She would have appeared tacky anywhere else. Even though the brothers had no prior experience in a bordello, they thought it odd that a Black woman was the madam.

"What are you boys looking for? I assume you want white women. That's all we have here."

"Yes, ma'am," Jim sighed.

Two mornings later, Earl woke the brothers. "Gentlemen, unless you have any more money, you will need to leave after breakfast."

Broke, all the money they'd found in Doyle's tent spent, the brothers considered working for bus fare to Oregon, but finding few work opportunities, they opted for robbery and car theft. Jim and Ben returned to the brothel at four in the morning. Miss

Flora, Earl, and the girls were asleep. Jim woke the madam with a hand over her mouth and said, "I will take my hand off your mouth. If you scream, I'll kill you. Nod your head if you understand."

She nodded.

Jim removed his hand from her mouth and stepped back. "Get up and sit in that chair." He pointed to an old rocker away from the door and window. Miss Flora glared at him with contempt as she sat her large body in the chair.

"We mean you no harm as long as you give us the cash."

"You best back away and forget this nonsense."

"Gimme the cash before I hurt you."

"No. I know who you are. Do this, and you be dead."

"How you gonna do that, old woman?"

"I don't own the house. I work for a group of Chicago businessmen. Even a white trash fool like you knows what that means."

Jim turned to Ben. "Get a girl, and be quiet."

"Whatcha want with one of my girls?" Miss Flora asked.

"You won't give us the money even if we beat you. But you will when we start breaking up the girls."

"You bastards, you'll die for this."

Ben returned with Rose, a tall, attractive, twenty-year-old redhead, Flora's best earner.

"Gag her." Ben did. "Now, put her on the bed and hold her down."

Turning to the madam, Jim continued. "If you don't give us the money, I'll show you what kinda bastard I am."

"Screw you, White boy."

With Ben still holding her, Jim grabbed Rose's right hand. Lifting the redhead's arm with his left hand, he took her little finger and bent it back. Rose screamed into her gag and began twisting and kicking. Her eyes seemed to bug out as tears streamed down her cheeks. Try as she might, she could not break Jim's grip. As Jim applied pressure, Rose bucked so hard one of her breasts came free of her nightie. The flimsy material ripped, exposing much of her body.

Jim faced the madam. "Well, Miss Flora, what's it gonna be?" The older woman spat. Jim pulled Rose's finger back until it snapped. The sound was like breaking a carrot in half. The young prostitute screamed into the gag.

Ben gave Jim a glance that conveyed a message. *I never thought you would do that.*

Jim repeated the process and broke the ring finger. The girl arched her back and fainted. Miss Flora whispered, "You're dead, you White trash."

Jim let out a long breath and sank onto the bed next to the now unconscious girl. "She can work with broken fingers, but she won't work for months when I break her arm and leg. Your bosses will be after me for their money, but who will they blame if she can't work? It'll be you."

"I'll give you the cash—you're dead."

"You don't need to worry about us, ma'am. Where's the money?"

"I'll get it. Now help me up."

Still held down on the bed, the redhead had come around. Ben let go of the sobbing girl and extended a hand to the obese madam. Once on her feet, she muttered through clenched teeth, "Pull the dresser away from the wall." As Jim moved the dresser, Miss Flora said in a soft but steady voice, "I swear, you'll die for this." She knelt and spun the combination on a floor safe. After a few spins, followed by a sharp click, she grasped the handle.

"Stop. Don't do it," Jim whispered, followed by "get back on the chair."

Ms. Flora hesitated a moment, used the dresser for support, and hefted herself upright before sitting back down.

Jim squatted and opened the safe, turned toward Ms. Flora, nodded, and said, "I thought so," as he displayed a snubbed nose revolver. "You would have shot me."

"Yes."

Turning back to the safe, Jim jammed the revolver in his waistband, reached down, and removed a white bank bag. It contained a large amount of cash.

Once they had the money, Ben tied Rose and slid her to the far side of the bed after covering her with a sheet. Jim moved Miss Flora to the bed, pushed her face down, and bound and gagged the madam. They took the only car at the brothel, Ms. Flora's flashy four-door Madame X Cadillac Cabriolet, painted pink like the house. Jim drove at a moderate pace, but Ben was anxious to get clear of Montgomery. "Can't you speed it up? We gotta get out of town."

"The car draws enough attention. I don't want to speed and make the cops curious about why two White boys are driving Miss Flora's Cad. They're probably her best customers. Who knows how long we got before the women get loose."

"We won't get far in this car. Every cop and gangster in the state will be after us," Ben said.

"Not much choice, either the Cad or on foot. We'll dump it in the river, and while they search for it, we'll be on a train. We'll steal another as soon as we get to the next stop."

"Why'd you do that?"

Jim glanced at his brother. "Do what?"

"Why'd you hurt the redhead?" It was more an accusation than a question. "She never did nuthin' to you except give you a two-dollar lay."

"Miss Flora was never going to give us the money. Putting the girl out of work for a few months was all I could think of to get the old lady to part with the money."

"Would you have broken Rose's arm?"

"Yes."

Ben mulled it over for several minutes, "I killed a man. You tortured an innocent woman. What've we become?"

"Shut up!" Jim's response was instant and harsh. Both men remained silent, buried in thought.

They drove north until they reached the Alabama River. A few miles further, the tracks curved over the river near a small town. Jim pulled onto a dirt road on the downstream side of the bridge, parked, got out, pointed to the tracks, and said, "Put our stuff over there and come back. We'll push the car over the edge into the river." While waiting for his brother, Jim put the top down. When Ben returned, Jim said, "It'll sink quicker this way."

"A waste of a great car," Ben said.

"I know, but we don't have a choice. I'll put it in first gear, jump out, and let it drive itself into the river."

"I can do that," said Ben.

The brothers bickered about who would jump out of the car for a few more minutes before Ben, who had remained in the Cadillac, put it in gear, jumped out, and rolled away.

Hunkered down in the brush near the tracks, they remained silent, remembering what they had done, while waiting for a freight train. Ben realized they were at the point where there was little chance of leading a normal, everyday life.

Shortly before dawn, a loud horn announced a train was about to pull out of the nearby station. Jim shook Ben by the arm. "Wake up, wake up. A train's coming." The cars moved slowly, not yet up to speed, when they reached the two fugitives. Spotting a boxcar with a side door open, Jim ran alongside the slow train. When he reached the back of the opening—he jumped and slammed against the behemoth. Lucky that he didn't fall under the wheels, Jim said, "I guess we gotta jump sooner." On the next try, he gauged his speed correctly and got aboard. Lying flat, he put out his arm to Ben, who now ran alongside the opening, "Grab my arm." Ben did, and Jim pulled him in.

After making sure they were alone, the

brothers settled down near the front of the boxcar, out of the wind. "Did you get hurt when you missed the opening?"

"My pants and coat are ripped, and my shoulder hurts like hell, but that might be from dragging your lard ass in."

"Hah, hah. Can we talk?"

"Sure."

"That woman back at Flora's. The way you hurt her, that's not how mother and father brought us up. Why did you do it?"

"Didn't have many choices."

"I know, but make me a promise. Promise me you'll never do that again. Killing Pete was one thing, but . . . that . . . it was wrong."

"I promise, Ben. Now we have to get some sleep, but one of us needs to watch for railroad cops or where to get off. I'll stay up and wake you when it gets dark."

"Okay, I'm ready for some sleep. But I don't think I can."

"Why not?"

"The walls and floor of this boxcar stink of manure or horseshit." Stink or not, the clickity-clack sound combined with the rhythmic rocking of the car had Ben snoring moments later.

After waking his brother when the sun set, it was only minutes before Jim was asleep.

Hours later, Ben shook him awake. Jim

asked, "You got any idea where we are?"

"No, but we've been headed north instead of west. Wherever we are, it's a long way from Alabama. The next time the train slows, we need to get off."

"Yeah, besides, I'm hungry and can't sleep."

Ben laughed, "I thought you were going to sleep forever." He rolled over and was out like a light.

An hour later, Jim yelled, "Hey, wake up."

Ben stretched and yawned, "Damn, I fell asleep. Why'd you wake me?"

"We've been slowing. It's dark, but the sky looks bright up ahead. We must be near a big city. We'll jump when we get closer." It wasn't long before the train slowed enough to jump, another new experience for the brothers. Blind luck saw them jump mere yards before an unseen bridge. They landed in tall grass, rolled, and came up laughing. A few yards away, they found a stream and cleaned up. They had no idea what time it was nor where they were.

Lying down on the grass, Ben said, "Brother, this grass shore does smell great, especially compared to the boxcar."

An exhausted Jim said, "I'm tired. Don't bother me." He was snoring within minutes. He slept the sleep of the dead.

Once Jim was up and had relieved himself, Ben told him, "While you were sleeping, I looked around. Found a road that way," he said, pointing, "and a village a half-mile up the way."

Ben told Jim about his visit to the village. "There's a small diner," he handed Jim an egg salad sandwich, "I got this when I visited with the waitress. She was lonely, bored, and wanted to talk, told me all about the place."

"The town's too small to boost a car. That big city with the lights we saw is Chicago."

"Chicago. Damn. We're way north," Jim exclaimed.

"Yeah, a bus comes through the village to Chicago in an hour, so eat up and let's get over to the bus stop."

Finished with the sandwich, Jim got to his feet. Feeling his pockets, he looked around the ground where he had been sleeping, shook his head, and shouted, "Shit," followed by, "damn."

Ben said, looking at his brother in surprise, "What is it? What's wrong?"

"The gun! It's gone. I must have lost it when we jumped off the train."

"We won't need it." *God willin' and the creek don't rise.*

Chicago was farther than they imagined. It took two hours on the bus to get to the downtown area. A fellow passenger told them, "The city lights are so bright they light up the sky for over a hundred miles." The passenger was talkative. Still tired, the brothers let him ramble. "Where you boys headed? You gonna try'n find work in Chicago? Ain't much to be had."

"We're passing through, headed west. Figured to spend the night and hop a train in the morning," Ben said.

"You ought to get a ways out of town before hopping a train. The railroad cops are mighty hard on folks around here. They'll beat you bad if they catch you. Word is they've beaten a few to death. My advice is to take a bus as far as you can. You gotta eat. Unless you got someplace to be, get off with me and get a free dinner at Capone's."

Ben said, "What's that?"

"You ain't ever heard of Al Capone?"

Ben answered, "No, can't say as I have."

"Where you been all your life? You live in a monastery?"

"Something like that."

"Why he's the biggest gangster in Chicago. It was his boys who killed seven guys in the Saint Valentine's Day Massacre. At least that's what they say. He's a gangster, but kinda like that English guy, Robin Hood. Hey, here's my stop, and that's Capone's."

The sign above the door read, "Free Soup, Coffee, and Doughnuts for the Unemployed."

The line stretched around the block. The brothers were famished and agreed the wait was worth it. An hour later, they were inside the hall with at least a hundred people. Men made up the majority of the people crowded around a series of long tables with only a handful of women and children. Each person who was already seated concentrated on a bowl of soup and a hunk of hard bread. The hall was filled with the sound of slurping soup raised to a chaotic level. The light-orange liquid was spooned into anxious mouths, accompanied by a combination of smells. The most prevalent was the stench of body odor. Servers ladled the same liquid into bowls that the next hungry soul in line seized. Another server handed each person a hunk of hard bread and placed a spoon in the waiting bowl.

Their companion told the brothers, "Looks like they got some squash for today's soup."

Food in hand, the three men found an open place at one of the tables and dug in. "This is good and thick," said Ben.

Finished with his bowl, Jim asked, "Are there seconds?" Before their newfound friend could reply, the sound of angry voices came from the direction of the serving line. "What's that?"

"They ran out of food." Both brothers

could see the first server pouring the dregs out of a large stockpot into the last bowl filled on the day.

After eating, Ben said, "I want a bed and a woman."

Jim agreed with the bed, but not the woman. "We got no idea if Miss Flora's owners are up here or not. We need to avoid whores for now." Instead of a brothel, they found a flophouse.

When they paid a disheveled man their twenty-five cents, he said, "Upstairs and take any open rack. Sheets are a nickel more."

"Bathroom?" Ben asked.

"There's one on each floor at the back."

The stairs were more of a dark tunnel with uneven slats. "This doesn't look much better than the shack back home."

At the top of the rickety stairway, they found an open room holding what appeared to be a couple dozen metal frame beds with thin mattresses. Ben pointed to beds and said, "Kinda reminds me of the beds we had in the chain gang tents."

The oppressive heat did nothing to diffuse the stink of body odor, dirty clothes, and stale smoke with a whiff of urine to complete the experience.

Unable to find two beds together among the men and a couple of women, they settled in for what they expected to be an uncomfortable sleep.

The following day, the Tuckers planned the next stage of their trip to Oregon. Jim wasn't sure how they should travel. Ben said, "We've still got a couple hundred bucks. Let's take the bus to Omaha. We rest on the way and figure out what to do next." It was agreed. Jim bought a newspaper; he hoped to read about this calamity folks called the Depression.

Walking to the bus station, they saw lines of men at a dozen or more soup kitchens. They stopped at one and ate next to two men deep in conversation. Both were wearing expensive but worn clothing. One wore a topcoat that must have cost at least a hundred dollars but looked threadbare—stained, frayed cuffs and missing a few buttons. The man wearing it said, "I've been out of work since the Crash of '29. My wife left me after we lost the house and car. Now she lives in Des Moines with her parents, not much better off. The famine's as bad in Iowa as here."

"Whatta you do besides stand in the soup line?" Ben asked.

"I'm an apple guy. Because I'm a Great War veteran, the Shippers' Association sells me apples for two cents. I sell them for a nickel. Eight hours on the corner of Wacker by the Mercantile Exchange, I make enough for a night in a flophouse."

Jim pulled Ben aside. "It's a good thing we're getting out of here."

"Let's finish eating first. Who knows when we'll get another meal once we get on the bus," Ben replied.

Settling in for the overnight bus ride, Jim wasn't surprised when Ben pulled the cribbage board out of his duffle bag; he'd held on to it for dear life when he jumped from the train. "How about a game? We haven't played since we left Georgia."

Jim said, "Sure." *Cribbage! It's the last thing I want to do.* "Two out of three, then I'm done." As expected, Ben won two straight games.

"Come on. Let's make it three out of five."

Jim refused and began reading the *Chicago Tribune.* The headlines were about the terrible economic situation facing the nation.

Two men sat across from the Tuckers when the bus stopped for passengers at the Iowa state line. They reminded Jim of his father. He could tell they were in their twenties, thirty at the most, but looked decades older. Each had deep lines etched in their faces by the wind and sun. One was tall, over six feet, the other no more than five-six. Other than height, they looked identical in bibbed overalls faded almost white with patches over the knees and backsides. Both wore shoes with soles held in place by tape, and old, knotted shoelaces and paper showed around the edges of the soles. *We'd be like them if we'd stayed on the farm.* Within minutes, the men were in an animated conversation about the effects of plowing in straight lines. The short one was Bill, the tall one Shorty. "I tell you, Shorty, they gotta change, or things will get worse. Plowing in the same deep lines year after year has weakened the topsoil. The wind blows it away."

"I know, Bill, but what can we do?"

"Don't know, but if us farmers don't change, we could end up like Pete Steinbeck."

"What happened to Pete?"

"Shorty, don't you know nothing? It was in the papers last week."

"You know I cain't read."

"Right. Pete's folks lost their farm—the bank foreclosed. Pete decided to get it back. He held up a bank and made a run for it. The sheriff caught up to him over to the county line. Pete put up a fight, and the sheriff shot him dead."

Jim and Ben exchanged sobering glances. Jim had picked up a copy of the *Des*

Moines Register at the last rest stop. The headlines were alarming. Ben settled down and went to sleep.

Iowa National Guard Called Up – Farms Auctioned

This past week eight more farms were foreclosed in Crawford County. These seizures bring the number of confiscations this year to forty-three. Bankers demand protection from violence at property auctions, as outraged farmers backed by the Farmer's Council of Defense have threatened them and potential buyers. The governor reacted to the threat by ordering the National Guard to active duty until the crisis is resolved.

Farmers cannot raise crops without rainfall, and cows die of starvation and thirst. Due to feed and water shortages, many are shot at the Des Moines stockyards to save the beasts from a slow death.

"The farms are surrounded by a sea of moving dust and dirt," Ben said.

"Those farm boys we talked to on the bus to Chicago told me they hadn't had a crop survive to harvest in two years. It's no wonder more don't join Al Capone in a life of crime."

Ben huffed, "Whatcha think we're going to Oregon for—work in a lumber mill?"

"It beats starving. Besides, plenty of otherwise honest people take the same risks and go to prison—or worse."

Renting a cheap hotel room in Des Moines, Jim was adamant. "We have to get to Oregon and out of this part of the country. Things are worse here than they were on Pa's farm. These folks are in worse shape than we ever were."

Ben said, "What of that kid who robbed a bank and got shot? I swear I'll never rob a bank. Let's get a car and get clear of this place."

"We'll pick one up tonight, but no farmer's car."

After dark and dinner at a soup kitchen, the brothers walked to an area noted for its well-to-do residents. "You sure this is the right place?" Ben asked.

"It is according to the fellow we sat with at the kitchen," his brother said.

They moved down an alley from one garage to another, located behind elegant homes. They found a 1930 Dodge in an unlocked garage near the top of a long incline. Pushing it out, Jim said, "We'll give her a shove and coast down until it stops, then we hot-wire it." They were well into Nebraska by sunrise and spent the night in

Hastings. As the sun set in the west the following evening, driving another stolen car, a Ford, the brothers left Nebraska, a distant memory in the rearview mirror.

Along the way, Jim picked up local papers and read more about the devastating effects of the drought and dust storms across the Great Plains. Families were losing their farms and homes—many starving. "The sooner we get through the plains, the better I'll feel. When we get to Cheyenne, Wyoming, we'll head north and leave this dust bowl shit behind."

It was noon but getting darker by the minute when Ben woke Jim. "You gotta see this."

Shaking himself awake, Jim said, "See what?"

"We're heading into a storm. It's getting real dark up ahead. I've never seen anything like it. Whatcha think?"

Jim stared ahead and looked to both sides of the road before answering. "How long has the wind been blowing? Is it getting stronger?"

"It started an hour ago and is getting heavy. Dirt has been blowing across the road for a few minutes. That's why I woke you."

"We're in for a dust storm. It was in the paper. Let's roll up the windows as tight as possible and get off the road."

The dust was so thick they could have passed a farm and never have seen it. "Jim, the dust is covering the road. Now, it's pushing the car sideways."

"Keep going. We gotta get under shelter."

The wind increased, and soon they were engulfed in a cloud of dust. Dirt came through every opening in the car, no matter how small. Soon it was impossible to see outside the windows. The brothers were coughing. Jim pulled two shirts from his duffle bag and handed one to Ben. "Here, put this over your face so you can breathe." He didn't have to tell Ben to turn off the car. The dust smothered the carburetor, and the car coasted to a stop. "Do you have any idea where we are?"

Ben said, "Yeah, we're still in Nebraska."

As the brothers fought to breathe, the wind rocked the stolen Ford side to side. "Jim, it feels like we're about to get blown over."

"Nothing we can do."

It wasn't long after that, a thunderous blow struck the Ford. It tilted dangerously and was hit by an even stronger gust of wind, knocking the car over on its side.

Ben was knocked against the passenger door with Jim falling the short distance and slamming into his brother.

"You okay?" Jim said.

"Yes. At least no windows broke, or we'd be dead."

"Yeah, but we'll be sitting for a while."

"One of us has to get in the back," Ben said. "I'll do it."

After what felt like hours, the storm abated. The car was stuck on its side.

"Can you see anything?" Jim said.

"No. The back window and the side are covered. There's a little bit of light coming in at the edges."

"I've got the steering wheel between me and the driver's door and window. Can you get to your door and give it a try?"

A few minutes later, Ben answered. "I can turn the handle, but there's too much dirt on the window. I can't get it to move."

With all the buildup of dirt piled on the windows, the weight prevented them from opening the doors. They were stuck fast.

5

THE ROBBERY AT THE El Camino Bank of America Branch added to Detective Smith's already unmanageable caseload. He wore a clean but worn, out-of-style sports coat and a frayed-around-the-collar dress shirt. In homage to the detectives of the fifties, Smith wore a fedora. There was much on his mind, much more than this bank robbery. If Smith were honest, he loved being a detective. Smith was eligible for retirement; his excuse for staying on the job was giving his two former wives half his retirement. Smith's first wife was after him for more alimony. Bert, his longtime girlfriend, was pushing for a commitment he was not ready to make.

The witness outside the bank had provided a partial license plate number for the getaway car. Smith sent a teletype to the Department of Motor Vehicles in Sacramento with a vehicle description and the partial license plate. A week later, a reply arrived by mail from DMV. "Holy Shit. There must be two-hundred possibilities."

"Whatta you yelling about?" Al's sergeant asked.

The search wasn't as bad as Al had anticipated. With help from the sergeant and another detective, they had it down to four possibles within two days.

The getaway car was a rental. It had been rented with false identification, paid for with cash, not returned, reported stolen, and recovered by California Highway Patrol. By the time Smith got his hands on the car, it had gone through several other renters.

Each time the car was returned, it had been cleaned, but all Smith needed was one latent fingerprint. He didn't trust anyone to do the job right except himself. His evidence collection kit—kept in an old briefcase—contained odd bits and pieces used to collect and preserve the residual morsels called evidence.

After taking photographs with his personal camera, a 1950 Crown Graphic 4x5, Smith went through the car with the proverbial "fine-tooth comb," finding nothing useable. The seat was pulled up close to the steering wheel. Moving it back as far as possible didn't help determine the robber's height because many others had been in the car. His next step was to imagine renting and using it for a day or so. *First, move the seat back. Then what?* His eyes turned to the two rear-view mirrors, the driver's wing window mirror and the interior one over the windshield. *Let's see. People almost always adjust the interior mirror, less often the exterior one.* His examination of the exterior mirror was unremarkable. The car had been washed so recently that there hadn't been time for any dust to accumulate. The interior mirror promised more. Smudges were visible on the mirror face. Smiling to himself, Smith dawned a pair of rubber gloves and used a Philips-head screwdriver from his evidence kit to remove the mirror, placing it in a paper bag for examination.

Back at the police department, Smith called his girlfriend. "Bert, I got a lead on the bank job. I'll be late for dinner."

"And as usual, no one but you has the skill to handle it," Bert replied. "And, of course, it's so urgent that it can't wait until tomorrow."

She was being sarcastic. Smith knew it but was in no mood to start an argument—they'd had too many of those lately. "I'll be over as soon as I can." He broke the connection without saying goodbye and knew there'd be hell to pay.

Smith liked to work in as sterile an

environment as possible and spread a sheet of heavy butcher paper on his desk. His fellow investigators always gave him a hard time about his rolls of paper. As a rookie patrolman in the fifties, Smith learned it could be used for most anything while investigating a crime. Rolled out on a table or attached to a wall, writing a chronological history of an investigation or any set of incidents was possible—all helpful in establishing the elements of a crime. There wasn't a name attached to the process when Smith learned it. In the seventies, this process was "invented" by some law enforcement executive and branded "Link Analysis." No credit was ever given to Smith or the old-timer who passed it on to him.

Smith examined the mirror from the rental car using his magnifying glass. The butcher paper kept the messy fingerprint powder from getting all over his desk while searching for latent prints not visible to the naked eye. Smith dipped a Magna brush into the jar of black magnetic powder, tapped it, swirled, and shook the brush free of excess. Finally, Smith passed the brush in a light swirling motion across the face of the mirror. The powder would adhere if the surface had latent prints on it and oils from fingers had transferred. If Smith were lucky, the result would be a visual fingerprint, palm, or partial. The smears were unlikely to yield useable prints. As expected, all the front of the mirror gave up were a few smudges. The backside yielded four complete or partial fingerprints.

Using the Crown Graphic, Smith photographed the mirror—front and back. With its 4X5 plate film, the old camera was being replaced throughout law enforcement by a small disposable thirty-five millimeter. Smith fought the trend. *I'll develop the film myself and get a better image of the latents.* The department had a small dark room where black and white film could be processed. An hour later, he wrote on the butcher paper, below one of the pictures taken of the mirror, the date, time, and location. To protect the chain of evidence, Smith wrote his name, badge number, and case number.

Once photographed, Smith placed lifting tape over the prints. Gently pressing the tape against the surface, then taking it up from the mirror, brought an image of the latent fingerprint, which the detective put on the blank side of a 3x5 index card. On the reverse side of the card, Smith duplicated the information written on the butcher paper. Releasing an audible sigh of relief, Smith sat back in his chair and lit up a Lucky Strike. Luckys were a habit Smith picked up in

Korea. Bert kept telling him to quit because people were beginning to understand how smoking cigarettes could lead to lung cancer.

Regardless of the detective's success with the prints, Josiah Cooper would be more concerned with appearance than substance—Smith was all about substance. His one concession to appearance—spit shining his shoes—was enough to survive the lieutenant's petty tyranny. Catching Smith smoking in the Detective Bureau would royally piss off Lieutenant Cooper.

The chief of police had been Smith's training officer and then his detective supervisor long before becoming chief. Smith was the real thing, the complete investigator, and the chief would do what he could, within reason, to keep him in the bureau until one of them retired.

Smith's pleasure at lifting the prints did not last long. Collecting useable latents is one thing, but finding a suspect with whom to compare can be a daunting task. Smith considered his options. *If I send the prints to the FBI laboratory without a name, the wait will be months or even longer. The State Lab, an even longer wait.* No technician would get excited about four prints from a small-town robbery. In the end, Smith elected to wait until they had a suspect to compare the prints.

6

WITH THE SMALL AMOUNT of light visible, the Tuckers could only distinguish day from night. They drifted off as darkness enveloped their small world and starved for food, water, and oxygen.

"Ben, Ben, you hear that?" Jim said between coughs as he cleared his mouth and nostrils of dust.

"What?"

"I heard talking. It woke me. You hear anything?"

"Sheriff, this is the third one in the last seven miles. I hope we find them alive this time."

"There, you hear it." Both Tuckers yelled and kicked at the windows.

They could hear the deputy telling the sheriff, "They're alive in this one. Grab the shovels." Soon the sound of their rescuers scraping dirt from the windows brought renewed energy to the brothers.

The officers pulled the men from the car and handed each a water canteen. "Easy does it, fella. Take small sips, and then wash the dirt out of your eyes. What's your name?"

"What happened? I never saw anything like that. It came out of nowhere."

"Dust storms. We call them dust storms. When a big wind comes along, ain't nothing to hold the dirt in place. I'm afraid the storm finished off your Dodge. You're lucky to be alive.

"Since the storm let up, we been out looking for stranded motorists. So far, found three cars along seven miles of the storm's path. One, an old open touring car, contained the bodies of a family, two adults, and three children—they choked to death. Sorry, but we gotta go. We're looking for others stranded on the road."

"Thanks, Sheriff, but what about my brother and me?"

"We'll leave you two full canteens. When we get to the next town, I'll send a tow truck back for you."

"Can't you give us a ride?"

"Nope. I got some dead people in the back. They were down the road a piece, not as lucky as you."

It was close to midnight before a tow truck showed up. "The sheriff told me where you boys were. I'd a been here sooner, but you're not the only ones I hadda tow into town tonight."

Town turned out to be not much more than a crossroads with less than a dozen homes. "We got no place for travelers to stay. Y'all are welcome to sleep here in the garage. I'll be back around sunrise."

Left alone, the brothers weighed their options. "As soon as the tow driver tells the sheriff the Dodge is hotwired, if he hasn't already, we'll be back in jail," said Jim. "We need to leave before that happens. If we get a car now, we should have a good head start."

A new Chevrolet was parked inside the garage with its key, and it started right up. Ben broke the lock on the gas pump and filled the tank. Five hours later, near the Nebraska State line, Jim said, "We need gas. I got two bucks left."

After filling up and robbing the next gas station, Jim said, "Sixty bucks. We'll change cars in Cheyenne. From there, we should have enough cash to get to Oregon."

They committed another robbery in Boise and stole their last car outside Ontario, Idaho, which they abandoned in Medford, Oregon.

"We don't want to bring any trouble with us."

Ben said, "You're right. Let's find a bus stop."

They bought one-way tickets to Marshfield, Oregon.

"Where are we supposed to meet this Ricci guy?" Jim asked.

"It's the Wicked Bar or something like that," Ben said, adding, "there's a cab. I bet the driver can tell where and drop us off there."

The cabbie dropped them off at the Wicked Eye a half-mile outside the Marshfield city limits. Even in the dark, it wasn't much to look at. The weather-beaten building was painted a dirty gray. The thing that distinguished it was a flashing eye with long black eyelashes over the front of the building. It sat, a large, dark rectangle in an unpaved lot covered with cigarette butts, used condoms, and more than enough empty beer cans to cover much of the lot.

The inside looked no better. Three walls were studded with semi-private booths; only half held customers. Three obvious hookers occupied one; the remaining side housed the bar and half a dozen small tables with chairs. Black paint covered the walls. Sawdust mixed with stale beer, cigarette ashes, and spit concealed the floor. The combination and a good dose of vomit blended in with the mess caused Ben to say, "The smell's making me sick. Hell, I might puke."

"Here, drink this beer down. It'll help," Jim told him.

A small stage with two poles for the performers occupied the center of the room. The platform was surrounded by chairs where the fans could ogle the dancers and place dollar bills in their G-strings. Patrons could enjoy a lap dance for fifty cents. Wooden stools, much in need of repair, were pulled close to a long bar.

Asking to join the brothers, a pair of the girls from the booth slipped in on each side for a drink. "Sure, we can do that." Ben was eager and said, "What can we get you ladies?" while quietly pulling his wallet from his front pants pocket.

"Just one," Jim said.

The woman next to Ben rubbed his crotch as she snuggled close. The other woman started the same maneuvers with Jim.

Almost broke, Jim declined the invitation, even after being offered a quick blowjob in the parking lot for a buck.

This is a high-class joint, Ben thought in disdain. "You sure this is the right place?" when the women moved away and immediately left the bar.

"Yes. How many joints named the Wicked Eye could there be?"

"Let's give it until midnight and leave."

The Ocean View Inn wasn't much better in appearance than the Wicked Eye but offered a room for forty-five cents a night. It was all Jim could afford. Ben's wallet and over a hundred dollars were gone.

The third night waiting at the Wicked Eye, Ben said, "I'm through waiting in this damn bar. We're broke. This place is depressing and makes me feel dirty. Every time we come here, I need a bath."

"Easy Ben, we'll give it another day or so. If we don't hear by then, we'll move on."

A few minutes before closing, a well-dressed, short, muscular man pulled up a chair. In an expensive business suit and tie, he looked out of place. "You the Tucker boys?"

"Who's asking?"

"Ron Ricci. You must be Ben."

"I am."

"I understand you boys vacationed down Georgia way with my brother."

"I guess that's one way of looking at it."

After some idle chitchat, Jim said, "If we're gonna talk, we ought to get outta here."

Ricci laughed, "Not to worry. I own the place, and once we close, we'll talk. For now, enjoy your beer. It's on me."

Jim later described Ronald Guido Ricci as an enigma who owned what could be best expressed as a seedy titty bar. The man always dressed in expensive business suits, looking more like the insurance salesman he had once been than a seedy club owner. Jim was not unique in his estimation of Ron. Many took him for Middle Eastern, a mistake. Italian, Ricci did not dissuade any from their opinion.

After the club closed, they were alone with their beers when Ricci came from behind the bar and joined them. "My brother tells me you two are short on experience but long on moxie. Says you killed a sadistic bastard who tried to turn you," nodding at Ben, "into his plaything. How'd you do that without getting caught?"

Ben started to reply when Jim silenced him with a frown before turning to Ron, "Don't matter. You got work for us or not?"

Ricci glared back. "I might, but I want to know who I'm working with. How can I be sure you're the Tuckers?"

Jim looked him in the eye. "I bet your brother gave you an idea or two."

"He did." Looking at Ben, Ricci commanded, "Take off your shirt." Ben looked surprised.

"Do as he says." Ben abided by Jim's bidding and removed his shirt and undershirt.

"Show me your back." Ben did as instructed, revealing a four-inch P-shaped scar. Ricci said, "I'm satisfied."

"Me and my boys have a thing for grocery stores. We do it smart, quiet—no one gets hurt or caught. I had four boys, but one of them decided to freelance down in San Diego. Now he's at San Quentin, doing five to ten."

"Thanks for the history lesson. What's that got to do with us?" Ben said.

"Before I bring you in or let you meet my boys, you'll have to prove you're not a couple of country bumpkins."

Ben started up, but Jim put a hand on his shoulder. "Easy brother, that's reasonable." Turning back to Ron, "Whatcha have in mind?"

"I want you to go up to Washington, Olympia—and pull a job."

"Why Washington?" Jim asked.

"You will be a long way from here, and if you're caught, it won't come back on me."

"Whatcha want us to hit?"

"Up to you. You tell me about the job ahead of time, so I know it was you. It has to be big enough to get in the papers. After it's done, wait a week. If you don't get picked up, come back to the club for a beer."

The brothers talked it over while Ricci went to get more beer. When Ricci returned, Jim told him they were in for the job. "Good.

Now where are you boys staying?"

"We got a room at the Ocean View Inn," Ben said.

Ricci sniggered. "Give me a minute." Ricci returned a few minutes later and said, "You boys are now staying at the Shelter Cove. Your stuff will be there. Shove off. By the way, you will find a little gift from me in your rooms. Be back here at noon tomorrow."

Ben asked Jim why he'd silenced him when Ricci brought up Pete while walking to the motel. "Let them think we killed him. It works to our advantage, but don't ever tell anyone it's true or how we did it."

"Why not?"

"If we tell him or anyone, they can use it against us—we lose our edge. This way, they'll always be a little afraid of us, especially you."

They were at Shelter Cove, getting the keys to their rooms twenty minutes later. The clerk said, with a smirk, "Your stuff and gifts are waiting for you." The brothers looked at each other with apprehension.

When Jim opened the room door, his meager possessions were lying on the moonlit floor. The bed unmade, he started to let out a "Damn it" when a shape on the bed moved. Startled, Jim flipped on the room light.

There sat a good-looking blonde wearing

a big grin on her face and not much else. "Hi, I'm Judy. Ron thought you might like some company."

Ben's gift was a redhead named Sally.

7

TIRED AND CRANKY, AL Smith needed a drink and was in no mood to chase tail. He and another detective had spent the last eight hours helping the San Mateo County Narcotics Unit execute a search warrant on a methamphetamine lab. It had been exciting, with hearts thumping, when they walked to the front of the dilapidated house. After complying with the requirement to announce they had a search warrant, one of the cons opened it in his underwear before the officers had a chance to kick in the door. They found the other two sound asleep.

The other detective badgered him. "It's not every night the Stanford ER nurses throw a party, and we get invited. Don't be a dick."

"Jesus Christ. I'm beat to hell."

"Look, you don't have to stay long. I don't wanna go alone."

"Okay, okay, where is it?"

"Follow me." Fifteen minutes later, they parked in front of a nondescript apartment building in Palo Alto.

"Whose place is this?" Smith asked.

"It's Patty Rosevear's. Several of her nurses are supposed to be there."

"Wonderful," Smith growled, "Damn it, one drink, and I'm outta there."

The apartment was well-appointed with stylish furniture, all in earth tones. *Can't imagine that light brown couch and the shag rug in my tiny place.* "Hear that music?" Jim said.

"Yeah, what is it?"

"Man, that's the great Carole King singing *I Feel the Earth Move.*"

"Is that new?"

"Fairly. It's from King's 1971 *Tapestry* album," Jim said before moving to Patty's sound system in the front room.

A nurse for at least twenty years, Patty was a good-hearted, unattractive forty-five-year-old widow. Every officer in the county knew her as the gal who ran Stanford's ER. She had trained more ER doctors than one could count. Smith loved her like a sister but had never been to her home.

When Patty saw him, she threw herself into his arms. "I was afraid you wouldn't show. Come on. There's somebody I want you to meet."

"No, not another perfect one. No, Patty, I'm tired. One drink, and I'm out of here."

"This one's different. You'll like Bert."

Al followed her into the kitchen. "Mind if I have one?" Al asked as he opened the lid of the large elephant cookie jar.

A game was going on with a plastic sheet covered with giant colored dots on the linoleum floor in another room. A woman on the sheet was twisting her hands and feet on four spots. A man on the floor spun a dial that pointed to red. "Red, okay, Bert, you gotta get a hand or foot on red."

The woman on the floor laughed as she fell on the sheet. "I give."

Smith stopped and stared. In front of him was the most striking woman he'd ever seen. *I can feel my heart tremble.* She was almost six feet tall, with short, straw-colored hair, a perfect complexion, and bright blue eyes. Her laughter filled the apartment. Her looks grabbed him like nothing he had ever experienced—pin-up beautiful. Taking in her physical appearance, Smith realized her dress was beyond skimpy. It was white with a slit up one side to her hip, no back, and a plunging neckline to her navel. That wasn't all. It took another moment to comprehend the dress was all she was wearing. Smith stood dumbfounded. Patty laughed.

Patty helped the woman get to her feet.

"Bert, get up and meet Al Smith."

Bert stuck out her hand. "Hi. Patty's told me all about you." One of the few times in his life, Smith was speechless. Bert took him by the hand and led him into the front room. Carole King was gone, and couples swayed to Frank Sinatra's "That Old Black Magic."

"Let's dance." After stepping on Bert's feet for the second time, Al suggested leaving the dancing to the others. They talked about their experiences working in the public safety arena. Two hours later, she said, "It's been great, but I've got an early shift."

"Where do you work?"

"Patty hired me when I got my RN license."

"Can I get your phone number?"

Bert smiled and asked for something to write on.

Al walked Bert to her car. She shook his hand, got in, and left him standing in amazement. *How could I have met such a wonderful person? Even more astonishing, how could I have monopolized her time?*

It was Monday before Al worked up the courage to call her. "Hi. It's me, Al Smith." They chatted for a few minutes before he asked her out.

Her response, "You're married," was a statement, not a question.

"Does it matter?"

"That's up to you, Detective Smith."

"All I know is I want to see you."

"Okay."

"Tonight?"

"Okay."

Smith told Bert he would call her back.

A friend in the Secret Service lived alone on a houseboat across the bay on the Alameda side of the Oakland Estuary. Over the last year, the agent had offered Smith the houseboat, telling him it was his to use anytime. It was time to use the key. A telephone call to the Secret Service office got him a call back within minutes.

"Hey, Al, what's happening?"

"I'm ready to take you up on the houseboat offer."

"When?"

"Tonight."

"Jeez, nothing like giving me a lot of notice. You're lucky. I have to go up to Reno for an interview. I'll shuffle things and head up today. I'll pack up, clean up, and be gone by five."

Smith called Bert, explaining he had to work until 7:00 p.m. but would give her the keys and directions to the houseboat if she could stop by the station. She said, "Okay." Smith was euphoric.

Late getting away from the office and an accident on the San Mateo Bridge delaying him even more, Smith arrived at the marina at a quarter to ten. Hurrying to the dock gate, it hit him—Bert's got the keys. Smith couldn't get the gate open, and no one came by. *I can go to a gas station and call her, except I don't know the houseboat's phone number.*

Beside himself with frustration, Smith opted to climb the dock gate and get past the barbed wire extending around the fencing. He made it with a few scratches.

Bert opened the door at his knock and led him to the front room. Double doors were open to the estuary across from Jack London Square. Flames from an actual fireplace lit the space. The deep white pile carpet fit in with the light-colored furnishings. On a low coffee table, set a bottle of an excellent cabernet. She drew him to her, "Hi, I'm Roberta Jordan. My friends call me Bert." Laughing, she pulled away, saying, "Take off your shoes and get comfy."

8

AFTER THE WOMEN LEFT the following morning, Jim and Ben walked to Mom's Diner, a neighborhood restaurant. They used their remaining money for steak and eggs breakfasts. "We might as well get into this on a full stomach. Ron doesn't strike me as the generous type."

Ben replied, "Yeah, Ricci didn't set us up out of the goodness of his heart."

They arrived five minutes late for their noon appointment. "I said noon. If you boys wanna work for me, you have to be on time," Ricci said.

Jim spoke up. "We don't know if we're gonna work for you or not, but we'll head on up to Olympia. The problem is we're broke and don't have a car."

"I'll front you a hundred for expenses. You'll have to get a car on your own, but not around here."

They took a bus to Portland, across the river from Washington State. In 1935, the city was already an important seaport with a population of over three hundred thousand. It was large enough for the Tuckers to go unnoticed getting off their bus before disappearing into the crowds.

They had listened and learned while on the chain gang. There were ways to steal cars that drew the least amount of attention. For the trip to Olympia, they chose a 1930 Ford pickup. Ben pointed out, "More trucks in Washington and Oregon than anything else on wheels. Driving one—God willin' and the creek don't rise—we'll pass for any other working stiff."

Jim added, "Even better, we switch license plates to avoid getting caught."

Finding a truck the Tuckers would steal proved to be complicated. Most men they saw with Ford pickups reminded them of their long-dead father—all hard-working men trying to survive the Great Depression. Growing up dirt-poor, working another man's land, had instilled an affinity for farmers. Once they found the right pickup behind a fancy house, they were off. They were on their second set of license plates and having lunch in Olympia four hours later.

After a few hours sleep, they got busy planning. Ben, anxious for a big score, wanted to find a liquor warehouse. "We steal a truckload of Scotch and deliver it to Ron."

Jim, realistic, frowned on the idea. "Look, Ben, if we hit a liquor warehouse, we'll piss off the mob. It'll bring trouble down on Ricci and us. We can't be sentimental about who we rob, but we can't take those guys on. We don't have to bring anything back to Ron. We have to make the papers, that's all."

Brainstorming was hard work for two ex-cons who were long on moxie but short on experience. Ben had long been a fan of dime-store novels, reading everything ever written about his heroes, Frank and Jesse James—old-time bank robbers. Ben asked himself, what would they do? *They would get people's attention, but how?* "We need to pull a job, get clear away, and make a big splash. We gotta get the newspapers to write about it."

They stewed over it for days, each putting forth ideas. Each time, they found the crime too risky or not splashy enough to get into the papers, much like when they planned Pete Doyle's demise.

On the third day, Jim had a plan. "I took a walk around today, and I got an idea. It'll make a big enough splash that Ricci'll hear about it, and we'll get back to Marshfield."

"Yeah, so. What do you have in mind?"

"How about this? A few blocks from here's a Sherwin-Williams store. I did some checking. It's the biggest store of its kind in Olympia. We could hit it."

"Do you think this will get us in the papers?" Ben asked.

"No. Stealing paint won't, but we can use it in a way that will."

"I'm listening."

"Here's my plan."

After Jim finished, Ben laughed so hard he thought he might wet his pants. Under control, he said, "Okay, might work, but let's spend a couple of days looking it over."

Three days later, and out of money, Jim called Ron Ricci. "You guys are nuts. If you pull it off, you won't have anything, but it'll sure make the papers."

That night they struck. Jim's surveillance had led him to a hidden key used by the first worker each morning. When the local cops were at the station house for the midnight shift change, he let himself and Ben into the Sherwin-Williams store. Jim went to the loading dock while Ben went to the front of the store and looked up and down the street to make sure no one was out. It was clear. Ben began his part of the caper—he had a message to deliver.

Jim loaded one of the store's delivery trucks with a half dozen fifty-five-gallon drums of paint using a forklift. *That should be enough.* Jim strapped the drums in place.

Ben joined him, "It's done. Let's get this show on the road."

After ensuring he was not being watched, Jim drove to the State of Washington Department of Social and Health Services headquarters, the agency running Washington's prisons. Jim said, "I'll meet you at the pickup," before Ben walked the two blocks to their stolen truck. After Jim joined his brother, they drove south for an hour before they could relax.

Ben pounded his brother on the back. "We did it. That'll make the papers."

The following week, the brothers walked into the Wicked Eye and asked for a beer. Not only had the job made the Washington papers, but also the national newspapers, even a few foreign ones.

"You boys may not have made any money, but you sure made the papers and snagged everyone's attention," Ricci said, handing them cold beers. "Take a gander at this." He held up a copy of the *Seattle Post-Intelligencer*.

The story was on the front page. The headline read, "Crooks Take Loot to Jail." The article had pictures of the store and the truck parked in front of the Department of Corrections.

"During the hours of darkness, thieves entered the Sherwin-

Williams store in Olympia, Washington. They stole a thousand dollars worth of paint which they put to use. The desperados punched holes in the bottom of six 55-gallon drums of paint strapped to the back of the store's stolen delivery truck and drove eight blocks to Washington's prison headquarters, spreading a trail. Each drum contained a different color creating a veritable rainbow. The miscreants provided what may be a clue to their identity. They painted names on the store window and truck doors. Across the front window, written in foot-high letters, were "The James Gang Rides Again" and "Jesse and Frank." On the driver's door was "Jesse." As you can surmise, "Frank" was on the passenger door. Police report they are investigating several leads. This reporter asked if the leads included the James Brothers. Chief of Police Cushman would only say, "No Comment." Unnamed sources in the police department consider it a prank by youths."

Ricci and the Tuckers enjoyed a good laugh. "Take a couple of days off. Enjoy yourselves. Your rooms at the Shelter Cove Motel are ready. Judy and Sally will stop by tonight."

They did not tell Ricci about the cash box they found with a little over a hundred in small bills in a desk drawer in the paint store's office, and it wasn't mentioned in any newspaper article. As Ben pointed out, with a smirk, "Why bother him with unnecessary details?"

Three days later, the Tuckers were back at the Wicked Eye. The place still smelled of urine-soaked sawdust and the permeating stench of tobacco smoke. Ricci waved the brothers over to a table near the back of the barroom, told them to have a seat, and ordered a round of beers. Ricci then indicated a table occupied by three men near the front door. "That's my crew. Let me tell you about them.

"The oldest is Buck." His face was pockmarked from chickenpox; standing at six-four and weighing three hundred pounds, he was an imposing man. "His prostitute mother abandoned him shortly after birth. Buck has no idea who his father was," Ricci said before explaining further that the brute was raised in a series of abusive foster homes. Buck despises anyone he considers too damned smart, rich, or of any color other than White. He's going on forty and has already done time for manslaughter at Walla Walla Prison in Washington.

"His crime?" Ricci raised an eyebrow. "Beating a blonde prostitute to death while in a drunken rage."

By the time Ricci was done, the Tuckers understood Buck to be an illiterate White man who was bigoted, full of hate and a bully who hated women, especially pale-skinned, peroxide blondes.

"Next in line is Steve. He's done time in California for burglarizing hardware stores," Ricci said. "After Steve, we have our newest and youngest member, Ed."

Ricci said Ed was related to Buck, but how was never clear. Six inches over five feet and almost bald, Ed sported an ugly comb-over. Weasel-like in demeanor and afflicted with dry skin, he scratched at himself nonstop. Many thought Ed was an addict. He wasn't—yet. A few years later, they would learn how much a weasel the man was.

9

IN THE 1970S, COMMUNICATIONS were better and more straightforward than what came later with computerization. More often than not, police agencies prepared informational teletype messages for significant crimes, whether solved or not. Julie Matthews finished her midnight records shift by collecting the teletypes and separating them by topic. Once in the appropriate piles, Julie clipped each bundle together and put them in Lieutenant Cooper's mailbox.

Lieutenant Josiah Cooper, a creature of habit, began each morning by closing his office door, reading the *San Jose Mercury News* from cover to cover, and glancing at the *Mountain View Voice*. Once finished, Cooper collected his mail and went through the teletypes. Although his investigative skills were nonexistent, the man knew enough not to throw them away. After scanning the messages, Cooper handed the entire stack to the sergeant closest to his door. Once this arduous task was complete, he retreated to his office, locked the door, and read the *San Francisco Chronicle* cover to cover before his much-needed first nap of the day.

Everyone in the department, even the chief, knew how much of his day Cooper wasted. Promoted by the previous chief, Cooper was protected by civil service rules and his uncle, the mayor. His detectives were happy the sluggard kept busy doing nothing. Their lieutenant was prone to interfere with real police work if not otherwise occupied. The chief would never place Cooper where the incompetent lieutenant could do serious damage.

Detective Al Smith religiously read the teletypes. Not only did Smith pay attention but saved copies of every serious notification that came through. Smith had a separate file for bank robberies he started during his first days as an investigator. These were not elaborate files, simply stacks with the latest teletypes on top. Generally, they got to the detectives as early as 10:00 a.m.

Years ago, Smith and Julie Matthews had had a brief fling. Both had moved on but remained friends. Julie knew what interested the detectives, just as she knew Cooper was useless and had less law enforcement skills than a meter maid. Julie copied the teletypes which would be of interest to Smith. Before leaving, she put them in an envelope on his desk.

Smith cleared his desk, opened his second pack of Lucky Strikes for the day, and lit up. *I have to identify my bank robbers.* With Bert working evenings this week, he could stay home and toil over his cases without distraction. Smith put his paperwork in his battered old briefcase and headed home. Smith always thought better at home with Jack Daniels—straight. *The devil's in the details.*

Smith's place wasn't much. He lived in a tiny one-bedroom apartment in a crime-ridden area of East Palo Alto. There was little money left over for a decent apartment after alimony leaving Mountain View outside his price range. The decaying apartment building was all that remained of a complex built with Works Progress Administration (WPA) money in the early years of the Franklin Roosevelt presidency. As Smith turned off the pothole-strewn street into the gravel parking lot, he suffered the melancholy permeating the lives of every occupant existing in the sixteen apartments. The stench, almost visceral, drenched the project. His door was at the rear on the bottom floor, allowing him to enter through the back.

As Smith stepped into his kitchen, the decades-old walls closed in on him. He stepped over the bag of garbage he had forgotten to take out while in a hurry that morning, his entire being wilted. After a few hours of work in the hot, stuffy, and dinky place Smith called home, the bag's rancid smell added to the unfortunate and sad atmosphere. Trash pickup was still days away, leaving the air laden with the stench of rotting garbage. All sixteen units shared one large Dempsey dumpster, and a bum was rooting through the overflowing container when Smith got there. Not a lot different from the smell of my apartment, Smith thought.

Smith had installed grates over the windows and double deadbolt locks on the doors. He made these modifications because of being burglarized within weeks of moving into the place. After the second burglary, Smith resolved to prevent any more of his valuables from being stolen. Smith removed a section of the floor from under his bed and installed a safe bolted to the cement foundation. Here, Smith stored the Japanese Type 14 Nambu and the Russian Tokarev TT-33 pistols taken off dead North Korean officers and brought home from Korea.

His leftovers and dirty dishes remained on the kitchen table. *Everything in this place depresses me, from the vomit green linoleum peeling from the floor to the nineteen-inch television with tinfoil-wrapped rabbit ears.* Bert rarely spent the night with Smith because she found his apartment repugnant. He had learned to accept his self-chosen prison. The one luxury Smith allowed himself was a fresh bottle of Jack Daniels every Friday. Unless they went somewhere, Al was usually out of JD by Sunday night. He checked the whiskey bottle and found the golden-brown liquid was pretty much used up, leaving enough for one tall drink.

Sipping his drink, Smith poured over every report written by the officers involved in the bank robbery's initial assignments. *The FBI has primary jurisdiction in bank robberies, but they never shared their reports.* Smith wrote notes:

1. Two men, one White, one Black (Doubt it)
2. They spoke in normal tones except to announce the robbery
3. Speech clear, direct, polite, but commanding (Accent?)
4. Ski masks
5. Large pistols (45s?)
6. One told patrons to lie on the floor
7. The other went from teller to teller
8. "Don't put the dye pack in the bag."
9. Brought an old doctor's bag

10. Escaped in a rental car, paid cash, used a phony name
11. Car renter described as 50+ White male, nothing distinctive remembered
12. They might have left fingerprints in the rental car
13. Taller one may have a bad leg

Al made a second list of assumptions to help guide the investigation.

1. The two are proficient - have robbed banks before
2. Their MO is distinguishable
3. White males in their 50s
4. Ex-cons

Smith made three stacks of the last five years' collection of teletypes. The first was of two-man robbery teams of a Black and a White man. There were two, and Smith set those aside as unlikely. The second stack was White men or men of an unknown race. The third contained those eliminated from consideration. The sorting took him well past midnight, stopping once to fix Spam and eggs and later to answer a call from Bert.

Bert, working a relief shift, told him, "I can get away for three days next weekend if you're interested." Smith was but was more interested in solving the bank robbery.

Smith promised to pick her up the

following Friday afternoon. "We'll drive up the coast to Fort Bragg."

Spam is getting pretty ripe. I better clean up the kitchen and take out the trash. The trip to the kitchen was to give his mind a break. Smith didn't get any rest. He was facing serious problems—the foremost solving the bank robbery.

Even more significant was his relationship with Bert. Ten years his junior and happy in her career as an ER Nurse. *Bert wants marriage and all that comes with it. I can't give her what she deserves or wants. Hell, I can't give her half what she deserves. Bert wants a home, a full-time husband, and kids.* Smith thought of it as the Big Trifecta for women. *I'll never be able to afford a house.* Smith's loyalty would forever be divided between his wife and the police department. *It's already cost me two marriages.* Smith had no desire to father a child at his age. Smith loved Bert but recognized the three things impossible for him to give. It would hurt terribly, but he would break it off—soon.

Smith glanced at his watch, "Twenty to two. If I hurry, I might get to the liquor store before it closes."

The next day, Smith arrived with a horrific hangover and again late for roll call. His sergeant was upset with him. Cooper was engrossed in the newspapers and had no idea when his subordinates came or went. Smith offered a lame excuse about working through the night on the robbery. His sergeant said, "Al, you have more than one case to work. Besides, you're hungover. You promised you wouldn't let the booze get in the way anymore."

"I know, Sarge, I'm sorry. Last night I had way too much on my mind. I slipped. It won't happen again."

"It better not. If Cooper catches you, he'll do everything possible to get you bumped back to the street. If it's over booze again, not even the chief will be able to save your ass. Now get back to work, and clear some damn cases."

On Smith's desk was an envelope in Julie's handwriting. He tore the envelope open. One teletype. Reading it made him smile. He grabbed the phone and dialed her number. After several rings, a woman answered, her voice groggy, "It better be good, whomever you are."

"Hey Julie, it's me, Al."

"Screw you. I was dreaming. I was getting laid by Ryan O'Neal in *Love Story*. You going to make it up to me?"

"The teletype you left might help solve the Bank of America robbery."

Still sounding pissed but softening up, she said, "That's not as good as getting laid by Ryan O'Neal. I'll forgive you this time, asshole, but you owe me. Now piss off, and let me get back to my wet dream."

Smith reread the teletype. It detailed a bank robbery in San Leandro that matched his. The MO fit his case to a "T." The bad guys were White males who appeared to be in their fifties, both armed with pistols, Colt .45s, and the getaway car a rental.

Smith whispered, "We gonna get you."

10

IN ONE OF THE Wicked Eye booths, after closing, Ron Ricci explained his operation to the Tuckers. "This guy Skaggs is a genius entrepreneur, and his success has allowed me to get rich. Here's the deal. Skaggs built an empire of grocery stores. Right now, there are three thousand of his stores across the country. Most are called Safeway."

Curious, Ben queried, "What's that have to do with us?"

"Let me finish. From the beginning, the stores have been cash only. Every night they put the money in the safe. Safeway's building new stores, mostly on the West Coast, using the same plans for all. We only hit these new design stores because each is identical, and we know exactly where the safe is kept. Here's how it helps us."

After Ricci finished, the brothers raised their beers in salute. Jim said, "It sounds like you got everything you need to get us all rich."

"Our next job is in a few weeks. I want you boys to go to Sacramento. There are a dozen or so stores, but I want you to concentrate on three. Check them out, come back and tell me the one to hit and why. You got one week. Can you do it?"

"You bet," Ben said. *God willing, and the creek don't rise.*

Jim, more reserved, said, "We'll see."

They took a regional bus from Marshfield to Grants Pass and Greyhound to Sacramento, arriving during the busy afternoon with plenty of crowds. They stole a Dodge Coupe and swapped the plates with a Ford.

After visiting the three stores, they eliminated one immediately. It was an older building, two blocks from the State Capitol. Cops were coming and going day and night. The second store, located on a highway running from Northern to Southern California with traffic twenty-four hours a day, held little promise. The third, built in the new design the previous year, was in a small commercial area away from most traffic. Better still, the closest police station was five miles away.

Jim watched as two cops pulled into a diner's parking lot. *They're going to be having coffee or a meal. Whichever, they'll be talking.* Inside the eatery, the cops took a booth at a wall the furthest from the cash register. The place was pretty full, but Jim got a booth behind the two without arousing anything suspicious.

One of the cops, upset about communications, said, "Can you believe it, the Sacramento Sheriff got those new two-way radios installed in all their patrol cars."

"Yeah, I heard. Those bastards get all the new stuff first," said the second cop.

As the cops' conversation continued, Jim learned that the local officers received messages over the air like a regular car radio but could not answer.

Ricci had given them a set of blueprints for the new store design. "Ben, we've four days left before heading back to Marshfield. You go grocery shopping at the Safeway store. When you come back, we'll go over the blueprints and make a note of any changes. Tonight, you drop me off near the store and pick me up after it opens in the morning," Jim said.

"It'll be risky. You ought to take the car."

"No, Ben, I'll do better alone and on foot. When the store opens, I'll buy a few things.

That'll give me a chance to check it out firsthand and verify what you saw. I'll sleep during the day and go back tomorrow night and the next."

"What do you want me to do while you're watching the place? Sleep?" Ben asked.

"Yes and no. Find out what time the cops change shifts and how they do it. It'll be dicey. Plan on being in place near the police station by 10:00 p.m., stay until at least 1:00 a.m., and then head back to the hotel and get a few hours sleep. Memorize everything. Don't write anything down in case you get rousted. Go back each night. We need to know if anything changes. I doubt it will, but we need to be sure. Be careful. I'd hate to lose you."

They finished four days later and drove to Redding. They dumped the Dodge before taking the bus to Medford, Oregon, where they separated and bought bus tickets to Marshfield arriving hours apart.

Ricci said, "I checked them out while you were in Olympia and came to the same conclusion. You guys are smarter than you look. Checking out the cops was a nice touch."

Jim's face turned red, and his fingers tightened into clenched fists as he barked, "What the hell!" Regaining control, he said in a quiet but strained voice, "If you'd already made up your mind, why'd you send us?"

"Relax, it was a test. I wanted to make sure you two were smart enough—you are." As Jim calmed down, Ricci continued. "None of these other guys can do what you did. I want someone checking out the stores besides me. You gonna be okay with that?"

Ben, who had remained silent during Jim's outburst, asked, "We get paid extra for our efforts?"

"If I send you on a scouting party, you'll get a bigger share. Now, let's have a beer."

It was nearly two weeks before Ricci announced, "We hit Sunday. They'll have more cash on hand than any other night of the week."

Two weeks later, Ricci and his gang, including the Tuckers, were in Chico on a Sunday morning. From there, it was three hours over U.S. Highway 99 to Sacramento. They looked like farmworkers dressed in flannel shirts and overalls. They drew little attention when they checked into the Clunie Hotel on K Street. After a breakfast of steak and eggs, they went to Ricci's room.

"Let's go through this one more time," Ricci said.

Buck chimed in, "Jesus, Ron, we've done this before. Except for these turds," nodding at the Tuckers. "We know what to do."

"Shut up and listen. Okay, Jim, you go first."

"I'll be at the police station an hour before their shift change. When the cops come in at midnight, I'll drive past the store and honk three times if everything looks normal. If not, I'll give a long blast on the horn, wait a minute, and repeat."

"Good. Steve?"

"At 11:00 p.m., I'll drive through the parking lot and make sure all the employee's cars are gone. I'll look through the window to see if anyone's still inside. If it looks okay, I'll pick up the others."

"Where?"

"Outside the all-night diner on L Street."

"Ed, Steve picks you up in the panel truck with the equipment. Then what?"

"He'll take me, Buck, and Ben over to the store. If no one's in sight, he'll drop us and the gear off behind."

"Right, and then what?"

"We wait in the trees with the ladder, rope, and tools."

Ricci nodded to Ben, "Once Jim gives the signal, Buck and I carry the ladder to the back of the building and hold it while Ed goes up with a rope. He pulls up the tools. Once Ed checks it out and gives us the okay, we climb up. Steve takes the ladder away." Ricci nodded his approval. Ben said, "After cutting through the ventilation shaft, we lower Ed and the bolt cutters to the floor."

Ed said, "I climb up the inside wall mounted ladder to the roof access hatch. I cut the lock, letting in Ben and Buck. Once they're in, I lower the tools and the rope down to Steve, who takes everything and heads for Chico." Steve nodded assent.

Then it was Buck's turn. "I know what to do, damn it."

"Tell me," commanded Ricci.

"The three of us hide until the manager comes in, usually between two and two-fifteen. Once he's inside and locks the door, we grab him and take him to the office. The manager opens the safe, we tie him up, take the cash, and out the back door we go."

Jim finished with, "At two-thirty, I return and park next to the back door. I keep the motor running. When all three come out. I pick them up and drive here."

That night, tule fog settled in the valley, making it hard to see fifty feet while driving. Jim arrived at the police station and couldn't find the parking lot. *Should I call it off? There's no way to contact Ron. Hell, I don't even know where he is. Besides, the fog will muffle any sound we make.*

The night wore on, and as the fog got

thicker, Jim had an idea. Shortly before midnight, he pulled in behind a police car, followed it into the parking lot, stopped, and waited. While police cars straggled in, Jim thought, I need an accurate count. As the parade slowed, he got out and walked to where the lot ended and the building began. As Jim neared what he hoped was his target, a burly cop accosted him. "Hey, bud, whatcha doin'? This lot's off-limits."

Feigning confusion, Jim said, "I'm passing through town, got lost in the fog, saw a police car, and followed him here."

"Why'd you do that?" the cop asked.

"I figured he would stop sooner or later, and I could ask for directions."

"Well, he's stopped, and you're out of your car in the police parking lot."

"Sorry, officer."

They had been moving while talking. Jim could see a dozen cops milling around and caught snatches of conversation. "This damn fog, I'll never get out to my beat." Another, "I'm headed over to Zack's Diner, knock back some coffee, and hope for no calls."

The cop gave Jim directions to the state highway, walked him to his car, and showed him the way out of the parking lot. Now Jim knew they would have no cops stumbling onto them. *I hope I can find my way back to the store in all this shit.*

The fog had thrown him off his timetable, and Jim knew he had to get to the store. Driving faster than prudent, Jim managed to find the Safeway and give the all-clear signal.

The Safeway manager accommodated the robbers' demands, especially the big one with the pistol, by opening the safe and turning over the weekend receipts. He told the thieves, "It was a good three days—over twenty thousand dollars."

Jim and the others watched Buck hold tight to the satchel all the way to Chico. Once they met with Ricci and handed over the money, he was brief. "Steve's halfway to Oregon. You four split up and meet me at my place on Thursday." Ricci was out the door and gone.

"What about the money?" Ben asked.

Ed spoke up, "He always takes it. The split will be Thursday. You might not like it, but don't worry, Ricci never skims anything."

They met Thursday morning, and Ricci explained the split. "On every job, I take thirty percent off the top and divide what's left among the rest of you. In this case, 6K for me and $2,800 for each of you. Don't like it, take a hike, find another job."

Jim and Ben glanced at each other—happy. It was more money than they had ever seen. It was settled—the Tuckers were part of the crew. There were no more gifts from Ron.

They could afford a place of their own.

Over the next three years, they knocked over three or four Safeway stores a year. Ricci always visited the target and did reconnaissance, sometimes sending Jim later. If so, Jim would get a little extra. The score varied from as low as nine thousand to thirty-one thousand. The rest of the time, they did as they pleased as long as they didn't get into trouble.

The Tuckers rented a cottage a few miles outside of Marshfield and settled in for what they hoped would be the easy life.

Ben had suffered occasional nightmares for years about the dog he had killed as a test before doing away with his antagonist on the Georgia chain gang. The dreams never woke him, so he hadn't told Jim about them. One day not long after moving into the cottage, a mangy stray with one eye wandered into the area near the house. Ben bought the Gaines Food Company dry dog meat meal and left a pail of water and a pan full of biscuits near the back door each morning. It went untouched for a few days and then was gone by evening.

"Why are you wasting your time with that ugly mutt? It's sure to die."

"That's my business." *The nightmares*

have gone away. I'm keeping it.

Jim was sure Ben still felt guilty about killing the dog in Georgia, so he said no more about it. Soon the dog allowed Ben to touch it, and before long, the dog gained weight and then allowed itself to be washed in a tub. The next step was visiting a veterinarian where Glover's Mange Medicine was recommended. Within six months, the Springer Spaniel, or Lucky as Ben called it, had a full glossy coat and the weight of a healthy dog its age.

11

OVER THE YEARS, BUCK became a liability, a nasty drunk who couldn't handle his money, women, or booze. One weekend the local trooper visited Ron. "Buck's causing more trouble than he's worth."

"What's he done now?" Ricci asked.

"He beat the shit out of two girls, putting one in the hospital." The trooper, a friendly non-paying regular at Ron's club, would be forced to act if Buck's brutality continued. "Don't worry. She won't talk, but she won't be turning any tricks for at least a month. Buck's out of control."

Ricci tried to reason with Buck. "You gotta stop this shit. It's bringing heat down on us."

"I got it under control. It won't happen again."

A few days later, Ricci stopped by the Tucker brothers' cottage. "Hey, this is an unexpected pleasure," Jim said without a smile.

"I'm not here for pleasure. I've got a job for you."

Jim glanced at Ben before speaking. "What you got?"

"Buck." They didn't need an explanation. Arrested again for beating up a prostitute, Buck needed to be handled.

"Whatcha want?" Ben asked.

"I want him gone. Now."

"We're not killers."

"Aren't you? Look, boys, I don't care how you do it or what you do with him. I want him gone from Marshfield, clear out of Oregon. There's a grand in it for you. Half now, the other half when he's gone."

"We'll give you an answer tomorrow," Jim said.

"I'll leave this in case." Ricci put an envelope on the table and left. They didn't need to open it or count it.

"Hey Ben, how are you doing? I need a drink."

Ben was happy to oblige and handed Buck a tall, dark drink. "Here, have this."

Buck took a long pull, burped, and said, "Tastes a little funny." A few minutes later, Buck was face down, snoring, on the bar. Ben had slipped him a Mickey Finn. Hours later, Buck shook himself awake and looked around. He was in a grove of trees with birds and squirrels all around. It would have been a peaceful scene if not for being tied hand and foot. It was morning. Naked and cold, Buck shouted for help until exhausted before falling back to sleep.

A few hours later, Buck was hot, sunburned, and thirsty. Once again, he shouted himself hoarse to no avail. Buck spent the second night shivering from the cold and sunburn.

The following morning, Buck woke to find he had shit during the night and rolled over onto it. "Help me. Somebody, please help me." He screamed until delirious. Later in the day, he heard voices. They sounded familiar, but, in his condition, Buck couldn't recognize them.

"Should we kill him and leave his body for the wolves?"

"Please don't kill me. Please help me." Buck had no idea how long he shouted, but the voices finally returned.

"Hey, Buck, what have you got yourself into?" Opening his eyes, he saw the Tuckers and was beside himself with joy.

"We've decided not to kill you, but you won't be happy," Jim said.

Ben poured water from a bucket over Buck, and Jim cut the bindings. Cramped and in such pain from the hours of being bound up, Buck could not stand. He couldn't even get to his knees but did manage to roll away from his shit. Ben came back with another pail of water and a few rags. "Here, clean yourself."

When Buck was somewhat cleaner, Jim handed him his shoes. "Put these on and follow Ben. Keep your mouth shut, or I'll kill you."

"Why? What'd I do?"

Jim did not answer. Instead, he hit Buck in the stomach with an ax handle so hard that the man fell to the ground gasping for air and rolling in pain. "Get up unless you want more of the same." Buck was up as fast as possible, stumbling after Ben.

They walked through the trees for a few hundred yards until they reached a cabin Buck knew belonged to his tormentors. Ben hosed him down. Jim told him, "Clean up and get dressed. Now." Once finished, they marched him inside.

Jim did the talking. "We ruled out killing you and agreed to give you a choice."

"You can't do this to me. Ron won't let you get away with it."

"Who the hell you think sent us? Ben, get the tool."

Ben returned, holding a strange-looking device. "What's that? What's it for?" Buck asked.

Jim stared at it for a long moment, then said, "It's for you." Buck cringed and shook, not wanting to know more.

"Jim, you want to tell him what's about to happen and why, or do you want me to?"

"You tell him."

"Buck, you have become a liability to Ricci and the crew," Ben said.

"Whadda you mean?"

Jim slapped him, "Shut up and listen before I do something you'll regret." Buck remained silent.

"You're a drunk, a coward, and a woman beater. Ron warned you to knock it off. Instead, you beat another prostitute and were stupid enough to get caught doing it in his place. The cops can't ignore it any longer, and neither can Ron. He hired us to make the problem disappear—that's you—you piece of shit. Jim wants to kill you and be done with it. I say we give you a choice."

"I got a choice?"

"You could take a bullet to the brain," a smiling Jim said.

"What's the other option?"

"You leave Oregon and never come back."

"I'll leave."

No longer smiling, "Ben, hand me the tool." Tool in hand, Jim turned to Buck. "You know what this is?"

Eyes wide, Buck shook his head.

"When Ben and I lived on our Pa's farm, we used these on bull calves. This device is a nine-inch Burdizzo. We put it over a bull's balls and squeeze it until it's closed. It castrates the animal by crushing and breaking the blood vessels in the testicles. The testicles shrink and sooner or later are gone. The bull becomes a steer." Holding the device inches from Buck's face, Jim continued. "Used on a man, he becomes a eunuch."

Weeping and shaking, Buck gasped, "Please, let me go."

Jim answered tonelessly, "It's up to you. Whatever you choose, you'll be gone, and you'll never bother a woman again."

"Oh, God, please let me go. I promise I'll leave Oregon. I promise I'll never bother another woman—I swear. Please let me go. I've got money, and I'll give you everything I have if you let me go."

"It's too late. You have ten seconds to make up your mind. Will it be a bullet or the Burdizzo? Ten. Nine. Eight. Seven."

"My balls. My balls. Don't shoot me."

Pushing him back into a chair, they tied his arms and strapped his legs to the chair after tugging his pants down. Buck began weeping and shaking. "Oh God, oh God."

Stifling an urge to gag, Jim put the clamps around one of Buck's testicles. "Why me?" Jim mouthed the words and used all his strength to close the jaws and crush the testicle twice to make sure he got the spermatic cords. Buck screamed an animal-like sound and passed out. Moving to the other testicle, Jim repeated the process. Still unconscious, Buck cried out again.

Ben never enjoyed torturing men or animals. So, when Buck regained consciousness, Ben gave him a hefty dose of Laudanum. "Take this. It has morphine in it. It won't do much, but it's better than nothing." Buck swallowed several table-spoons before sobbing.

"You bastards, I'll get you if it's the last thing I ever do."

"Now, Buck, remember you made a choice. If you ever come back here, we'll kill you," Jim reminded him.

Ben said, "I'll drop you off at your place. Take one day, two at the most, to get on your feet. Then disappear." A day later, Buck loaded his car and left town.

12

ED, ALWAYS A WEAK link on Ron's gang, developed an addiction to heroin, making him a much greater liability than Buck had ever been. Buck had introduced him to opium on occasional trips to Portland. "You should give this a try. It can't hurt you. It makes you feel like everything's perfect."

"I heard you get addicted to it."

Buck told him, "Look, I've been using this stuff for years. Every time I come to Portland, I visit an opium den. It hasn't hurt me. I'm not addicted."

Ed thought and almost said aloud, Maybe that's why you have so much trouble with women. Not wanting to be the brunt of one of Buck's rages, he thought better of it and shut his mouth. Ed had dabbled in marijuana use for years but never seriously. He told Buck, "What the hell, I can handle it. Why not enjoy myself?" Ed liked how it made him lose much of the dread that consumed him every day. Soon it was weekly trips for the drug, then his stays in Portland became days at a time, and before long, he graduated to heroin. Ed now had an ever-increasing habit costing more than he could afford. Even with the vast sums of cash garnered from the Safeway robberies, Ed soon needed to go elsewhere for a way to pay for his addiction.

Ed decided jewelry store heists would be the solution to his drug needs. He didn't even head out of state—Portland would do. He robbed two jewelry stores with his face bare, bursting into the stores midafternoon, the day's busiest time. At least a dozen witnesses got a good look at him, and his car parked in front. Within days he was identified, located, and arrested. Even before booking, Ed demanded to talk with a detective. "I've got something you want."

Shortly before arraignment, he talked to one.

"You want to talk to a detective? Talk, I don't have a lot of time."

"I work for Ron Ricci over in Marshfield."

"So, who's Ron Ricci?"

"Ron has a gang. They, er, we, rob Safeway stores," Ed said.

The Portland detective had been around a while and knew of the Safeway heists. "Go ahead."

"We've been robbing them for years. Me and a couple of other guys go in through the roof. We wait for the manager. He comes in, we jam him up and force him to open the safe, tie him up, take the cash, and go out the back."

The detective told Ed, "Wait here."

"Like I got a choice. Leave me a cigarette."

The detective called the Oregon State Police and asked for Detective Paul Carter. After a brief conversation, the two called the Attorney General's Office.

Ed worked a deal. Not able to fence the jewelry, it was all returned, making the victims whole. The arrest did not make the papers.

With pressure from Safeway, the prosecuting attorney approved a plea bargain. Ed would get probation if he could deliver up the crew. Names and information would not be enough. They needed to catch the gang in the act. Ed was given a suspended prison sentence with the understanding that if he didn't deliver, he would serve ten years at the Oregon State Penitentiary in Salem.

By the time Ricci assembled his gang for the next score, the Portland detective and Detective Sergeant Paul Carter knew everything about him, the Tuckers, and the other gang members. They even had suspicions about Buck's disappearance and Pete Doyle's death.

Early in August, Ricci summoned Jim to the club. "Jim, it's time for another job. You ready?"

"Always."

Ron's instructions were simple, "I want you to go down to Oakland for a little scouting trip. Here are the addresses of four Safeway stores. Check them out and let me know which one we should hit on Labor Day. It'll be a big haul."

"Got it. Is next week soon enough? Ben and I have a place rented for the weekend in Grants Pass, and we were planning to do a little steelhead fishing on the Rogue River."

"Enjoy your weekend, and then get to work. And don't mention this to the others."

"Okay."

The following week, Jim took off, and Ben busied himself around the cottage. Ed noted Jim's absence and asked Ben. "What's Jim up to? I haven't seen him around for a few days."

"He's busy."

"So, is he around? I need to talk to him." Ed pushed for an answer.

"Why, what do you want? Tell me. I'll give him the message." Ed did not learn anything from Ben but suspected Jim might be on one of his scouting trips for Ron.

Ed drove to the Salem OSP Field Office and met with Detective Carter. Ed did his best to convince him a robbery was in the making. "Look, Ron relies on Jim Tucker to scout the stores and the cops. Jim's gone, and no one's talking. That means Ron's getting ready for a job. It'll be soon."

Frustrated, Carter wanted to shout at the despicable weasel, "Drag your ass back to Marshfield, and don't bother us until you've got something useful."

Once Ed was gone, Carter called the prosecutor and relayed what the informant had said. "The little shit may be onto something. I'll ask my captain to update the Superintendent and see if we can't get a couple of undercover detectives to nose around Marshfield, even snoop around inside Ron Ricci's club." Even though his captain agreed and forwarded the request up the chain of command, office inertia drowned the request in the agency's bureaucracy.

Returning from Oakland, Jim gave Ricci a thorough report, eliminating two stores and keeping the other two as possible targets. One was a little closer to an Oakland police substation than Jim liked, especially since Oakland was more progressive than most law enforcement agencies. Jim told Ron, "For one thing, they have radios in all the patrol cars and are bringing in two-way radios. Another problem is how they change shifts. Instead of all coming in at once, half stay out in the field until half of the next shift comes out. Oakland always has cops on the street. To make it even worse, they use two-man cars."

Ricci said, "So what are you suggesting?"

"There's a small town bordering Oakland. Piedmont is the moneyed part of the Bay Area, and they have a new style Safeway store. In the twenties, they called it the "City of Millionaires." They've got more millionaires per square mile than anywhere else in the state. It's a rich, quiet, and smug little place with a tiny police department. They have one cop on duty at night, and he sleeps a lot."

"Are you telling me you checked it out already?"

"Yes."

Angry, Ricci stood. "I didn't tell you to, so why'd you go against my orders?"

"I did what you told me to do and a little extra."

"Okay, let me think. Now beat it."

Weeks later, the two men met at the club. "Jim, you're right. Oakland would be tough. Are you sure about Piedmont? Do I need to go down for a second look?"

"You're the boss. It's up to you. Oakland is doable, but Piedmont is less risky."

Ricci brooded over it for a week and then gathered the crew for a morning meeting. "It's time. We're going to hit a store."

Ed pushed for details. "When? Where?"

Ricci put up his hands, palms out. "Whoa, hold your horses. Jim, fill them in on everything except when and where."

Once Jim finished, Ed had one question. "When?"

"We go when I say." The rest were surprised by Ron's reluctance, but not Jim. Ron trusted him, but he'd never approved a job he hadn't checked out himself.

13

THE ORIGINAL PLAN WAS to hit the Safeway on Labor Day, 1937. Ron Ricci always liked working at the end of a three-day weekend because the take was bigger. Because of his unease about Piedmont, Ricci decided to hold off until later in the year, not telling anyone about his decision, not even Jim Tucker. Although his gang pressured him, Ricci told them nothing.

Ricci vanished for a few days the first week of November, and Ed reported to his handler at the Oregon State Police. The detective's response frightened him. "If you don't get something pretty soon, the deals off, and you're headed for Salem and the general population." Ed knew as small and weak as he was, survival in gen pop was not a risk to be taken if there was any other option. Ed couldn't do anything, but as Detective Carter told his captain, "Hey, why not put a scare into the little bastard?"

In 1935 President Franklin D. Roosevelt issued a proclamation designating the fourth Thursday of November as a Day of National Thanksgiving. Thanksgiving 1937 was November 25th. Ricci thought, "We'll have a bigger haul than usual."

On Monday the twenty-second, Ricci, in good spirits, called a meeting at the club. Optimism had replaced his doubts about the Piedmont job. *After all, aren't there more millionaires per square mile? That means more people with more money to spend on a Thanksgiving celebration.*

Once they all had a drink in hand and were quiet, Ricci announced, "It's time to work."

None was happier than Ed. "That's great, Ron. Where?"

"You'll know soon enough. Now let's get to work. Ben will take Buck's place inside with Steve and Ed." Once Ricci finished, they all knew their jobs. The one thing missing was the location.

"We need to know where we're going," Ed persisted.

Ricci growled at Ed. "All you need to know is what I tell you." Then in a more neutral tone, "Now take off. Get some rest. Be here at 7:00 a.m. Friday."

An hour later, Ed left for Salem. When he arrived at the Oregon State Police Headquarters, an officious desk officer told him,

"Detective Carter's on vacation."

"You've got to find him. It's important."

"He's on vacation. We got no way to contact him, even if I wanted to."

Ed got a room, shot up, and calmed down. A fresh shipment of heroin on the streets was more potent than any Ed had ever previously used. Within minutes of injecting the drug, the little man was unconscious and remained that way for over twenty hours. When he woke up, Ed faced the same dilemma. He didn't know what to do. The detective in Portland was no longer involved because Marshfield and Ron's gang were out of his jurisdiction. Ed didn't know how to locate anyone he could trust. At wit's end, he returned to the State Police Office and asked for Carter. Ed approached the desk officer, "I have to talk to Detective Carter. It's an emergency."

The officer laughed at the disheveled and insignificant pint-sized man. "You're in luck. Detective Carter is here."

Five minutes later, in a windowless interrogation room with Sergeant Carter, "I thought you were on vacation."

"I am. I stopped by for my paycheck."

Ed was crying. "We're gonna hit a Safeway."

"When? Where?" He had the detective's full attention.

"Ron won't tell me."

"What do you mean, won't tell you?"

"All Ron said was, 'We'll hit this, Sunday.' I can't guess where. We're supposed to meet Friday morning."

"Shit. Wait here," Carter exclaimed. Carter telephoned his captain, who put him back on the clock. Hours later, Carter finished his third interview of the day with Ed. "Okay, get your ass back there and find out what you can."

"If I ask too many questions, Ron will get suspicious."

"Keep your eyes and ears open. You learn anything. You get word to me."

"How do I do that? If it's a job, we'll hit the road right after the meeting on Friday morning."

"Do your best, and don't act like you know me if I show up somewhere."

With Ed on his way back to Marshfield, Sergeant Carter and his captain began putting a plan together. "Paul, you got anyone you trust in Marshfield?"

"No, sir. The local trooper's a good guy but close to Ricci, and the strip club's his hangout. It's a small town, and strangers stand out."

"Where does the snitch live?"

"He's got a house, more like a shack, on the outskirts of town."

"Can you get inside without being spotted? Because that's what I want."

"Yes, sir."

Friday, the twenty-sixth, Paul Carter hunkered down thirty yards from Ed's shack. Around five in the morning, or as Paul liked to say, "O-dark-thirty." At 7:00 a.m., the snitch came out and walked about fifty feet to a shabby wooden outhouse behind the cabin. A few minutes later, smoke and sparks came from the chimney, followed by the smell of coffee. Not long before eight, Ed rushed to his car and took off toward town.

Ed returned a few hours later, slammed his car door, kicked an empty beer can, and banged the front door so hard Carter could hear it from the back of the house. *He doesn't look too happy.*

Carter tapped on the shack's back door, satisfied his snitch was alone and unlikely anyone would join him. He knocked twice before the door opened with an angry, "What the fuck? What are you doing, trying to get me killed?" Carter thought the man might faint from shock.

Carter stepped through the door, pulling it closed behind him. "No. I need to know what Ricci's got planned."

Ed slumped in a chair. "He didn't tell us much other than to be at the old Sailor's Hotel in Vallejo tomorrow night by seven. I have to pick up Steve in an hour. Ron told me to drive to Chico and spend the night." He ate a slice of cold bacon before continuing. "The Tuckers are taking the 99 and stopping in Redding. We never know how Ron travels. When we meet at the Sailor's Hotel, he'll tell us the target." Ed hesitated, then went on. "We have to go over the plan, and he'll do it again before hitting the place. I'm sure the job will be Sunday night. The store will have four days' receipts. It won't be in Vallejo because we never meet where the store is."

"Okay. Stick with the plan and pick up Steve. We'll be in touch before Sunday."

"How?"

"Let me do the worrying." Carter slipped out the back door, leaving Ed to his fears.

The captain assigned four other detectives to work with Carter. He persuaded the Safeway attorney to make four of their store detectives available. Carter set up a command post in Ashland at the Ashland Springs Hotel. It took him two hours to get there. The Safeway detectives had already arrived and paired up with the Oregon State Police detectives.

Paul Carter briefed the detectives, who all agreed the store had to be within three hours of Vallejo, no more than seventy-five miles. San Francisco was ruled out.

Sacramento to the east and south to San Jose were the target area's farthest limits. Removing those stores and the as-yet-to-be-modernized stores brought the list down to seven, too many for the small group to watch.

Carter observed, "In all the previous jobs, they met Ricci between the store and Marshfield. We forget those stores that don't fit the pattern."

"Brings us down to five, and we only have four teams," a Safeway man remarked.

A trooper from the area, who had remained silent, put in his two cents worth, "He's right, and these guys are good at surveillance. We can't be too close. We can't ask five different police agencies to go poking around. We'll get blown for sure."

After further discussion, they decided one of them would have to get a room at the hotel in Vallejo and contact Ed. Mike Morgan, a former dockworker who looked more like one than a cop, would fit the bill. No one would ever mistake Morgan for a cop.

Following a call to the captain, Carter and Morgan left for Vallejo. Taking turns driving and sleeping as best they could, they made it to Vallejo in twelve hours. Carter dropped Morgan off at the Sailor's Hotel and found himself a place to stay a few miles away. He called his captain with the location and then slept until dawn. When Carter woke, the rest of the team had all checked in. They grabbed a few hours sleep and then waited in the dining room. After a hurried breakfast, they went to his room to plan their next step. Carter said, "I got nothing until we hear from Mike. Any suggestions?" None of the other detectives spoke up. "Okay, get a little more sleep, but be back here by 1:00 a.m. If we don't have anything by then, we'll set up surveillance on them around the clock."

For Carter, past exhaustion, eleven came all too soon, and with nothing new to work with, he checked in with his captain. "The captain hasn't heard from Mike. We'll set up surveillance at 6:00 p.m. Here's what we'll do."

By 9:00 p.m., they were restless after three hours of sitting on the stakeout with no word or movement. Carter called the captain.

The response shocked him. "Where the hell have you been?"

"What?"

"Morgan called an hour ago. It's on . . . a place near Oakland . . . a town called Piedmont. Piedmont has one Safeway store. It fits the picture, built less than a year ago."

"Great news. When?"

"Sunday night."

"We'll be there, skipper. We need help we can trust. It wouldn't hurt having you here," Carter quipped. "Besides, you'll get your picture in the paper." His captain hated publicity, but his rank would influence the locals.

"I'll be there."

Sunday afternoon, Carter had a plan and the manpower needed. Oakland was more than willing to support OSP in taking down the infamous Safeway Gang. Piedmont was too small to conduct an operation of this size. Their chief, glad for the help, was happy to let Detective Sergeant Carter take the lead. By six, Carter had managed to infiltrate four detectives into the store. A loose tail was set up at the Sailor Hotel. The detectives would stay well back as the suspects made their way to Piedmont. After the gang was on the road, other detectives would follow Ricci. and keep him under observation until the robbery went down. Once the heist was in progress, they would take Ricci into custody and book him into the Oakland jail.

At 11:00 p.m., Jim parked a short block from the Piedmont Police Station. Ten minutes to midnight, the two police cars assigned the evening shift pulled into the police parking lot. He waited until the lone midnight shift officer drove from the lot.

Jim knew the cop would meet an Oakland officer at an all-night diner on MacArthur. When planning the robbery, Jim had discovered the officer started his shift by spending an hour visiting with an Oakland officer. Then at 2:00 a.m., the cop took an official meal break. *We shouldn't have to worry about an interruption.*

While Jim was checking on the police, Steve checked the store. *It looks clear.* Satisfied, he picked up Ben and Ed and dropped them and their equipment behind the store. Buck hadn't been replaced. The two would enter the store alone.

A few minutes after midnight, Jim drove by the Safeway store and gave the all-clear signal. He was to return at 2:30 a.m. and pick up Ben and Ed. *I wish it were me inside instead of Ben. I might as well watch the police station and make sure the cop went in for his meal.*

The only change in how they carried out the robbery was the entry. As small as Ed was, it still took two men to lower him to the store's floor. Steve would follow the other two up the ladder. Once Ed was on the floor, Steve climbed down and put the ladder back in his truck.

Inside, Ed climbed up to the roof access door and cut the lock. Ben lowered the tools back down to Steve, who drove happily away from the store. The detectives allowed Steve to get to Richmond before they pulled him over.

At 2:10 a.m., a plain-clothes detective, posing as the store manager, entered the store and walked to the office. The detective made enough noise, knocking over a pallet, that Ben had no doubt the manager was in the store. When the detective opened the door, Ben stepped forward with a pistol in his left hand. Much to his surprise, the man stepped aside as two other men pointed shotguns at him. "Freeze! You're under arrest. Drop the gun before I blow your head off."

At 2:30 a.m., Jim drove to the rear of the Safeway store and parked beside the rear door. *Where's Ben?* Before the thought was complete, three cars materialized as if out of thin air. Two pulled to a stop in front of Jim, the other behind him. Even before they shouted, "Police," he knew who they were. The Tuckers were armed with Colt .45 pistols. Ricci had an old thirty-eight revolver. Neither Steve nor Ed was armed.

The following day, Jim Tucker was taken from a cell to a small room with a table bolted to the floor and a metal chair behind the table where he was instructed to sit. Two detectives sat across from him, and a third lounged against the wall next to the door.

The youngest one introduced himself. "Mr. Tucker, I'm Detective Paul Carter with the Oregon State Police."

"Why are you here?"

The detective shrugged and said, "Just visiting."

Cigarettes were passed around and lit up. Jim declined. "I don't smoke."

Within minutes the tiny room was filled with acrid smoke. Then the questioning began. Detective Carter didn't say much. Jim refused to answer any questions, not even to confirm his identification. The cop leaning against the wall pulled a sap from a pocket. Without a word, he stepped close and hit Jim's left arm. The blow from the flattened lead and leather-covered weapon almost knocked Jim off the chair.

"What the hell," Jim shouted.

Carter stood up and repeated, "What the hell."

"You want him to talk, don't ya?"

"That's not the way I do business. You hit him again, and you'll have to deal with me."

A jailer was called, and Jim Tucker was returned to his cell. Ben asked, "What's wrong?"

"One of those assholes nailed me with a sap and would have done it again, but some dick from Oregon stopped him."

All five were charged with burglary and armed robbery in the local court. Ronald Guido Ricci, booked and charged, denied any knowledge of the robbery. Apart from Ed, they refused to talk. With no evidence other than the testimony of Ed, a convicted felon, the police didn't have any evidence linking the gang to any other Safeway robberies.

Ben used his phone call to ask a woman he had occasionally dated to take care of Lucky. "I don't know anything about dogs." After some cajoling, she agreed to pick up the dog and give it a try.

Lucky, I think you're on your own—again.

At their first court appearance, the Tuckers found the judicial system in California was quite different from what they had experienced in Georgia. As soon as the judge finished reading the charges against them, she asked if they had an attorney.

First Jim and then Ben said, "No, ma'am."

"Can you afford one of your own, or will you need the services of the Public Defender."

"What's a Public Defender?" Ben asked.

"You're lucky. Since 1926, Alameda County has provided lawyers to criminal defendants who cannot afford to pay for one," the judge replied.

The Tuckers pleaded poverty. The judge referred their case to the Public Defender's office and continued it for ten days.

The Tuckers were each provided with a public defender. But they insisted on having one attorney represent them both. The PD explained they faced a sentence of fifteen to twenty years because they were felons in possession of a firearm during the robbery.

Ben spoke for him and Jim. "Get us a decent deal, and we'll plead. They got us cold, so there's no reason to sit through a trial and end up with the maximum sentence."

The PD agreed that would be the best course for them. Jim added one requirement to any plea deal. The brothers would do their time together.

Because the Tuckers were ex-cons and armed, they took the heaviest hit. Even with a plea deal, their sentence was five years at California's oldest prison, San Quentin.

After the Tucker's arrived at the prison, they had time to think about how the cops knew about the robbery. "What do you think happened?" Ben asked.

"It's obvious. Someone set us up. Think about it, no one, except Ron Ricci, knew where we would hit until a day before the job. Right?

"And Ricci got off easy, except for losing his crew."

After thinking it over, Ben said, "Ed. It has to be that little weasel. He was the first one to get out of jail. Where'd he get the money for bail? He's been doing that dope shit and is always broke."

"You're right, little brother. When we get

out, he's gonna pay."

Steve was lucky—two years. Ron Ricci, even more fortunate—a year in county jail. Ed went back to Oregon, where his plea deal was unhappily honored. Released from custody, he returned to his heroin habit. The Oregon State prosecutor was apoplectic. Oregon could not prove a case against any of the gang members except Ed, who was freed under the plea agreement conditions.

On the positive side, the robberies stopped. Safeway was happy.

14

THE TUCKERS SERVED THEIR prison sentence, and with time off for good behavior, they walked out the gates of San Quentin in early 1941. Not yet free men, they had to complete a period of parole. Forbidden to associate with other felons, they were sent in separate directions. Ben went to Oakland, Jim to Redding.

One month after they were paroled, Paul Carter learned Ed died with a needle in his arm. The medical examiner ruled his death an accidental heroin overdose.

Now, the lieutenant in charge of detectives, Carter wasn't so sure. He believed the Tuckers killed Ed as revenge for being the informant in the Piedmont Safeway robbery and arrests.

The Tuckers had learned harsh lessons on the streets, chain gangs, and prison—trust no one except themselves. With this in mind, they resolved never to commit a crime with anyone else. They focused on Bank of America, one of the largest banking systems in California with over a hundred branches. As spring slipped away and signs of summer appeared, Jim went to work planning a robbery at a downtown Los Angeles branch. The turn-of-the-century building seemed a good choice where ten teller windows were always staffed.

Pretending to open a savings account, Jim spent an hour watching the teller line. The middle-aged woman with no wedding ring who helped him was an easy mark. Pointing to a picture of the woman and a teenage girl, Jim quipped, "You're not old enough to have a daughter. She must be your sister."

Blushing, she replied, "I'm afraid not. Jenny's sixteen."

Jim glanced at her nameplate. "Oh, Mrs. Stevens, you're much too young."

"Oh, please, it's Muriel." They chatted as Jim discussed opening a savings account with a small deposit. Before long, Muriel agreed to meet him for dinner. "Jenny's dad has her this week, so I'm free to get out this evening." A smiling Jim assured her they would have an excellent time. He never got around to opening the account. She handed him a business card with her address on the back.

Jim said, "I'll pick you up at seven." Muriel flushed with anticipation. She had not been on a date since her husband walked out on her over a year ago.

Dinner was at a swanky downtown restaurant. "My ex-husband never brought me here."

"He should have," Jim quipped. He was a perfect gentleman and pretended interest in her.

"I grew up in Oxnard and went to high school there. I won't tell you what year I graduated."

Jim smiled. "Who cares? You're a beautiful woman and fun to be with."

Muriel knew she would get this man into her bed before the night ended. They moved to the lounge. She continued to tell Jim the story of her life and all about her job. Muriel told him everything she knew, almost, about the bank and how she fit into the operation. "Someday, I will be a branch manager."

"I'm sure you will be. You're a bright and beautiful woman. Nothing should stand in your way." Jim doubted she could balance her checking account.

On the way to her place, Jim continued to compliment her looks and her sure-to-come success. At the apartment, she invited him up for a nightcap. Jim feigned shyness and hesitation to impose on her. Muriel insisted and took him by the arm. She closed the apartment door, moved to Jim, put her arms around his neck, and kissed him.

Stunned by the intensity of her desire, Jim returned her kisses with a gentleness that surprised him. Pulling away, he said, "Not here."

"You're not as shy as I thought." She took him by the hand and led him to her bedroom.

Jim surprised her. "It's been a long day, and I want to please you."

"Don't worry. I'm sure you will."

Later in her bed, they cuddled and talked. Muriel confessed she had rarely found intimacy enjoyable. "Don't worry. It was pleasurable tonight."

They talked more before they fell asleep. Sometime before dawn, Jim woke and sat up on the side of the bed.

"Where are you going?" she said.

"I've got to get to work."

"Get back here! You can't leave yet."

"I'll be right back, lady."

Before Jim left, they had made love, cuddled, and talked more about Muriel and her work until well past sunrise. Jim didn't care what Muriel thought their future held—he knew. *The next time we meet, I'll be wearing a mask.*

Ben was anxious to hear all about it when his older brother returned after his night with Muriel. Jim filled him in on what he had learned about the bank. The rest was none of Ben's business. "There are two merchant windows. Most of those transactions are cash, and many are large deposits. The last Friday of the month is the biggest day for the bank, and they often bring in uniformed guards. The other Fridays are not as big, and no uniformed guards."

"Then we hit on a different Friday," Ben said.

"When we hit the place, we won't waste time on the other eight teller windows. There should be plenty of cash at the merchant windows, cutting down on the time we have to be inside." As ready as they ever would be, Jim told Ben, "We'll hit it on a Friday at closing and get a good haul."

At work, Muriel found it hard to concentrate. She kept thinking of what she had done with a stranger. Jim was a gentleman and a fantastic lover. Beyond that, she knew nothing. *I don't even know his last name, for God's sake. I hope he calls.*

After a week went by without a call, she fretted. *Did I do something to offend him? No, Jim enjoyed it as much as I did. I hope he's all right.* Soon she began to worry that she had told the stranger too much about how the bank operated. Muriel feared she had shared secrets better left unsaid. Did she tell him anything that could cause her problems? *Yes, I surely did.* She struggled over what she should do. *Should I tell someone? If I tell anyone, I'll have to tell them everything.* Remembering the night, she blushed. She kept it to herself. As she relived their conversations, she grasped that there was one thing she had not told the stranger. Muriel hadn't told Jim that because of the likes of John Dillinger and Bonnie and Clyde, her bank hired private robbery investigators and had armed plainclothes detectives placed in many of the larger branches.

"I've checked and rechecked everything at the bank. Tomorrow's the time to hit it," Jim said.

Ben agreed. "If you say so, we go."

Friday began according to plan as the brothers walked up to the bank's double doors while scanning the outside area within a hundred yards. Satisfied the immediate area contained no threat, they stopped. In a movement almost invisible, they glanced through the doors and took in the lobby scene. As expected, there were no uniformed guards. The merchant tellers were without customers. Customers were conducting business with most of the other tellers.

Ben said, "Let's go," as they pulled on ski masks.

They entered the bank, walked straight to the merchant windows, and pulled their jackets back, revealing matching .45 caliber Model 1911 pistols. Jim spoke quietly but loud enough for the tellers to hear, "This is a robbery. Put the cash in the bag."

Ben handed over a dark black bag. "Put it all in here and make it quick." Both tellers did as told. First one and then the other stuffed the cash in the bag. Once finished, they slid it back to him. "Thank you. Don't say anything until we're outside." The brothers turned and started toward the door.

"Stop, or we'll shoot." Two armed men blocked the doors. They would have been described as nondescript if they had not held revolvers pointed at the Tuckers.

The brothers drew their pistols. The other men fired first. Their shots, deafening in the confines of the bank, went awry. Jim fired back. Screams filled the air. Customers crowded for the doors. One bank man was down. The other fired again, hitting Jim, pushing him back on his heels as the bullet slammed into his left arm. Blood splattered both brothers as Ben hit the other bank guard over the head, knocking him to the floor. He grabbed both guards' revolvers, placing them in the black bag. They ran for the door, pushing through the fray and making good their escape.

The Tuckers were lucky. Jim's wound was through and through, but he lost a lot of blood. Ben cleaned and bandaged his brother's wound when they were back in their cheap hotel room.

Muriel Stevens saw the robbers pull off their ski masks as they left the bank. The way the shorter one carried himself reminded her of the man she now thought of as the stranger. Muriel knew she had told him too much. *Even if I tell what I know, they won't be able to identify him.* She thought, Some things are best kept secret.

The brothers stopped in Goleta, a small town outside Santa Barbara, until things cooled down. As Jim rested and regained strength, Ben wandered around the picturesque village until he found the local public library. He borrowed several books using a fake ID card, including his all-time favorite, *Riders of the Purple Sage.* One day, at lunch, Ben listened as two old men talked at the next table. One pointed across the street at an old bank building. "I'm not kidding. The robber walked in as bold as day with a big-ass six-shooter."

"When was that?"

"I told you afore, ten years ago, 1931. The first bank robbery in Santa Barbara County of modern times." For emphasis, the old man pointed, "Occurred right there at the County National Bank."

"Come on, Walt, there's more to the story."

"Well, the guy got less than fifty bucks for his troubles, and they never caught him."

"What'd they do about it?"

"They didn't do nothin'," Walt snorted.

"Whadda you mean?"

Walt finished, "I mean nothin'. They didn't put in alarms or hire a guard or anything. Still haven't. And the fools have a lot more money now that so many Hollywood stars have homes here and Montecito."

Ben told Jim about the conversation he had overheard. Jim mulled it over for a few hours before saying, "I've got plenty of free time while my arm heals."

"What do you mean?"

"I want to hit the bank."

"Are you out of your mind?"

"Look, this one should be easy enough to figure out. I'll take a few days, put it together, and if you don't like it, we'll head on up north."

Their most significant obstacle in Jim's planning was the getaway. Santa Barbara is situated against the coastal mountains. The only escape route was U.S. Highway 101.

"If we go north or south, the cops will set up a roadblock and stop every car. We wouldn't have a chance of escaping," Ben said.

"I've got it figured. The cops will be looking for two guys in a getaway car, right? So we boost a fancy rig, drive it a few blocks and switch to a second car. You throw your coat away and walk back to the motel. Instead of a robber wearing a dark coat, you'll be wearing a fancy cowboy shirt and a ten-gallon hat."

"Okay, what about you?"

"I take the second car three or four blocks and switch to a third one, another three or four blocks. I park and change my shirt, walk a block to a bus stop, and come back here."

"Then what?"

"Our same routine for a couple of days, then we take a Greyhound bus to Frisco."

Ben returned his library book and checked out another Zane Grey and *The Log of a Cowboy* by Andy Adams. Close to four hundred pages long, he hadn't finished it by the time Jim's arm was healed. Jim's plan was similar to that of the 1931 robbery, except for two robbers. The Tuckers took it over when they robbed the Goleta Branch of the Santa Barbara County National Bank. Jim's plan went off without a hitch.

From San Diego up the West Coast to Eureka, newspapers reported the recent Los Angeles and Goleta bank robberies. An Associated Press reporter in Los Angeles picked up on the similarity in the robbers' descriptions and their modus operandi. His story went out on the wire to every state in the Pacific Northwest.

Paul Carter was enjoying his morning coffee when his captain walked in unannounced. "Hey, Paul, you seen *The Oregonian* today?"

"Nope."

"I'm sure the Tucker brothers are hitting banks down in California."

"How's that?"

"Take a look at the Associated Press story on page two."

Carter spent less than a minute examining the article before slapping a hand on his desk, spilling his coffee. "Damn, Captain. You're right. That has to be them."

15

DETECTIVE LIEUTENANT CARTER REACHED out to the Tuckers' parole officers. "I know they killed Ed and are robbing banks, but I can't prove it." Not anxious to roust their well-behaved parolees, both agreed to conduct a parole search in a half-hearted effort to find evidence tying the Tuckers to the death of Ed, Carter's old informant, and any bank robberies.

Carter wanted to be in on both parole searches, but it wasn't to be. The parole officer in Redding and the local police had no history with the Tuckers or Detective Carter.

"I don't see any reason to have an out-of-state police officer along on a search of a California parolee. I talked with Redding PD. They don't want you either. If we turn up anything connected to Oregon, I'll let you know."

Oakland was a different matter.

Inspector George Cramer, who had helped

Carter in Piedmont, remembered him and welcomed him with a smile and handshake. "Hey, you know these guys better than anyone else. The Oakland Oaks are in town, and we'll take in a ballgame."

"What about Ben Tucker's parole officer?"

"He's a good guy, and I'll give him a heads up."

"Thanks, George. I'll be down next week. I haven't seen the Oaks play in a year or so."

The searches turned up nothing. Had they searched the attics, the results would have been different—cash and guns. Rifling the Tuckers' apartments accomplished one thing. It confirmed what the brothers thought; someone was gunning for them.

Carter couldn't leave things alone; the teletypes describing the Los Angeles and Santa Barbara robberies intrigued him. *The Tuckers could be the robbers*. He reached out to both police departments. They expressed interest but did not waste energy trying to solve their cases. The FBI's response was similar. "These guys have no history of bank robbery. You got a hard-on for them?"

Bank of America was interested. The bank lost a sizeable amount of cash, somewhere around five thousand, and one of their robbery suppression investigators had been shot. So, they assigned bank detectives to investigate both robberies and sent teams to surveil the Tuckers and see if they did anything criminal. When the brothers were away from their homes, the bank detectives broke in and searched them. Although pros who did their best to leave no trace, Jim knew someone had been through his place when he saw a slight disturbance in the dust around a reading lamp. On the way to his barber, he spotted a tail and several other surveillance team members. After a haircut, Jim went home, recovered his stash of money and guns, lost the tail, stole a car, and drove to Oakland. He waited until dark before slipping up to Ben's back door.

Ben, likewise, had found signs of a search at his place. "I don't know who's onto us, but it's getting a bit warm around here." They talked all night. At first light, Ben located a tail of his own. It was time to disappear. The papers were filled with talk of war. Everywhere people looked, they could see preparation for the inevitable hostilities. As convicted felons, they could not join any of the armed services. They figured if they gave false names to a recruiter, they could get into one of the services and vanish.

Jim had an idea. "If we get birth certificates for dead men, we could enlist together."

"They'll take our fingerprints. Sooner or later, they'll find out who we are," said Ben.

"Yes, they will, but they, whoever they are, should have given up looking for us by then. All that will happen is we'll get kicked out."

They slipped the remaining tail and took a bus to San Diego the following day. They split up and arranged to meet at a coffee shop at noon.

Jim visited Holy Cross Cemetery and searched for a grave marker of an infant or young child born and died the same year and within four years of his birth. Jim figured the odds of being local were good with such a young child buried in San Diego. Jim found a marker for James Dean, born July 9, 1914, who died three months later. *Perfect.*

Ben chose the city-owned Mount Hope Cemetery. The first grave marker he checked looked good, but the next looked even better. Benjamin Alexander had been born the same year as Ben and died within months. *This should do the trick. God willing, and the creek don't rise.*

Jim arrived at the coffee shop first. "Coffee, please, black." The waitress looked him over, head to toe, and smiled before hurrying off.

Returning moments later, she smiled and said, "Here you go, good-looking. You live around here?"

"No, visiting."

"How nice. I get off at six."

"Sorry, I'm waiting for my brother."

"Fantastic. My girlfriend's off tonight." She turned with a flip of her hair and an exaggerated sway of her hips as she sashayed away.

Ben came in a few minutes later, and they compared names. "We're lucky we found dead boys with our first names," Jim said. "It'll make things easier."

"What should we join?" San Diego, a Navy and Marine town, gave them options. "If we join up, we disappear right away." Ben continued, "I don't know how to swim, and I sure as hell don't want to be on a ship." They chose the Marines.

When the waitress brought their lunch orders, her blouse revealed more cleavage. "He's even cuter than you. You wanna go out tonight?"

Ben responded before Jim could open his mouth. "It sounds good. Where do we meet you?"

"I'll write it down for you. We'll see you boys at seven."

Finished with lunch, they headed to the San Diego County Clerk's office. It turned out their choices had been born in the county. Ben had been in line a few people ahead of Jim. When he requested a certified copy of the birth certificate for Benjamin Alexander, the clerk questioned him. "Who are you, and why do you want a copy of this birth certificate?"

Caught off guard, Ben stammered, "What do you mean?"

"I mean, who are you? Why do you want a certified copy of this birth certificate? Do I have to spell it out for you?"

"I'm his uncle. Ben died, and we have the death certificate. Now we need the birth certificate."

"Why?"

"It turns out my father, his grandfather, took out a small life insurance policy on the boy. The insurance company has a copy of the death certificate, and now they want the birth certificate."

The clerk softened, "Sorry. That'll be $3.25. Do you want a receipt?"

He handed over the money. "A receipt would be fine. I hope the insurance company will give it back to me."

"Don't hold your breath. Those insurance guys are all scavengers. It'll be ready for pick up after nine tomorrow. Sorry for your loss."

Jim had a story in place but didn't need it. The clerk said, "That'll be $3.25. You want a receipt?" He was told to return the following day for the certified copy.

Their next stop was a Marine recruiting office. The Marine sergeant was happy to get a pair of healthy men eager to join. Down on his quota, these two would help get the lieutenant off his back.

"Can we stay together?"

"Yes. If you enlist as buddies, you will go to boot camp together. You must bring your birth certificates and be ready to get on the bus. If you're here by 10:00 a.m. tomorrow, we'll have your enlistment papers complete by eleven, sworn in by lunch, and by one, you'll be on the train." The Marine Corps had recruit training at Parris Island, South Carolina. "Boot camp starts as soon as you get back there."

They met the waitress and her girlfriend as planned. After dancing and drinking, they took the girls to a cheap motel and spent the night. They were at the county clerk's office when it opened, at the recruiting office an hour later, and in the Marines by lunch. The recruiter said, "You'll remain together through your first assignment."

Boot camp was challenging but not as severe as the brothers had anticipated. To the drill instructors, they were ordinary Marine recruits. Four weeks into the seven-week boot camp, they and the other recruits in the training battalion, packed up their equipment and marched with full packs to the rifle range. With a month of strenuous training behind them, the recruits covered the distance with no discomfort. Ben, a southpaw, learned to fire left and right-handed.

Decades later, Ben described what they found at the camp to Detective Smith. "We covered the distance at double time. The tough part was a half-mile in dry sand. As we approached a low rise, the camp came into view—old and worn."

"How big was it? I understand they had something like fifteen to twenty different rifle and pistol ranges?"

"Nah, that was later, during the war. We had a thirty-nine-target range, and it was pretty well beaten up. The tents for us recruits were all in one area. They had buildings for the officers and drill instructors. Did you have DIs in your officer training?"

"Yes, we did. Our DIs were like yours, but they took immense pleasure in humiliating officer candidates," Smith replied. "How many of you were at the rifle ranges, Ben?"

"Back then, it was small. The Corps increased in size after Pearl Harbor. Our training battalion was made up of four companies. Fifty recruits formed a platoon with a DI and an assistant."

"How did the two of you do at firearms training?"

"We qualified as expert marksmen with

the M1 Garand and the Colt Model 1911 .45 pistol. We thought we were hot stuff."

"What happened after boot camp? Did you get the usual thirty-day leave?"

Ben laughed, "I wish. A couple of days before we were scheduled to graduate, reveille sounded at oh-two-thirty, and the battalion assembled at oh-three-hundred. All the officers, NCOs, and even the major were there. As soon as we fell in ranks, the major told us training was over. Everyone, including officers and NCOs, was now part of a provisional battalion assigned to the 4th Marines. The major ordered us to get some chow and report back by oh-five-thirty ready to deploy. "We didn't know what to think. Nobody did. We were on parade at oh-five-thirty and aboard buses by oh-six-hundred hours."

"What happened?"

"We were assigned to the 4th Marines and shipped to the Philippines."

"Shit."

"Our battalion rode buses until they put us on a train to New York and then on an old passenger ship. I don't know the name. We sailed to Panama, through the canal, and then to the Philippines."

"How was the trip?"

"I was fine, no problem, but my brother was seasick all forty days."

"Shit!"

"Tell me about it. We wound up on Corregidor. December 7, 1941, the Japs attacked Pearl Harbor—we were in World War II."

Months after the Tuckers enlisted, a newly assigned sergeant at the San Diego Marine Corps recruiting station received an official notice from 8th and I, United States Marine Corps Headquarters, Washington, D.C. The fingerprint check on enlistee James Dean showed he was a convicted felon named James Tucker. A few days later, a similar communique arrived identifying enlistee Benjamin Alexander, real name Benjamin Tucker, also a convicted felon. Not sure what to do, the sergeant asked the officer-in-charge, a recently minted reserve second lieutenant. "Sir, these FBI notices are for two men who enlisted together. They've finished boot camp by now. What should I do with the notes?"

The OIC said, "Give them to me. I'll handle it." The FBI notices went to the bottom of his pending stack and were still on the pile when the young lieutenant was transferred six months later.

The new OIC, an experienced and efficient officer, went through the pending file. The pair had been sent to Parris Island. He forwarded the notices with a note, "Discharge these men." The staff officer who received the documents was busy transforming a peacetime training camp into one at war.

"Private Dean, I want you to take a patrol out, probe the Japs' strength to the north. And while you're at it, bring back any food you come across."

"Yes, Sarge. Who do I take?"

"Pick three volunteers."

Jim Tucker selected his brother and two other Marines. Three hundred yards into the jungle, the men spotted a Japanese machine gun. "Ben, move forward and see if they are supported. If there are no other Japs, let me know if we can kill or capture them."

Ben crawled to within ten yards of the machine gun nest before reporting back. "Three, and they are not on the alert. One's asleep. We should be able to get within a few yards of their rear."

Jim Tucker took his team to the rear as Ben had suggested. On his signal, they attacked with bayonets and killed the three Japanese soldiers without firing a shot. After searching the bodies for any intelligence formation or maps, they disabled the Nambu machine gun, gathered up the soldiers' packs, and searched for food. The only food they found was in the enemy soldiers' packs. Each contained a kilo sack of a rice and barley mixture and a small amount of the mixture in an open bag. In one pack, they located two bottles of sake.

While returning to their lines, they were pinned down by another machine gun.

"Ben, take the others and work your way behind the gun. Try to take them out like the other nest. I'll keep them busy."

"How you gonna do that?"

"Don't worry. In exactly fifteen minutes, oh-four-thirty hours, they will be busy. You attack."

Giving Ben time to get in position, Jim kept up intermittent fire. At oh-four-thirty, he exposed himself to the enemy fire and ran forward. The three other Marines attacked. The attack was successful, but Ben was stabbed with a bayonet in his left hip, and Jim suffered a grazing wound to his right arm.

One of the soldiers found a Zippo lighter with a Marine Corps logo stamped into its face in a Japanese sergeant's pocket. "Bastard killed one of ours," he said.

The patrol made it back to their unit. Jim's wound was cleaned and bandaged, and he returned to duty. Ben's wound was more serious.

"Private Alexander, your hip will never be the same. I'll clean your wound, stitch it up, and have you rest for a day before we send you back out. I'm sorry, son, you'll have a slight limp." Defending the island fortress, Corregidor was a twenty-four-hour-a-day job for the Tuckers.

A few weeks later, on May 6, 1942, General Jonathan Wainwright surrendered all the U.S. Troops in the Philippines to avoid the massacre the Japanese threatened if they refused. The Tuckers were prisoners of war.

"Let's run for it and join the guerrillas," Jim said.

Ben agreed but wanted to talk to their platoon's one remaining officer. "Captain, we want to run for it and keep up the fight."

"Boys, I sympathize with you, but we have our orders. Colonel Howard ordered all 800 of the 4th Marines to comply with General Wainwright's orders."

"What about you, sir? You're wounded?"

"Not as bad as you, Private Alexander. Besides, I intend to collect the remaining men of the platoon and lead the way wherever the Japs take us."

The 4th Marines joined those forced to walk 85 miles with only a cup of rice a day. It took six days. The captain's wound was worse than thought, and he couldn't maintain the pace. "Captain, Jim and I'll help you. Put your arms around our necks, and let's go."

By the fourth day, the captain was dead weight, barely alive. Even with the Tuckers' help, the officer was slowing the pace. A Japanese sergeant walked up behind the three men and shot the captain in the back of the head. The captain lay where he fell. At bayonet point, the Tuckers were forced to leave their murdered comrade and continue their journey into hell.

Surviving the Bataan Death March, they were held at the Cabanatuan Prisoner of War Camp. Aside from the meager portion of rice during the march, the Japanese did not feed the POWs. The only other food was what brave Filipinos managed to throw to the men whenever their guards were otherwise occupied, usually beating or murdering POWs. At Cabanatuan, their diet consisted of a cup or less of filthy rice a day and anything the men could scrounge or steal. Once or twice a month, their captors fed them a bowl of thin chicken or fish stew.

The Tuckers remained in the POW camp until early 1943, when the Japanese shipped them to Japan. Their reward for staying somewhat healthy was to become slave labor. Transported on an overloaded "Hell Ship" to Japan, they were assigned to the Hosokura labor camp near the town of Miyagi-Ken. This

POW camp provided slave labor for a Mitsubishi Materials mine. They remained there until liberated in August 1945.

Ben still carried his hand-carved barrel-stave cribbage board from their Georgia chain gang days. It was weather-worn and grayish-white from age. He had never stopped using wooden match sticks for pegs. Ben gambled with his fellow POWs, winning enough to keep the brothers in cigarettes and enough food to stay almost healthy.

Returning to the United States on the U.S. Navy Hospital Ship Hope (AH-7), they arrived in San Francisco in November. Rehabilitated at Oak Knoll Naval Hospital, found fit for duty in January 1946, they were discharged.

Three weeks before his discharge, orders arrived at Oak Noll Naval Hospital for PFC James Dean. He had been promoted to Sergeant days before May 6, 1942, when U.S. Lieutenant General Jonathan Wainwright surrendered all U.S. troops in the Philippines to the Japanese. This gave Jim a considerable amount of back pay.

A month later, the FBI notices arrived. The hospital corpsman acting as company clerk read them. He checked and found the brothers had been released with honorable discharges. Their files revealed both suffered wounds at Corregidor and survived the Bataan Death March, the Cabanatuan POW Camp, and slave labor in Japan. Both men were long gone; the corpsman tossed the notices in the burn bag.

The day the FBI notice to discharge James Dean arrived, orders came through that Sergeant James Dean had been awarded the Purple Heart Medal and the Bronze Star. The citation read in part:

. . . pleasure in presenting the Bronze Star Medal to Sergeant, then Private First Class, James Dean for heroic achievement in action against hostile Japanese forces on April 17, 1942 . . . his unit encountered intense hostile fire. Sergeant Dean directed his unit to a location from which to attack the enemy position. Sergeant Dean then exposed himself to the enemy fire enabling his unit to destroy the threat. His personal bravery and devotion to duty are in keeping with the highest traditions of military service and reflect credit upon himself, his unit, and the United States Marine Corps.

Taking a cab from Oak Knoll to San Francisco, the brothers got a room and prepared for a night on the town. "What's it like being a civilian named Ben Tucker?"

"It's the best day of my life, and having

four years back pay in my pocket doesn't hurt."

"Amen. Best we keep our Marine names, at least for a while."

A few weeks of the good life found the brothers low on money. "Well Ben, what do you think we ought to do? Should we get back to work or go straight?"

They had few options with no trade other than as criminals, Marines, and slave labor miners. "We rob banks, and I'm ready to get back to work." Within months, they had robbed several local banks. The banks were easy targets but produced small takes. Ben was restless. "We're beating ourselves to death and not making enough to live on. We need a big score."

"What do you suggest?"

Ben responded, "We got more from Bank of America in Los Angeles than any of these piece-a-shit neighborhood banks."

Jim wasn't anxious to take on the bank that had not only got him shot but had detectives itching for the chance to shoot him again. "The risks are worse than with the local banks."

Ben insisted. Jim caved. "Okay, but we have to plan like never before."

Secure that they were no longer wanted, Jim went to work planning a robbery. Avoiding Los Angeles, he selected a Bank of

America branch in San Diego. "The big branches have more money but are likely to have armed detectives. This branch has six teller stations and one merchant window, not big enough for detectives."

"You're probably right," Ben agreed and, as usual, when Jim reconnoitered a bank, went off to visit a library.

On the day of the robbery, following weeks of planning, they strolled up to the front door and looked in. With no danger in sight, they donned their masks. Ben said, "Let's go." From the second they entered the bank, Jim felt something was wrong.

Ben walked to the commercial teller and announced the robbery after showing his forty-five. The teller did something neither brother had ever seen. She dropped to the floor behind the counter. Ben, stunned, glanced at Jim. "What the hell?"

Jim felt a gun at the small of his back. "Don't move, or I'll kill you."

Another man accosted Ben with a sawed-off shotgun, saying the same words. "Don't move, or I'll kill you." Within seconds, they were on the floor, their masks removed, hands cuffed behind their backs. Uniformed San Diego police officers came through the door. FBI agents arrived an hour later and took them into federal custody.

The bank anti-robbery detectives moved from branch to branch throughout the state using three or four-man teams. Bad luck was following the Tuckers, and a four-person crew was in place.

Jim's assumptions had proven wrong, terribly wrong. The first time the Tuckers robbed Bank of America, Jim got shot. This, their second Bank of America robbery, resulted in a lengthy prison term.

Booked into jail as James Dean and Benjamin Alexander, they thought they had a chance at bail. But the FBI was quick in getting their fingerprints matched. Jim and Ben were charged under their true names before their bail hearing. The brothers faced state and federal charges for armed robbery, possessing a firearm by a felon, and having prior felony convictions. They had no chance of acquittal and faced a potential sentence of forty years to life. They asked their court-appointed attorneys, "Can you get us a deal if we cop a plea?" The offer was twenty-five years in federal prison. The deal did not allow them to serve time together. Separated for the first time in their lives, Jim was sent to McNeil Island, Washington, and Ben to Leavenworth, Kansas.

16

DETECTIVE NOAH BECKER INVITED Al Smith to meet with him in San Leandro. The two detectives couldn't have been more different; Smith, older, college-educated, and a Marine veteran of the Korean War. Still in his twenties, Becker was a Navy veteran of the Vietnam War with no college. Yet the two were alike where it mattered. Both wanted to solve crimes and put bad guys in jail.

Becker should have known something was awry when telling his boss, Detective Sergeant Rodney Murphy, about the invitation. Instead of him and Detective Smith sitting at the sergeant's desk in the bullpen, Murphy said, "We'll meet in the chief's conference room."

Murphy told Becker that he was taking on the old San Leandro case now that it had a connection to the San Mateo robbery. "Becker, this is beyond your experience. I don't want you getting in over your head. I'll run the investigation. You watch and learn."

"No sweat, Sarge. I'm here to learn. I'll do whatever you want." Murphy didn't notice that Becker was pissed.

Murphy had in mind taking the credit if the investigation succeeded in the robbers' arrest. *If it turns to shit, the kid takes the hit.*

Smith sized up the situation in minutes. He was experienced enough to realize Murphy was like his lieutenant—in for the glory, out for the work. The minute Murphy finished an account of the San Leandro robbery Smith said, "Your holdup sounds much like ours, Sarge. I'm happy to run through the details for you, or if you wish, Becker and I can grab a cup and see if there are any differences." Murphy nodded, and Smith continued. "Your call. We go through it now or save you some time and have Detective Becker update you later."

Murphy replied, "Sounds good. I've got plenty to do." Without another word, he left the two alone.

They were sitting in a booth at Emil Villa's twenty minutes later. Becker told Smith he had put one over on Murphy.

"Well, kid, I don't have time for his type. Let's get down to business. I read the old teletype. It was interesting."

"How'd you find it?" Becker asked.

"I didn't. One of our records gals did. When I wrote the teletype for our robbery, I sent it out, hoping someone would call. No one did. But our midnight records gal remembered seeing one from years before. She's smart, found a copy, and here I am."

"After you called, I pulled the old case and told Murphy."

"What'd Murphy say?"

"He says reading teletypes is a waste of time. Murphy took the case away from me when I told him you called with a similar robbery. I get to do the leg work, and he'll get the credit if we solve the case."

"Well, kid, do you care who takes credit, or do you want to get these fuckers?"

"I want to get 'em."

An hour later, Smith and Becker agreed—the robbery team was experienced, and there was a good chance the same pair had committed both robberies. They had little doubt these guys had done time. Smith believed it went beyond doing time. "From the way they hit the bank, I'm sure these two have done hard-time, and they've done it together. They didn't talk much, but one witness said something about a southern accent."

Becker agreed. "With that accent, I doubt they're West Coast. It could make things tougher. We should go back at least twenty years looking for two guys pulling jobs together. If I'm right, there'll be breaks when they served time. Hell, we might even find an arrest record. What about Murphy? What do we tell him?"

"Tell him I'm doing some research. I've promised to keep him in the loop through you. Should give us a little time to get copies of the robbery teletypes for the last twenty years." They headed to their respective offices with a promise to meet in a week.

When Becker returned to his office, reached his desk, and took a seat, Sergeant Murphy asked, "What'd you two talk about?"

17

EVEN AS LONG AS their sentences were, serving time in federal prison wasn't hard on the Tuckers. Compared to the brutality of the Georgia chain gang and the Japanese POW and slave labor camps, Jim described it as a walk in the park in a letter. Ben wrote back, "If I didn't have my cribbage board and a good prison library, it would be boring as hell."

Ben Tucker was paroled in 1966 after twenty years, and Jim was released six months later, with time off for good behavior. The Tuckers were still bank robbers. Free again, they plied their trade, robbing banks, working undisturbed for four years.

Hoping for a big haul, the brothers decided on a Crocker National Bank. There were three branches in Alameda County. By process of elimination and ease of escape, they settled on the Bay Fair Mall Branch in San Leandro. The location of a stand-alone structure in a large parking lot gave the

Tuckers options. "We have seven escape routes, but the sheriff's office is only four blocks away," Ben said.

"San Leandro has its own police department, and the station is three miles away. The alarm will go to the police, not the sheriff. We'll have time."

Always the restless one, Ben suggested, "Let's hit the place now and take our chances."

Jim rejected the idea. "I'm not rushing ever again. From now on, we need to learn everything possible before we hit a place."

Over the next three weeks, Jim became an expert on Crocker National. He visited local libraries and read every article he could find on the bank and the police. Ben went along with his brother but spent his time reading westerns and finishing Owen Wister's *The Virginian*, even though the story and the passage of time were a bit slow before Jim had a plan for their next robbery.

Jim learned that, unlike Bank of America, Crocker did not have robbery suppression teams.

An article in the Oakland Tribune detailed modern police technology and modernization in law enforcement communications that were unavailable when they went to prison in 1946. All police cars had two-way radios. One article said, "Although police communication is improved, and with it the public's safety, there is a vulnerability. It's possible to keep track of the police with scanners."

A visit by Jim to Radio Shack gave them an edge they never expected. "What can you tell me about police scanners?"

The young store clerk was a wealth of information. "Motorola recently came out with a new transistor-equipped police radio, and San Leandro has them in their police cars. They have two channels."

"And the sheriff?"

"If you want to listen to the San Leandro Police and the sheriff, you'll need a scanner with three crystals."

"Okay, set up two of your best scanners with all three crystals."

After a week of eavesdropping on the San Leandro Police scanner, Jim told Ben, "The cop working this area eats around 1:30 p.m. The good news is all six of the cops on duty go to the police station at 3:45 p.m."

No longer as anxious, Ben wanted to go to a concert at the Fillmore Auditorium before hitting the bank. "Otis Redding is playing on the twentieth, and the Grateful Dead on the twenty-first." Jim agreed, but only because they would have a final day of surveillance on the twenty-second if they hit the bank at 3:45 p.m. on Friday, December 23.

"Doesn't the bank close at three?"

"Nah, that's the beauty of it. They're open until four to accommodate the Christmas customers," Jim said. "The mall will be swarming with shoppers, and the parking lot will be full."

Ben added, "It might slow us down, but we'll get lost in the crowds with all the police at the other end of town."

Hours later, "Jim, you gotta hear this." Listening to the scanner, they heard officers talking on the investigation channel.

"I-29 for I-31."

"Go ahead for I-31."

"I am set up on the north side of Macy's. Where are you?"

"I-31, I'm on the east side by Round Table Pizza. I'm high enough to see most of the cars in the East 14th Street parking lot."

"Jim, what the hell's going on?"

"I'm not sure. Let me listen."

A few hours later, Jim had it figured out. "The mall has complained about customers' cars broken into for Christmas presents. The cops take reports of thefts every day. It looks like they're staking out the place in unmarked cars." His eyes drawn into a hawkish glare, Jim added, "Three weeks of work down the drain."

Ben usually followed his older brother's lead, but this time, he disagreed. "Before we chuck it in, let's think it over for a day or so." Listening the following day gave them hope. "Pay attention to this." Jim was ready to move on when Ben explained what the cops were saying. "Look, a couple of times a day, they spot some dumb shit breaking into a car."

"So, what?" Jim demanded.

"Both cops swoop down and grab them."

"So?"

"When they make an arrest, they take the dummy to the police station."

"Like I said, so what?"

"Jim, listen to me. Each time, they're gone for at least an hour. We wait until they make an arrest and go to the police station. That's when we hit."

"Son of a bitch. It might work." Jim's anger vanished.

For three days, they took note as the cops arrested car burglars. Each time the cops went to the police station, they stayed for an average of ninety minutes. "Ben, you hit the nail on the head. We go Friday."

Friday morning, the Bay Area was clear and cold, but by noon heavy clouds filled the sky. Besides the scanner, the Tuckers kept the radio on, listening for any hint of rain. Usually, the rain was welcome, but not if it stopped thieves from breaking into cars. Moreover, if the thieves came, the cops might not see them in a downpour. The two plainclothes cops would remain in the area if that didn't happen. At 1:00 p.m., the rain began in earnest with intermittent wind gusts.

Jim wanted to put the job off for a week. Ben objected. "If we go today, they'll have a lot of cash from the merchants. Next week will be after Christmas and before New Year's. They won't have as much on hand."

Jim agreed to wait until 4:00 p.m. but no later. "After four, the other cops will be on the streets. We could have three or four of them around here."

"Yeah, okay. If we don't go by four, we don't go," Ben conceded.

The day dragged on with no let up in the foul weather. With nothing happening, the plainclothes officers chatted, bored. At 2:00 p.m., they drove across the street to Winchell's Donut shop. Thirty minutes later, they returned to their hiding spots.

At 2:45 p.m., Jim, long accustomed to the drudgery of surveillance, portrayed a calmness belied by the inward pressure he wrestled to keep under control. *Are we doing the right thing? Should we pack it in and get out of here? No, we need to hold on for another hour.*

Ben couldn't conceal his agitation. "Time's running out. We have to hit the bank or call it a day."

"No. You need to relax. Keep your ear to the damn scanner. We hold until four."

By then, it was 3:15 p.m., and the rain had increased. At 3:30 p.m., Jim was beginning to think they should pack it in. "We should wrap it up and come back next week."

"You said we wait until four," Ben reminded him.

Before Jim could respond, the scanner crackled to life.

"I-31 for I-29." After a brief exchange about two possible suspects peering in a late model Cadillac window, the radio remained silent for what seemed an eternity but was less than three minutes.

"I-29, we have two in custody. No cover is needed. We've talked with the owner of the Cadillac. She's on her way to the station. We're following with the suspects." Both Tuckers heaved a sigh of relief. Within seconds, the day shift officers began announcing they were out of service at the police station for the shift change. Looking at each other and nodding, Jim and Ben started for the bank. It was 3:46 p.m.

Soaked to the bone after walking less than

fifty feet from the getaway car to the entrance, Ben said, "Let's go." Pulling on their masks, they entered the bank. A half dozen people were lined up in front of the teller windows in the lobby. Ben walked to the merchant window.

Jim proclaimed in a commanding voice, "This is a robbery. Everyone down on the floor." One of the customers started to object, drawing his attention. Dealing with the teller, Ben seemed unmindful. Able to handle any problem within the bank, Jim strode to the loudmouth, the solitary person still standing. The man towered above him and became louder. When within arm's reach and raising his pistol with lightning speed, Jim hit the man across the left side of his head, knocking him to the ground. "You stupid shit." Then he stepped back to the door. The other people were spread out across the bank floor. The distraction allowed an alert teller to push the alarm.

The robbers were in and out in less than ninety seconds. They heard the sound of sirens through the downpour. Letting out a sigh, five minutes later, Jim drove away at the speed limit. "That was too close."

Ben laughed, "It ain't over yet, brother."

Fifteen minutes later, they were in Hayward and had pulled off Mission Boulevard into the large, out-of-sight parking lot behind Frenchy's Nightclub. They rubbed down the rental car to remove any fingerprints, then hopped into a second rental they'd stashed earlier and drove south in the heavy Nimitz Highway traffic. Ben, flush with excitement, held up a wad of bills. Jim scowled at him, "Are you out of your mind? All we need is for a highway cop to see you holding a handful of cash. Every cop within fifty miles is looking for us."

A few minutes later, they drove into an underground parking lot. After wiping the car down, they walked up one level where Ben's old Dodge station wagon, complete with a kiddy car seat, was parked. Thumbing through the money later, Ben commented, "Not bad for an afternoon's work."

Still upset with his brother for flashing the cash in the getaway car, Jim retorted, "You mean more like a month's work for some of us."

After a moment of glares, then almost in unison, "Screw you." It wasn't often the brothers argued so vehemently. Jim was the most upset. "I'm getting out of here." Leaving the hotel room, he slammed the door.

Ben thought, He'll be back.

Jim didn't come back that night, and Ben could not sleep until the room phone rang around two in the morning.

"Hey brother, I'm sorry," Jim said.

Ben said the same thing and then, "You coming back?"

"Nah, I'm hunkered down at a cheap hotel, the Washington, in San Leandro. Meet me down the street at Chuck Burgers at nine."

"I'll see you there, and I'll bring the money. I'm done with this place."

After breakfast, they went to the Washington Hotel and finished counting. They were surprised. It was one of the biggest hauls they had ever taken, and each walked away with over $10,000.

Ben was excited. "I like Fremont, and once I have enough money put away, I want to buy a house."

"Why?" asked Jim.

"I've never owned a place of my own. I want a place to come back to. Don't you?"

"I'll think about it after I get back up to Oregon. I always liked Marshfield, and besides, by now, anyone who ever knew us up there is either gone or dead."

Jim headed for Oregon, and Ben started a small landscaping business. It gave him a legitimate source of income through which to launder his money. Once the small business was flourishing, Ben made a sizeable down payment on a new tract home in Fremont, a considerable one but not large enough to raise eyebrows.

Back at Marshfield, Jim was surprised to find the town's name had changed during his twenty years in prison. It was now Coos Bay.

Not wanting to appear flush with cash, Jim bought a used Ford pickup truck. Picking up a tent and camping gear, an outdoorsman at heart, Jim drove to the Paul Bunyan Park, where he had occasionally camped before going to prison. Even it had changed names in the intervening years; it was now Mingus Park. Using a small-time real estate agent, Jim found a medium-sized hunting cabin built of logs with electricity and running water on a seldom-used road five miles east of town. Jim Tucker purchased it for cash using his Marine Corps name, James Dean.

Over the next four years, the Tuckers robbed banks throughout California. For no reason they could explain, they did not ply their trade in Oregon. Never greedy, they lived low-key lives. Jim had no neighbors closer than a half-mile. Aside from an occasional visit to the whorehouses in Portland, he lived a quiet life. Ben didn't cultivate friendships with his neighbors. Always a quiet man, he ran his landscaping service and did his own yard work. Whenever a neighbor inquired about his services, Ben had one of the Mexicans working for him—most illegal aliens—give the neighbor a reasonable estimate. Ben dated but never entered into a serious relationship.

"I need to get to the animal shelter," Ben said. "It's my regular day. You know that."

"I know. I don't know why you continue to volunteer after all these years. It was only a mangy cur." Jim had never felt sorry about the dog they sacrificed those many years ago while serving time on that dreadful Georgia chain gang.

Ben had been helping out at the animal shelter since buying his house in Fremont. "I used to have nightmares about that damn dog we killed. Helping save Lucky and other dogs keeps the visions away."

"Aren't you afraid you'll be spotted and arrested?"

"No, I've been there so long. Besides, no one knows where I live, and most folks only know me as Ben, the friendly guy who mops and keeps the kennels clean." Completing the call, Ben hurried off for his weekly attempt at redemption for killing the dog in Georgia. An act for which atonement would never be possible. The thought of adopting another dog had crossed his mind, but a bank robber's erratic life made caring for an animal difficult at best. *I could never put a dog in a kennel for weeks at a time. It's too much like a prison.*

"Okay, Ben, I'll let you go, but don't forget we have a reservation at the Stardust next week. I'll pick you up on the way."

Twice a year, Ben and Jim vacationed together. In December, they spent time in Las Vegas. They gambled, whored, and enjoyed the shows. They went on guided big game hunts in the Wyoming and Montana backcountry during the summer months. Neither had lost their expert skills with long guns or forty-fives. After an expensive few weeks in Las Vegas, they decided it was time for a decent score. "Jim, it's cold and damp in Oregon. Why not stay with me?"

"Okay, I got nothing planned, and the cabin's already closed up." Jim suggested they pick a target in the Bay Area.

Ben said, "I don't mind, but no bank anywhere near my place."

"You're right. How about across the bay?" Jim agreed.

When they got to Ben's house, Jim decided to stay at a motel on the peninsula. "No sense in drawing attention with a stranger at your place, and I'll find the right bank and work easier if I don't have to fight the traffic back and forth."

18

IT WAS IN 1936 when Ed had been Detective Paul Carter's informant. And with the help of the Piedmont and Oakland California Police Departments, they had taken down the infamous Safeway robbery gang. Carter still smarted from the light sentence the Tuckers received.

"Joe, I know the Tuckers killed Ed within a month of his parole in 1941."

"You may be right, but the coroner ruled the snitch's—I mean, Ed's death was an accidental overdose," said Captain Doll.

Carter knew that around 1932, the brothers had been suspected of the mysterious death of a violent convict who had assaulted Ben while the Tucker brothers were serving time on a Georgia chain gang.

"Over the years, I've done my best to keep track of the brothers. I lost the trail shortly before World War II. After the war, the brothers were arrested and sent to federal prison until paroled in 1966. The brothers jumped their parole after a few months. There had been a few bank jobs that sounded like them, but none in Oregon."

Doll said, "Paul, you gotta let it go."

"I can't."

Carter's rise to become Assistant Superintendent of the division was phenomenal. Spurning further advancement, he remained with the job and the investigators he loved. Sixty-three, approaching the mandatory retirement age and responsible for administrative duties, Carter still read the daily teletypes and put the information to good use. He had indoctrinated his secretary and Captain Joe Doll so well that they helped fill his notebooks with material from the 1930s to the present.

Not that Carter held a grudge—or maybe he did. Why else keep a separate file all these years for those sounding in the least like the Tucker boys?

Returning from a long overdue vacation in Hawaii, one his wife had insisted they take, Carter had to admit February on Waikiki Beach was far more pleasant than Salem that time of the year. He made up for the lost time by reviewing every felony case CID had picked up in his absence. It wasn't necessary as his heir-apparent, Captain Joe

Doll, had been in the division for a dozen years and was an outstanding investigator. *Besides, Joe's the best administrator in all OSP.*

Doll stopped by Carter's office to give his boss a concise but complete briefing. After they chatted for a few minutes over coffee, Doll left him alone.

The following morning, stopping in again, Doll said, "Hey, Boss, if you're caught up on the administrative crap, I've got a few things you might find interesting."

Peering over the top of his bifocals, Carter gave Doll a questioning glance.

"I've been keeping up on the teletypes in your absence and might even have one for your Tucker Brothers file."

"Joe, you always have had a better handle on those damned pieces of yellow paper than I ever did. Whatcha got that'll make me happy?"

"The Tucker boys hit a bank in California while you were laying around soaking up the Hawaiian sun," Doll replied, handing Carter a teletype.

ATTENTION ROBBERY UNITS
BANK ROBBERY
OCCURRED: 1520 HRS FRIDAY, FEBRUARY 13, 1970
VICTIM: BANK OF AMERICA, MOUNTAIN VIEW, CALIFORNIA

SUSPECT #1: UNK RACE MALE
MEDIUM HEIGHT WEARING SKI
MASK AND LONG SLEEVE "FREE
HUEY" SHIRT
SUSPECT #2: WMA MED HEIGHT
WEARING SKI MASK AND MAY
HAVE A LEG INJURY
WEAPONS: SUSPS ARMED WITH
.45 PISTOLS
VEHICLE: RENTAL CAR ABAN-
DONED NEARBY
LOSS: UNDETERMINED CASH
M.O.: SUSPS ENTER THE BANK
LOBBY WEARING SKI MASKS.
SUSP #1 ORDERS EVERYONE TO
GET DOWN ON THE GROUND.
SUSP #2 GOES TO THE BUSINESS
WINDOW: "DON'T PUT THE DYE
PACK IN THE BAG." BAG WAS AN
OLD BLACK BAG.
ANY INFORMATION CONTACT:
DETECTIVE AL SMITH
MOUNTAIN VIEW PD
TEL: (415) 555-3232

Carter read the teletype and slapped his
hands on his desk before opening a file
drawer and pulling out a thick, well-worn
folder. He glanced at the stack of teletypes
and said, "Joe, this could be them. Why
didn't you show me this yesterday? Never
mind. You did the right thing. I needed to get

caught up. Have you talked to this Detective Smith?"

"No way would I ever deny you the pleasure of reading this on your own. Put the phone on speaker when you call. I want to be part of the conversation."

"Thanks. Let's call them but hang on a second. I want to take a look at my Tucker file first."

Five minutes later, Smith came on the line, and Carter said, "Detective Smith, I'm Paul Carter with the Oregon State Police. Joe Doll's here with me on speakerphone."

"What can I do for you?"

"We're calling to share some information that might be of help. Have you heard of Jim and Ben Tucker?"

"I can't say as I have. Why do you ask?"

Carter explained he had been a detective for a while.

An amused Doll added, "If over forty years is a while."

"Okay, Joe, let me give Detective Smith the short version."

Once Carter finished, Smith agreed it was a good chance the Tuckers were his guys and told them about the 1966 San Leandro robbery. "I'm working with a San Leandro detective, Noah Becker. We're trying to tie the cases together."

Carter told him the San Leandro case

sounded like the Tuckers who were paroled earlier in the year.

Doll spoke up. "You got any physical evidence or good eyewitnesses?'

"We don't have a lot. I did get a few prints off the getaway car. They might or might not belong to them. Without a name to compare, I've held on to them."

Carter asked, "Can you take a ride over to Oakland PD? That's not far from you, is it?"

"Nah, less than an hour. It's a ten-minute drive for Becker."

"Good. They should have prints for the Tuckers from 1937 when we arrested them doing a Safeway job."

"Thirty-seven? Damn, you are old."

"I'm still young enough to come down and kick your butt." The three enjoyed a chuckle. Carter continued, "The newest photographs will be from 1966 when they were paroled out."

Smith gave Becker a call. "I may have a lead on our suspects. I got a call from some dicks in Oregon." Becker agreed to arrange to pick up the fingerprint cards from Oakland. Because the latent prints were for the Mountain View case, Becker would bring them and copies of the old booking photographs to

Smith the next day.

When Becker arrived at OPD, a reluctant old-timer worked the Identification Bureau Help Desk. "First off, you don't waltz in here and get our prints. You can request a fingerprint comparison from the lab, but they won't want to waste time on your caper."

Becker persisted and found his way to OPD's Robbery Detail. He ran into an inspector who had been an instructor when Becker attended the police academy. Now the young detective had to again put up with the familiar, "Whadda you need, kid?"

"I'm working a bank job with Al Smith over in Mountain View."

"Shit. Why didn't you tell me you're working with Al? Tell me what you need." The inspector was more than ready to help the young detective.

Even with the inspector's help, it took time. OPD had reorganized the entire department in the early sixties. Everything—prints, photos, evidence, anything from before 1960—was in storage. It took a week to find the case file, fingerprints, and photographs from the 1937 robbery. Once in hand, Becker called Smith. "I have the prints, copies of the reports, even the photographs, but there's a problem."

"What now?" Smith asked.

"Sergeant Murphy knows what I've been

doing. He knows about the stuff from OPD and wants to take charge."

After talking it over, they agreed Becker couldn't buck his sergeant. Smith said, "I'll call the prick and tell him I appreciate all he did getting the prints. I'll even mention how grateful my lieutenant is for his help. I'll explain that my district attorney wants the comparison done here because the latent prints are on a Mountain View case. I'll ask him if he wants to be there for the evaluation. I'll tell him it shouldn't take more than three or four hours."

"What does that do for me?"

"Maybe nothing, but I doubt Murphy will carry the prints over here and wait around. I bet he'll send you." And that is what happened.

Mountain View's expert had been comparing fingerprints for twenty years. When Al Smith came to him with the Tuckers' prints, the tech said, "Look, Al, I understand what you want. Half the other detectives are asking for the same. Everything's a rush, top priority. Leave them. I'll give you a call when I get to them." It took the promise of a bottle of Johnny Walker Black, but he agreed to do the examination. "It could still take hours. I don't want you hanging around. It'll slow me down. When I finish, I'll call." The tech ushered them out of the remodeled garage he called his lab that had once housed a police ambulance.

"How about lunch while we wait? My girlfriend's off today. We can meet her. You like Italian?" Smith said.

"Sounds good to me."

Smith called Bert, who was happy to meet them at Frankie, Johnnie, and Luigi Too! "After what you've told me about him, I want to meet this young man you think has a bright future as a detective," Bert said. They enjoyed an excellent lunch, as always, at this old family-owned restaurant. Bert noticed Smith didn't have his usual glass of wine, opting instead for iced tea. *This young man is a good influence.*

When they were leaving, she hugged Noah. Pulling Smith close, she kissed him and whispered, "I like him." Something she didn't do for any of Al's other friends or co-workers.

Back at the police station, Smith learned that the print tech had gone to lunch. They waited. Returning a short time later, he motioned for the two detectives to follow him to the lab, where he looked at the two with a huge grin. "Where's my Black Label? I have a good match and a so-so match on one of your guys. I compared all four with James Tucker and didn't get a match. Then on the third latent, I found six points of comparison for Benjamin Tucker. Still, we need at least twelve points for me to testify it's a positive identification."

Becker exclaimed, "I thought you had a good match?"

Smith glanced at him, "Ignore him, Noah. He doesn't get much done and always has to drag it out. So, if there is something, he takes his sweet time trying to impress."

"Okay, okay. I compared the fourth latent, the one at the top of the back of the mirror, and matched it with Ben Tucker's right index finger."

"And. What'd you find?"

Thrusting his chest out and raising both hands with fists closed, the technician almost shouted. "Eighteen ever-loving points, as clear as can be. You got your man."

Smith broke into a grin, gave the tech a bear hug, thanked him, and promised to have his Black Label on payday.

Back at Al's desk, Becker was in a great mood. Smith wasn't. "Al, what's wrong? You made one of them on prints?"

"Yes. We placed Ben Tucker in the getaway car, a rental. It might give us probable cause to arrest him, but it doesn't put him in the bank. It doesn't give us enough to prosecute. We gotta get more."

Smith called the Oregon State Police. "Assistant Superintendent Carter here."

"Al Smith calling. Hey, you never told me you're the Assistant Superintendent and me a pooh-butt detective."

"Don't worry, Al, we're all detectives at heart. I've got Joe here."

"Detective Noah Becker from San Leandro PD is here with me."

Carter interrupted before Smith could say anything else. "Noah, glad to meet you. I'm Paul Carter, and I've got Joe Doll here."

Smith and Becker explained what they had been doing and where they stood on the prints. All four agreed the Tuckers were responsible for the robbery but lacked the evidence to prosecute.

Carter spoke. "We know they've gone by their Marine Corps names at least once. They may be using those names. I'm betting they're living either in California or Oregon. Joe, can you get a statewide property search for these guys using their real and Marine Corps names?"

"Yes, sir, I can. I'll make it a priority assignment. It will take time, but we have troopers in all thirty-six counties. We should have answers back within a week."

Assistant Superintendent Carter directed his next question to Smith. "Can you do the same down your way?"

"We don't have an organization like yours. I'll do what I can, but I doubt we'll get any help from other agencies. I'll handle the counties here on the peninsula. Noah, could you take your side of the Bay?"

It's starting to come together. Smith was excited.

19

LUNCH WITH BERT AND Noah had been fun. Smith hadn't even needed a drink. Over dinner, telling Bert about the print results, she didn't express much interest. "That's nice. Are you staying over tonight?"

"I'd planned on it. Do you have something going on? You want me to go home or stay?"

"It's up to you."

Bert had been a little distant for a few weeks. She was still loving and caring, but something was missing. Their lovemaking was okay but lacked the passion they once shared. Over dinner, she responded to him but didn't lead the conversation. Smith loved how she could talk about the most trivial things and how she kept him interested and involved. She was a left-leaning Democrat, while Smith remained a staunch conservative. They often had heated debates over the way the politicians ran the country. There were fewer of these thought-provoking discussions, and he blamed himself. *I'm drinking too much. Bert wants to start a new life with a husband, home, and children. I've got to do something, or I'll lose her.* They finished dinner in silence.

"Hey, let me help with the dishes. Your choice, wash or dry?"

Bert smiled. "I'll wash. You never could get a dish clean."

Helping with the dishes—enjoying himself—Al made a life-changing decision. *It's time. I'll have to take the first step and see how it plays out.* Looking at the apartment kitchen, with hardly enough room for the two to work without bumping into one another, Smith knew. *It doesn't get any better than this.* He bumped Bert with his left shoulder, almost tipping her over.

"Uh," her head jerked back. "You trying to kill me?"

Al laughed, and she got angry before he said, "Roberta Jordan, I love you."

"I know," she said as she scrunched her shoulders up and forward. "Why the formal announcement? You've never called me Roberta."

Smith set the dry plate and towel on the countertop, took the dishrag from Bert's hand, and laid it next to the towel. Bert tilted her head to the side as Smith inched closer, their bodies almost touching. "Al, what is it? What's going on? What is it?"

His face aglow, his appearance was confounded by the beads of sweat on his forehead. "This isn't the right time. It's the wrong place, not the way it should be, but will you marry me?" Taking her silence as rejection, Smith went on; his voice squeaked. "I know I'm not much. I drink, I smoke, and I'm a workaholic. You could do a lot better."

Smiling, Bert looked into his face. "I see the man I want to spend the rest of my life with. Now shut up, you big lummox. Let me get a word in. It's my turn to talk."

Al started to back away but stumbled and reached for the sink top for support. He looked like a man on the verge of collapse. "Okay."

"Will I marry you? You bet I will." They began to cry as they hugged and kissed. An hour later, laughing, crying, kissing, and hugging on the couch, she said, "I want a church wedding."

"Jesus, Bert. We gotta start that now?"

"Hey, this will be my first and last wedding. I want it to be what I've always dreamed of."

Al knew better than to argue. "Yes, dear. Whatever you want. Dear." She punched him. "What a way to start a marriage. Getting the crap kicked out of me by a girl. Let's go to bed and celebrate."

"Because I agreed to marry you doesn't mean you can get me into bed anytime you want."

"Tonight it does." Smith added an exaggerated, "Dear." Enjoying a rare weekend off work together, they slept in and enjoyed an unhurried breakfast. Bert wore her regular sleepwear, a floor-length flannel nightgown.

After the night they met at Patty Dean's, Smith had never seen her wearing anything but modest attire. "Hey, honey, you remember the night we met at Patty's?"

Bending over to refill his coffee mug, she looked him square in the face. "Yes, I remember. Why?"

"You recall the dress you were wearing?"

Bert turned a bright red and stood straight up. "Yes."

"Well, I was curious." Unable to keep from staring, Smith said, "You're blushing."

With an indignant, "So," Bert turned to the coffee pot.

"So, what happened to the dress? I've never seen you wear it or anything like it again."

"Do you really want to know?"

"Yes. I wouldn't ask if I didn't."

Bert poured a cup of coffee, taking twice as long as usual, mixing in cream and sugar.

Once finished, she looked across the table at Al. "That wasn't the first time we met."

"Um, uh, are you sure?"

"Your memory is unbelievable. You honestly don't remember when we met?"

"Whadda you mean? I remember. I've never forgotten it or the way you dressed."

"That may be, but it was the third time we met."

"Nah. No, Bert." His mind was churning. "I'll never forget the night I met you."

"Oh, you found me forgettable, you big lummox. You think you can remember that far back?"

"Yes. Like I said, I'll never forget."

"Okay, what'd I tell you?"

"You told me you were an RN working for Patty."

"You're almost right. I said I got my RN, and Patty hired me."

"So, what's the difference?"

"The difference! I worked in the ER as a student nurse for a year."

"So?"

"Because Patty introduced us twice. You couldn't see a student nurse as anything but a kid."

"You sure as hell were no kid. You were all woman, and then some."

"No shit, Sherlock. You ought to be a detective."

"So, what does this have to do with the bloody dress?" Smith asked. "Look, I spotted you and asked Patty who you were."

"For a year, I tried to get your attention. As far as you cared, I was invisible."

"I must a been sick or something. How could anyone miss or forget meeting someone as fantastic as you?"

"You did, you big dummy."

"Okay. I must have been blind. How could anyone miss a girl as great looking as you?"

"You did, dummy. Anyway, I returned it to Macy's. You know I don't wear dresses like that."

"So, why'd you wear that dress?"

"Got your attention, didn't I?"

20

TROOPER KILPATRICK FOUND CAPTAIN Doll's suggestion to search for property owned by the brothers was reasonably straightforward in Oregon. He found three properties owned by someone named James Tucker and one belonging to Benjamin Tucker, then searched for James Dean and Benjamin Alexander. Kilpatrick found a listing for James Dean in Coquille, another in the rural area outside Coos Bay. There were four listings for Benjamin Alexander; one in Bandon, two in Charleston, and a fourth in Coos Bay.

Sometime later, "Ma'am, I have ten names with addresses. How do I make sure they are the current owners?"

"We put the cards in archives whenever there's a change of ownership. What you have should be correct."

Finished at the Tax Assessor's office, Kilpatrick called Captain Doll.

"Hi, Captain. This is Trooper Kilpatrick over in Coquille."

"Whatcha got for me?"

"I found ten properties owned by the four names you sent. That's a lot of possibilities for the people you want to find, but we can eliminate four right off the get-go. The same man and wife have owned those properties for over twenty years. I doubt they're who you want."

"Right. That leaves six. What do you have on the others?"

"I know the James Dean in Coquille. He's around twenty-five. He went to Marshville High School over in Coos Bay with my wife. He's not involved. I don't recognize the other five."

"Good work, Trooper. Check out those five and get back to me?"

"I'd love to, skipper, but I'm not sure my sergeant can spare me. It could take a full day."

"Okay, who's your sergeant? Is it Bill Whitmer?"

"Yes, sir."

"Okay, I'll call him. One of us will get back to you within the hour. If this turns out the way I think, Steve, you better be careful. These are dangerous men."

"Yes, sir. I will."

An hour later, Kilpatrick got a call from

Sergeant Whitmer. "What have you got yourself into, Stevie?"

"Following up on the assignment you gave me, Sarge."

"Sounds like good work and that you are definitely making headway. I'm off tomorrow, so Captain Doll gave me the okay to ride with you, so you're stuck with me. Check out an undercover car, wear casual clothes, and pick me up at home at eight in the morning."

Kilpatrick arrived at his sergeant's house at eight sharp. The young trooper was a former Marine, a recruiting sergeant's dream, a poster boy for the Corps, and now for the Oregon State Police. At six-five, he weighed an even two hundred pounds, and there was not an ounce of fat on the man. He was intelligent and what Hollywood called "ruggedly handsome." His plainclothes included a Stetson.

"Hey, Tex, are we going on a cattle roundup?" Whitmer joked. "Let's stop at Mom's Diner. I'm hungry, and we need to talk about the case."

Over breakfast, and before getting down to business, Whitmer said, "You know the history of Mom's?"

"Just the sign painted on the upstairs side facing Fulton Avenue. It says it was established in 1910 and has that on the menu." Turning and giving Whitmer a quizzical look, he added, "The food's good. I've eaten here a few times. I usually go home for lunch."

"Morag Riley opened the place and named it for her mother, a Scottish immigrant who married an Irishman. It caused quite a stir when those two got married. Her daughter took over the place when Morag got too old to run it. Now, Morag's granddaughter owns it."

"Interesting." *But what's this got to do with our investigation?*

"Well, lad, what's the first thing you think of when you think of Mom's?

"Nothin'."

The sergeant shook his head and was about to speak when Steve blurted out, "Wait. I know. It's the scones. Homemade and smothered in honey butter."

"Aye, bet you don't know it's the original recipe that Morag brought with her from Scotland. Now that you've had your history lesson for the day, let's get down to business."

"Yes, sir."

Whitmer waved the waitress over and asked if Miss Morag was working.

"She's in the office. Would you like to talk with her?"

"Please."

Waiting for the restaurant owner to join

them, Whitmer explained to Kilpatrick that the woman knew just about everyone in the county.

When the current Morag came out, Whitmer asked her to join them for a minute.

"Why, Sergeant Whitmer, it's good to see you. It's been a while."

"We've trying to find a guy who goes by the name James Dean. And I don't mean the dead actor." Morag didn't recognize the name, nor could she identify the photos of the Tuckers.

After he thanked her and she returned to work, Whitmer said, "Okay, so tell me how you plan to handle this. I'm here to help."

"Thanks, Sarge. There's one house in Bandon. We should hit it first. I'm sure we can scratch it. OSP records show the guy who owns the place has filed seven complaints about his neighbors over the last ten years. It doesn't sound like he's hiding out."

"Good. Go on."

"Then we have two in Charleston and two in Coos Bay. I suggest we swing by Charleston and then double back to Coos Bay. One's in town, and the other's a small place five miles out."

Kilpatrick was right about the owner of the house in Bandon. The owner wanted them to quiet the neighbor's dog. Young couples owned the properties in Charleston.

Both were recently married, with the property titles still in the husbands' names.

After checking the fourth house and eliminating it, Kilpatrick and Whitmer returned to Mom's in Coos Bay for lunch. Over thick pot roast sandwiches, they discussed the final place they would check later in the afternoon. They had nothing to show that either of the Tuckers lived there but agreed to approach this last place with caution. Checking with the Coos Bay Police, county sheriff, and the OSP Field Office, they learned James Dean had filed no reports. They found no record of any calls for service from the property on Old Creek Road. There had been a few calls over the years from landowners on either side of the property, but none involved Mr. Dean. Nor had any of the calls required contacting him.

"Sarge, I don't see any reason to expect trouble, but this is the kind of place a guy could hide. I'd like to talk with the neighbors before checking out the suspected Dean property. We ought to call the sheriff's office and speak to the deputy who works in that part of the county."

They met the deputy assigned to the area surrounding the James Dean property. The deputy needed a shave and a haircut, and stains spotted his loose-hanging tie and untucked uniform shirt. It was clear to both

OSP officers he held little respect for the job or his appearance.

Without going into detail, Kilpatrick said, "We're looking into a couple of pieces of property out on Old Creek Road. We understand that's your beat?"

"Yup, it is. Nothing ever happens out there, ever."

"Do you know any of the owners?"

"Nope."

"You ever see any strangers or new people?"

"Nope. I like to keep a low profile. I don't bother them, and they don't bother me."

"Can you tell us anything about Old Creek Road?"

"Nope. What're you looking for?"

The trooper lied. "No big deal. The taxes on the land haven't been paid in years." Turning to Whitmer, Kilpatrick asked, "Sarge, you got any questions?"

"Nope. Let's hit the road."

They thanked the deputy who didn't volunteer to go along or assist, and the troopers were on their way. "I'm glad he didn't ask to help. He'd have only gotten in our way. Talking to him was a waste of time, Sarge."

Whitmer agreed. "He's one of those who respond to calls—unhurried—does as little as possible and wouldn't last a month in OSP."

The closest neighbor to the east was helpful. He had lived there for thirty years. "Old man Crockett died eight or nine years ago. His kids sold the place through a realtor three or four years ago. I've never met the man who lives there."

"Can you tell us anything about the place?"

"Well, the gates are always locked, even when he's around. I know because three or four times, I saw him locking the gate before driving up the road. The cabin sits back a mile from the county road."

"Can you describe him and his vehicle?"

"He drives an old white Ford long bed pickup, could be a fifty-five or six. He's usually alone, but one time another man was with him, both White. I'm fifty-eight, a little over six feet. They looked younger and shorter. That's all I can tell you about them."

"Do you know if anyone's up there now?"

"I couldn't swear to it, but I don't think so. The road's shaded year-round, and there's snow on it now. I haven't seen any tire tracks for the last couple of weeks."

21

Smith checked property ownership in Santa Clara, San Francisco, and San Mateo counties. He drafted a teletype for the Southern and Central California Sheriff's Offices detailing his request and took it to Julie Matthews. "Yes, I'll get them out for you. Whatcha gonna do for me?"

"You still on your *Love Story* kick?"

"Hey, it ain't a kick, but what if I am?"

"Should I get you the soundtrack?"

"I already have one, but it's scratched. You got a deal."

The responses disappointed Smith, with fewer than a dozen counties acknowledging the request. Most replied they didn't have time, and one officer even suggested calling their assessor's office. *That's a good idea. Why didn't I think of it?*

Becker had the same results. Frustrated, he called Smith, who said, "I feel your pain, brother. I'm getting the same over here. The Los Angeles Sheriff's Office called a few days ago. They have over two hundred potential properties."

"Two hundred? Jeez, Al, you think we ought to put this on the back burner for now? Have you talked to Paul or Joe lately?"

"No. Let's get together tomorrow and give the guys in Oregon a call. Your place or mine?"

"Sergeant Murphy is all over me. He wants me to close the case. Any chance you could you come here?"

Assistant Superintendent Carter and Captain Doll were discussing current projects when the phone rang. Carter answered on the first ring. "It's interesting you guys called," followed by, "Joe's here with me. I'll put him on the squawk box and have him bring us all up to speed."

"Hey, guys, Joe here. We got this sharp trooper in the Coquille Office. Coquille is the location of the Tax Assessor's Office. He and his sergeant took a day and checked property records. I don't remember how many names they came up with, but he found one who could be our Jim Tucker." After Doll filled in the details, the California detectives expressed admiration for the young trooper's work.

"Smart of him to suggest backing off and letting the detectives take it."

"Especially since the kid was a Marine," Doll chuckled.

"Hey, once a Marine, always a Marine," said Smith.

Carter said, "You're a Marine, Al, so's Joe. That's why I'm sending Joe over to work this with the trooper. Joe will do anything to get away from me."

"You're right. I threatened to call the superintendent to keep Assistant Superintendent Carter from going himself." Doll paused. "I'll be over on Monday and stay as long as necessary. The trooper, Steve Kilpatrick, and I'll follow up the way he suggested. I have two photo spreads with Jim and Ben Tucker. We'll show them to the neighbors and all the shops selling ammo within twenty miles of the property."

Smith asked the Oregon officers. "We have our robberies to investigate. You don't have any you can tie to the Tuckers, do you?"

Doll replied, "No, aside from the fact the Assistant Superintendent wants their asses in jail. We have Oregon gun laws prohibiting felons from owning firearms, much the same as in California." Doll promised to keep them in the loop. "After I meet with Kilpatrick, I'll call the boss and let him know where we stand. I'll get a search warrant for the property as soon as we confirm one of the Tuckers owns it. My gut tells me he's our guy."

22

THE TUCKERS CONTINUED ROBBING California banks, staying clear of Oregon to avoid Paul Carter and his unwanted attention into the 1970s. This did not keep the brothers out of the sights of the Oregon State Police's Assistant Superintendent. Carter still lamented that the brothers received such a short sentence for the Safeway robberies.

"There's no doubt in my mind. The Tuckers are robbing banks in California," Carter said to Joe Doll, now Captain of Investigations.

"I agree, Boss, but there's nothing to suggest they work here in Oregon."

"It's only a matter of time. That's why I had you assign that young trooper, Steve Kilpatrick, to look around. I had another thought about that."

"What's that?" Doll asked.

"My old partner and mentor, Bill

Whitmer, is stationed at the same barracks out at Marshfield. He'd be an asset to Kilpatrick. If you could ask the area commander to free him up for a few days, it'd be a favor to me."

The neighbor to the west of the suspected Tucker property with the cabin set back from the road had never seen the man nor a vehicle coming or going. "There were tracks in the snow around Thanksgiving. There was another thing. It might not mean anything."

Kilpatrick took the lead. "What'd you see?"

"Sound carries pretty far out here. Last summer, I heard gunfire coming from over there," the man said, pointing toward the Dean or most likely Tucker property. "It sounded like more than one person was shooting. One of the weapons was a forty-five; I'd bet my boots the other was a Garand."

"Why do you say a forty-five and a Garand?"

"I fought in World War II and then got called up for Korea, a Marine. I know the difference between the lower crack of a forty-five and whistle and whoomph of an aught-six downrange."

"Why do you say more than one person?"

"I know how long it takes to switch out the clips on the M1 and the magazines on the forty-five. The M1 clip holds eight rounds. Once or twice, shots overlapped. I counted as many as twelve reports in a row. The forty-five magazine has a capacity of seven rounds. It takes three seconds to eject an empty mag, insert a new one, and chamber a round before firing again. Sometimes a forty-five fired the same time as the Garand with overlapping shots."

The troopers returned to the main road and drove a quarter mile to the driveway leading to the neighbor across the road. This one said he had heard gunshots several times over the years but didn't think anything of it. "Gunshots are common before hunting season when the locals fill their freezers." The man claimed to have never seen who lived across the road. "The gate's always closed and locked. I haven't seen any tire tracks in the snow since Thanksgiving."

Back on the county road, Kilpatrick said, "Sarge, I don't see any sense in charging up to the place right now. The gate's locked, and we would be trespassing."

"Yeah, anything else we should be doing?"

Kilpatrick responded, "We could check all the gun shops in the county to see who has been buying forty-five and aught-six ammunition. Lots of folks buy aught-six, even me. Aught-six is what the Garand fires. I trained with it before I went to Vietnam."

"Anything else?"

"We ought to show photos of the Tuckers to the neighbor and at the gun shops."

"Don't you think that's work for detectives?" Whitmer asked.

"It is, Sarge, but we've talked with the neighbor. He might be more receptive to us. As for the gun shops, if we ask around, we should have pictures with us."

"You have some good ideas. Now let's get out of here."

The following morning, Whitmer made a phone call to the captain of investigations. "I spent yesterday with Steve Kilpatrick. He's a bright young man. You should keep an eye on him. Kilpatrick and I checked out the Tucker and Dean properties yesterday. We believe it's quite possible Jim Tucker owns the last place we visited under the alias James Dean."

"Okay, Bill. Tell me what's going on."

"Okay, okay, you're the boss. The property is secluded, a mile off the county road. Neighbors have seen a man fitting Jim Tucker's description with another guy who could be the brother. And the sound of gunfire coming from the property has been heard several times. One of the neighbors is a former Marine, World War II and Korea. He's sure more than one person fired weapons and believes the weapons were a forty-five and an M1 Garand. He carried both in the wars."

"Bill, everyone out there owns a gun. Why does this mean anything?"

"The Tuckers were Marines. They qualified as experts with the Colt .45 pistol and the Garand."

"Okay, you got my attention."

"Kilpatrick will suggest you send investigators over here with photos of the Tuckers. They would show the photos to the two neighbors and ammo dealers. If any of the neighbors identify a Tucker, it'll confirm one of them lives there. Here's the part that impresses me. Steve reminded me both are two-time losers. If we can put ammo in their hands, we'll have enough for a search warrant for the property."

Captain Doll was silent for a moment.

"Joe, are you still on the line?"

"Yeah. Let me put you on hold. No better yet, give me a callback number." Captain Doll copied Whitmer's number and broke the connection without another word. Doll walked to Assistant Superintendent Carter's office, knocked, didn't wait for an answer, and walked in.

The boss was on the phone and held up two fingers to signal he needed two minutes, then pointed to the chair in front of his desk. Closer to ten minutes went by before Carter finished the conversation. "Sorry, Joe, that was the Superintendent. To what do I owe this interruption?"

When Captain Doll finished briefing Carter, he asked, "What do you think?"

"Kilpatrick's on the right track. These may not be the Tuckers, but I'm willing to invest a few days to find out. We'll wait until four-thirty for the trooper to call. If Kilpatrick hasn't called by then, you call him.

"Once Kilpatrick lays it out for you, especially the ex-con in possession of firearms as a crime and the grounds for a search warrant, tell him you'll call him back within the hour," Carter said.

"Why?" Doll asked.

"I want to hear what you think after talking with him. If nothing changes, we'll have enough time to discuss how we respond."

"Okay, sir, I understand." Captain Doll left to wait for the phone call.

Kilpatrick called long before the Assistant Superintendent's deadline. "Captain Doll here."

"Hi, Captain, Trooper Kilpatrick here. I'm calling about the Tucker case." Kilpatrick related the same information Sergeant

Whitmer had shared earlier in the day. Captain Doll did not mention the call.

"Good work, Trooper. It sounds like you're on to something. What do you suggest we do?" He listened with interest—*Whitmer's right. Kilpatrick has potential.*

When Kilpatrick wrapped up, Captain Doll told him, "Nice work, Trooper. We'll take it from here. Whatever our decision, I want you to know how much I appreciate what you have done."

"Thank you, sir. Thank you very much."

Two hours later, Doll called the young trooper back at home. "Hi, Steve. Joe Doll here. You got a few minutes?"

"Yes, sir."

"Good. Here's what we've decided," Joe said.

Finished updating Kilpatrick, Joe Doll called Bill Whitmer. "Hey Bill, you were right. The kid has potential."

"I told you."

"Yeah, yeah, you always did know more than me. Remember, I'm the captain." The two old partners enjoyed the moment before Captain Doll went on. "We want to use Trooper Kilpatrick on this." His use of the formal "Trooper Kilpatrick" told Whitmer it was all business from here on.

23

CAPTAIN DOLL DROVE TO Coquille the following Monday morning. Assistant Superintendent Carter arranged for Trooper Kilpatrick to work with Doll for the rest of the week. He and Sergeant Whitmer met at Mom's Diner for lunch. After sitting, Doll said, "Bill, I appreciate you loaning us Steve this week. I promise I won't teach him any bad habits."

"It's not like I had a choice, sir."

"Hey, I told your commander it's your decision, I—"

Whitmer interrupted, "Jeez, Joe, I'm busting your balls. Steve's a good officer, and I'm happy he's getting a chance to work with you." Kilpatrick walked in as Whitmer said, "After all, I taught you everything you know."

Kilpatrick shook his head at this display of audacity and familiarity by his sergeant. "Bill, you're embarrassing the kid." The superior officers slapped each other on the shoulder. They hugged before Sergeant Whitmer walked to the coffee pot behind the restaurant's counter.

Captain Doll said with a smile, "Bill was my training officer after the academy. When I went to Investigations, he was a senior investigator. We were partners until he screwed up and made Sergeant. Bill still thinks he taught me everything I know—where to get coffee and the best Chinese in town—that's all he had." The old friends enjoyed another good laugh. "Now, let's order and get to work. How long can you spare Steve?"

"We're shorthanded, but I'll make it happen this week. I can't promise next week."

"If we don't have our work finished in a week, we'll never get it done. The Assistant Superintendent has authorized overtime if necessary."

Kilpatrick spoke up for the first time. "Excuse me, sir, but what am I supposed to do?"

"You want to fill him in, Bill?"

"Will do, Skipper." Whitmer, now all business, said, "Steve, how you handled the captain's request to check for property showed initiative and good police work. He appreciated what you offered when you briefed him and the Assistant Super-intendent. Especially your suggestion a detective take over."

"Hey, Sarge, I wasn't alone. You guided me all the way."

"No, I watched, listened, and provided you with a sounding board. It was all you."

Doll added, "He's right, Steve. We have some serious work ahead of us. Bill says you're up to it. His recommendation is more than enough for the Assistant Superintendent and me. Now, let's get down to business."

Whitmer laid out what was expected of Kilpatrick and the captain. Steve could tell his sergeant knew what he was doing. Captain Doll shared Kilpatrick's opinion. Whitmer turned to the captain. "That about cover it?"

"It does. If we need backup, can you provide it?"

"Yes. The area commander warned our guys to be on the alert for any requests from you or Steve. The desk officer will call me with any news. I'd appreciate it if you or Steve could touch base with me as things progress. I need to keep the lieutenant in the loop and happy."

"Thanks, Bill. Will do."

"Thanks, Boss. I have to get out and do some real police work. Oh, and another thing, Mary and the kids know you're in town. Unless you're in a shootout, you're expected for dinner tonight, around seven."

"I'll be there."

"Good. I would not want to face Mary if you said no. Steve, you and your wife are invited as well." Whitmer left to return to his duties.

Doll said, "I have some administrative chores. Don't you have a shift to finish?"

"Yes, sir, I do."

Doll said, "We'll meet here at 7:00 a.m. tomorrow. I'll catch up with you at Bill's later tonight."

24

KILPATRICK AND HIS WIFE discussed the dinner invitation to his sergeant's home. He wanted to beg off. "Honey, Bill and Captain Doll are old friends. We should give them time to catch up."

"You need to be there, Steve. Getting to know Captain Doll will be good for your career."

"I don't care about that. I'm doing fine."

"True, but you could do better with Captain Doll in your corner."

"Okay, honey. We'll go, but I don't want to stay late."

Arriving at the Whitmer's, Kilpatrick was surprised Captain Doll's car wasn't in the driveway. Even before the trooper had a chance to knock, Bill Whitmer opened the door. Tears were in his eyes, and he looked shattered as he ushered the couple into the kitchen. Mary Whitmer was seated at a booth in a breakfast nook. Windows on three sides provided a spectacular view of the snow-covered forest and iced-over lake in stark contrast to the distraught woman. Slumped over the tabletop, she held a large highball glass in shaky hands. Crying and sobbing, she tried to get up. Bill put his hand on her shoulder. "It's okay, baby. Sit."

Turning to the Kilpatricks, he waved them to the bench across from his wife.

"Let me get you a drink, then I'll explain. Bourbon and water, okay?"

Steve looked at his wife before saying, "That'll be fine, plus a little ice, please."

Once they had their drinks, Mary Whitmer pleaded with her husband. "Please, Bill, I can't."

Bill hugged his wife and turned to the young couple. "It's Joe's son. He's three and dying from an incurable brain tumor."

"Oh, Jesus, we had no idea," Steve said.

Bill explained. "The boy has been sick for at least six months. Last month he underwent surgery to reduce the size of the tumor. When the surgeon got inside, the tumor was larger and more advanced than they had thought.

"They couldn't get it all. The doctors had said they never would. Joe and his wife knew it. A few more months were all they could hope for." Bill paused and took a long pull on his whiskey.

"With all that going on," Steve said, "why'd the captain come out here? He could have sent a detective."

"You're right. The captain could've. His son has been doing well, so Joe thought he could get away for a few days. The Dolls are very private people. The few OSP people who know are the Assistant Superintendent, Joe's secretary, and us. We're the boy's godparents."

Mary looked up. "A few hours ago, Joe's wife found the child lying behind his bed with his favorite teddy bear in his arms—in a coma. Joe left to meet her at the hospital." Sobbing, Mary pushed her husband from the nook and hurried from the room.

"I'll be right back," Bill whispered as he followed his wife.

Mrs. Kilpatrick put her drink down and said, "Let's go. They need some time."

Two weeks after the funeral, Captain Doll called Bill Whitmer. It was the first time they had talked since the service.

"Thanks for understanding, Bill. I'm sending an investigator down tomorrow. Jennifer Collins should be there by 9:00 a.m. The Assistant Superintendent and I want Kilpatrick involved. He'll be on loan to Investigations for a week, maybe longer. You okay with that?"

"I'll miss him, but this is a good opportunity for him."

Trooper Kilpatrick met OSP Criminal Investigator Jennifer Collins at Coquille Division Headquarters at eight-thirty the next morning. Arriving early, both considered it a good sign. She offered to skip breakfast, but Kilpatrick, who had eaten, did not want his temporary partner to start the day off on an empty stomach. After she ordered, he asked for coffee and toast.

Jennifer Collins was a forerunner of change within the OSP. As the first woman on the state police, she was unique—a true pioneer—a short, stout woman with dark curly hair a shade darker than the OSP patrol cars. Her entry into a room lightened the mood. When she smiled, it was as though her whole being was smiling. Hired into an all-male organization, her chances of survival were slim, but she beat the odds. Her short stature, barely five-seven, was another strike. She was a good four inches shorter than most of her male counterparts. Her energetic personality, coupled with a fearless strength, overcame all obstacles. Troopers who were opposed to a woman learned to trust her. Collins never shirked her duty. Five years on the job qualified her to take the investigator examination. Placing first and being promoted came as no shock.

Sergeant Whitmer knew Collins and wasn't surprised when Captain Doll called to tell him he was sending her. "She learned the job in record time and was accepted as an equal. It wasn't always an easy road, but this woman was up to it. Kilpatrick will learn from her."

Over breakfast, Kilpatrick filled her in on what he and Sergeant Whitmer had uncovered. Collins told him the history of Jim and Ben Tucker. She had photo spreads for each of the Tuckers. "The photographs are old, from 1966 when Jim Tucker was paroled out of McNeil Island, Washington, and his brother Ben from Leavenworth, Kansas." Each group consisted of six photographs with five white males of a similar age to the Tuckers. Collins explained the photo spreads. "We used to take five or six photographs and hand them to the witness."

Kilpatrick replied, "I've done it a few times. It seems easy enough.

"You're right, but the Assistant Superintendent has been studying photo lineups. Investigators often subconsciously or intentionally influence a witness. By preparing the spread in advance and varying where we place the suspect's photograph, we reduce the chance of that happening."

"If I wanted to, Detective, I could still draw attention to the suspect."

"Yes, you could, but training should help you do the right thing. Another possibility the Assistant Superintendent's considering is having an officer unfamiliar with the case, and the suspect, show the lineup. He told me we aren't big enough, too few officers, to do that yet."

"Makes sense to me."

"The Assistant Superintendent thinks bad case law is coming down soon. He wants us to be ahead of it. Steve . . . is it okay if I call you Steve?"

"Sure, Detective."

"Call me Jennifer. We'll work as partners on this. You know more about the situation here and the way around. Now, how do you think we should handle this?"

"I've got a suggestion on what to do this morning."

"Go ahead. I've had my coffee, and I'm all ears."

"We have a dozen firearms dealers in Coos County. Six between here and the Dean property. My suggestion is to visit them on the way."

"Sounds good. Let's go. I'll drive if you don't mind. It'll give me a chance to learn the lay of the land. Besides, my seat won't go back far enough for you. How tall are you anyway?" *We make for an odd couple—a short woman and a giant. My God, he must be close to a foot taller than me.*

None of the gun shop owners in Coquille recalled selling .45 caliber and 30-06 ammunition to the same buyer. Nor could they remember seeing any of the men in the photo spreads. The officers had the same results at the fourth business.

The fifth shop was a mile off the main road in a rundown area. It looked like a converted barn; it had been one fifty years earlier. The peeling paint and the warped siding from past storms gave proof of years of neglect. County records listed the place as Mike's Gun Shop. Mike Ritter had died years ago. Phil Ritter, his nephew, inherited the store, but not Mike's industrious streak or morals.

"Phil's a loser. It's plain luck he's never been convicted of a crime. Some think he buys and sells stolen property. I'm not so sure. We would have busted him years ago if it were true," said Kilpatrick.

The interior was as rundown as the exterior, with walls once covered with lath and plaster. Now entire sections were missing. The animal stalls had been converted to small rooms or open alcoves. Formerly glass-topped mahogany display cases, obviously later additions, stood beyond repair. Each sported cracked or missing countertops and fronts above a floor thick with dust and years of grime. The place reeked of gloom combined with misery.

Phil Ritter fit in thinning red hair, a comb-over hung in wisps of dirty strings. Clad in filthy bibbed overalls, he was a walking advertisement for stale whiskey and tobacco. As kind and friendly as Anthony Perkins' portrayal of Norman Bates in Alfred Hitchcock's 1960 thriller, *Psycho*, Phil hated everyone.

"Whatta you want? You ain't here to inquire after my health."

"And a good morning to you, Phil. This is Detective Collins."

"When did the state police start hiring broads?"

For an instant, Collins thought Kilpatrick would bash Ritter in the face with an enormous right hand. Although turning red and stepping toward the man with clenched fists, the young trooper held himself in check. *Excellent. Good for him. He can control himself.* Collins stepped up to Ritter with a smile. "When they figured out some of us are much smarter than the average cracker. Trooper Kilpatrick has a few questions for you."

"Phil, we're interested in someone buying quantities of forty-five and aught-six ammunition."

"Hell, half the men in this county are

veterans. If they aren't, their daddies are. Most of 'em have an aught-six, and plenty of them have forty-fives. Ain't no law against it."

"No, but buying more than a box or two of ammo isn't usual. The person we're interested in is likely buying Army surplus aught-six in pre-loaded eight-round clips. He likely bought surplus forty-five ammo as well."

"Why do you want to know?"

Collins looked him in the eye. "Why's not your concern. Answer Trooper Kilpatrick, or I'll haul you in for being a low-rent piece of shit."

Ritter took half a step back. "Jeez, lady. You don't have to get your panties in an uproar."

"It's not lady! It's Detective Collins to you."

A somewhat cowed Ritter said, "Okay, okay." Looking back to Kilpatrick, "Look, I don't sell a lot of anything. I got one guy who comes in once or twice a year and buys both."

"Okay, what's his name?"

"I never asked, he never said. The guy drops by, tells me what he wants, and I order it."

"What's he get?"

"Four cases of forty-five, each holds 600 rounds, twelve boxes of 50."

Kilpatrick did the math. "Twenty-four-hundred rounds." Turning back to Ritter, he said, "Tell us about the aught-six."

"About the same."

"What do you mean about the same?"

"Well, officer, here's the thing. He wanted the aught-six in eight-round clips for a Garand—easy enough to get. After World War II and Korea, there were billions of surplus rounds. To get it in eight-round clips, I have to order GI cans. Each can holds 280 cartridges in thirty-five clips. The smallest order is ten cans. The guy said, 'Go ahead and order ten cans.' That's 2800 rounds. He paid cash, half then, and the rest on delivery."

Collins and Kilpatrick exchanged glances and shared the same thought. *This could be our guy.*

She continued to defer to Kilpatrick for questioning.

"When did he pick up the ammo?"

"Three months ago."

Changing direction, Kilpatrick asked, "What else have you sold him?"

Looking at the filthy floor, Ritter said, "Whatta you mean?"

In a soft but menacing tone, Kilpatrick got Ritter's attention. "Look, Phil, we do this now, or we close up the store and take a ride to the OSP Barracks. Your choice. Be straight with us, and we'll get out of your hair."

"Okay, okay. This is the third time I saw him. The first when the guy came in three or four years ago, wanted two Garands, two forty-fives, and a boatload of ammo."

Now we're getting somewhere, thought Kilpatrick.

"I sold him two Garands but couldn't sell him the forty-fives."

"Why not?"

"You don't need ID for rifles, but you gotta fill out a form and show ID for pistols. He didn't want to, and I wouldn't break the law."

"No, you would never do that, Phil. What'd the guy look like?"

"Average, just average."

"Phil, I'm not playing games. What'd the man look like?"

"White. He's White and way shorter than you, five-ten or so, hair like some guys get before they get all grays. I'm not sure what you call it, pepper or something."

"You mean salt and pepper?"

"Yeah, that's it."

"How old?"

"It's a funny thing, Trooper. It looks like he's in his forties, in real good shape, but my guess is he's older, in his fifties."

"Did anyone ever come in with him?"

"No."

"What'd he drive?"

"A ratty old white Ford F-100. The last time he came in, another guy waited in the truck."

"Phil, what'd you call him?"

"I called him mister."

"I don't believe you."

Ritter whined, "You gotta believe me. There's something about this guy. He's polite and quiet but scary. I don't know why."

"Would you recognize him if you saw his picture?"

"I doubt it."

"Phil, you're lying to me. You don't get many customers who buy as much as this guy. You remember the good ones. Now, can you identify the guy?"

"Honest officer, I don't think so."

Collins said, "Take a look at this." She opened the photo spread with a picture of Benjamin Tucker in the top right position. Ritter spent a few moments looking at the spread. Neither Collins nor Kilpatrick noted any sign of recognition.

"Not here," Ritter said. Collins picked up the folder and opened the second spread containing the photo of James Tucker. His picture was in the bottom left position. Ritter flinched, and his eyes locked in space for an instant.

"Do you see him here?" Kilpatrick said.

"No, nope," Ritter answered too quickly.

Kilpatrick asked, "Anything you haven't told us about this guy?"

"No."

"Have you ever seen him around town or at local spots?"

"No."

Collins pulled a business card from her pocket and handed it to Kilpatrick. "Write your name and number on the back." Taking the card back, she passed it to Ritter. "We'll leave our numbers. If you think of anything, anything at all, you call—understand?"

"Yes, ma'am."

In her car, Collins said, "He's not a very good liar, is he?"

"No. Did you spot Ritter's reaction to the spread with James Tucker?"

"Doesn't want anything to do with Tucker. He's scared."

They stopped at the sixth gun shop, where the owner was of no help in identifying the Tuckers. Collins asked him where someone could buy unrecorded handguns. He denied ever selling any but acknowledged it was common knowledge that a couple of dealers in the county might help a guy who didn't want a record of gun purchases—Phil Ritter was one of the two.

The following morning, they visited the neighbor who lived east of the property. After Kilpatrick introduced Detective Collins, she went over what the man had told Kilpatrick on his previous visit. He remained consistent in what he recalled. Collins opened the photo spread with Ben Tucker first. "Do you see anyone who looks familiar to you?"

The older man looked for a few minutes. "Can I pick this up for a closer look?"

"Sure."

A minute or two later, he told the officers, "None of these guys are familiar. Sorry."

"Not to worry, if you don't recognize anyone, that's fine," Collins said. "Please take a look at this set."

The old man pointed to the photograph of James Tucker. "He looks familiar, but I can't be sure."

A few days later, Captain Doll met with Detective Collins. "Jennifer, I've read your report. Is there anything you can add to help get a search warrant?"

"Captain, I have no doubt that James Dean is James Tucker. But I don't believe we'll get a warrant based on what we have so far. If we did convince a judge to sign one, it would get thrown out for lack of probable cause."

"If you took another shot at the gun dealer, do you think you could get any more from him?"

"He's so discriminatory against women, sending me would only make it worse. Even if you were to interview him, I doubt we'll get what we need. No, we need more to make this work."

"I'll brief the Assistant Superintendent and get back to you. Thanks for a good job, Jennifer."

"Trooper Kilpatrick carried the load, Captain."

25

"GOOD MORNING, DETECTIVE BECKER and Detective Smith." The detectives looked at each other. Not the usual "Hi guys, Paul and Joe here." Assistant Superintendent Carter's use of titles signaled this would be a formal meeting."

Becker responded to acknowledge their understanding of Paul Carter's lead. "Good morning, Assistant Superintendent." *I wonder what's so serious about this call.*

"Thanks for being available today," followed by, "Captain Doll, Detective Jennifer Collins, and Trooper Steve Kilpatrick are with me."

That must be the reason. Carter has two junior-level officers with him today.

Carter continued. "Trooper Kilpatrick is from our barracks in Coos County. He got involved when we started looking for property owned by the Tuckers and did some work identifying a place we believe Jim Tucker owns."

"That's great. Smith and I have not been so successful."

"Hold that thought, Detective. Let me run through what we have first."

Once Carter finished, Collins added she thought they lacked probable cause for a search warrant.

Becker praised the trooper and detective. "Some mighty fine work." He said, "I agree. It has to be Jim Tucker, no doubt. But, as Detective Collins points out, we don't want a warrant that fails to meet the test. We need more, but I'm not sure what we can do."

Assistant Superintendent Carter slipped back into a more familiar tone. "Thanks. Noah. What are your thoughts?"

"It might sound farfetched, but I have an idea."

"Damn it, Noah, get on with it."

"Okay, here it is. I've been helping one of our other investigators. He's a real old-timer, should be retired, but can't afford it. The point is he works checks and forgery crimes. I've learned a lot from him. One of his favorite axioms is it only takes one print to convict a bad guy."

"How does that help us?" Carter asked, his tone softening.

"There may be documents we can use

to identify Tucker."

Smith glanced at Becker with a questioning look and conversation buzzed on the OSP side of the call. It was all Becker could do to contain his excitement. With a grin in the direction of Smith, he said, "Can I go on?" Without waiting for an answer, Becker said, "First, a question for the trooper. Who does the property title show as the owner?"

"James Dean. Why?"

"I assume you all either own or are buying a home?" All but Smith were. "Here's the thing. In California, you have to fill out and sign dozens of forms for a home loan and close the sale. Is it the same in Oregon?"

"It's the same if you take out a mortgage. Tucker paid cash for the property. There won't be any loan documents," Carter said.

Becker said, "Regardless of how he paid, Tucker left a paper trail. He had to sign something with a realtor. There's the deed and other documents, and the buyer had to provide an address for the tax bill."

Carter jumped in. "I appreciate where you're headed with this, but Captain Doll looks perplexed. Please educate him. He's been an administrator for far too long."

Becker continued, "We have plenty to go on. We'll go to the Marine Corps if necessary, but we have everything we need at the Oakland Police Department and the prisons where they did time."

"Noah, I think I've got it figured out, but let's hear the details," huffed Doll.

"We all agree there isn't enough for a search warrant," followed by a chorus of yeses. "If we tie either Tucker brother—and I'm betting it'll be Jim—to the property, we're in the door. First, we collect the deed and other original documents on file at Coos County and then contact the realtor. He should be able to identify the person who bought the property and still have some of the original documents in his possession. If he identifies one of the Tucker's photos, that'll be enough."

Carter came on the speaker. "True, but I'd like to make the affidavit a little stronger."

"I agree," replied Becker, "and here's how we do it. It may take a while, but we need to get their original enlistment papers and any documents the Tuckers signed in jail, court, or prison. The originals will be needed later. Certified copies should work for a search warrant affidavit. Any questions so far?"

"Okay, so we assemble all these documents. What next?" asked Carter.

"Ninhydrin and handwriting comparison."

Trooper Kilpatrick spoke up. "This is new to me. What do you mean, ninhydrin?' I've never heard of it."

"Most people, including cops, haven't. It's

a process to develop unseen, latent finger-prints on paper, documents, and the like. It's been around since 1954, but you wouldn't know unless you work with documents or in a crime lab.'

"So, how does it work?" the trooper asked.

"The lab guys spray it or use a vapor in an enclosed container to get it on the document. It reacts to amino acids left when a person handles paper. The reaction develops an image of the latent print. You with me so far?"

No one spoke up.

"The image fades over time, so the lab guys take photos. They compare the fingerprint to known prints. What do you think?"

Kilpatrick wasn't the only one unfamiliar with the ninhydrin process. Becker went on. "We won't need the Marine Corps documents. Every fingerprint card they ever signed has their signatures. When they were released, they signed for their property and accepted parole. Those are identified handwriting samples, which we call exemplars. We compare their fingerprint to the latent prints we get from ninhydrin to anything related to the sale of the property."

Kilpatrick raised another question. "What if dozens of fingerprints from others are on a document?"

"You need one fingerprint to convict the bad guy. If I find a hundred prints belonging to others, say the deed, but we find one for Jim Tucker, we have him."

Assistant Superintendent Carter accepted Becker's recommendation. "Unless someone has a better idea, here is what I would like to happen. Detective Collins, the warrant will need to be issued in Coos County. I want you to be the affiant and co-ordinate the efforts of the other investigators. Can you handle it?"

"Yes, sir, I can."

"This may take a while, Trooper Kilpatrick, so you return to your unit."

"I understand, sir."

"Don't worry. You'll be included when the time comes to serve the warrant."

"Thank you."

"Detective Becker, we'll need you to get your hands on the fingerprint cards from the old Safeway heist arrest. Certified copies will be fine for now."

"I'll try, sir.

"Good. Detective Smith, will you be available to back him up if he has a problem with OPD?"

"No sweat. We got the print cards once, and we'll get them again. My fingerprint guy made copies. They should be good enough for the search warrant," Smith said.

"The warrant will be served in Oregon, so the handwriting and fingerprint comparisons should be made by OSP. Does anyone see a problem?" Carter added.

Captain Doll offered to help with the Feds. "Jennifer, if you don't mind, I'll reach out to the federal prison system. I've got a friend in the Federal Bureau of Prisons headquarters who should be able to get us certified copies of the Tuckers' documents."

"Once we get the documents coming in, should I take them to the lab piecemeal or wait until we have everything in hand?" said Collins.

"Detective Collins, what do you suggest?" asked the assistant superintendent.

"Well, my take is the documents will come in from several organizations. Some could take a long while. If you approve, I'd like to take things to the lab as they come in."

"I agree. I'll notify the lab to give your requests precedence over everything except homicides. They won't like it, but they'll do it. If you get any shit, er, I mean flack, let me or Joe know."

"Yes, sir, will do."

Smith broke in. "I've stayed active in the Navy League. It's an organization for Marines and sailors. I've got friends in the right places in the Corps. I'll do what I can on the Tucker boys' Marine prints and signatures."

Carter ended the call with, "I'll brief the superintendent today. The rest of you keep Jennifer abreast of your progress." After a pause, "Jennifer, I'll expect you to brief Captain Doll at least once a week, sooner if necessary. Joe, you update me as appropriate. Thank you all." He added, "You're all professionals. I don't have to remind you, I don't want any talk about this case leaking out."

Trooper Kilpatrick was the first to report to Collins. "I talked to the assistant county clerk at Coos County. She arranged to assemble all the records related to Tucker's property. I stressed the importance of protecting the documents from unnecessary handling."

"It's always who you know," Collins quipped.

"Amen. The clerk collected the documents, and the county clerk certified they are original documents maintained in the normal course of business."

"Um, smart. It'll help us identify the documents for the search warrant affidavit and suppression hearings. Now, all we need are handwriting exemplars and prints for comparison. Thanks, Steve."

Captain Doll was the next to report to Detective Collins. "The Bureau of Prisons is proving to be difficult. My buddy tells me they have a strict policy of not releasing original print cards. I got the same from the FBI. Both agree to compare anything we send them, but the turnaround time is sixty days to six months. They'll provide certified copies if we send a subpoena, but they're talking sixty days for delivery."

"Seems to be severe treatment by the Feds towards a state law enforcement agency."

"That's for sure. I got the same explanation at both places. This policy comes straight from J. Edgar Hoover. Anyone violates it, and he'll crucify them."

"I hear you, Captain."

"Anyway, I'll submit a formal request to both agencies today. I'm sorry. It's the best I can do."

Al Smith was the first to come up with a positive result. "My old commanding officer, General Lew Walt, is the Assistant Commandant of the Marine Corps. When I explained what we were trying to do, he promised to check into it. In less than twenty-four hours, I got a callback."

"Al, these boys might be crooks, but they were good Marines. Do you have any idea of what they went through?" said the general.

After General Walt finished, Smith was impressed and spoke. "They were good

Marines. I'm not sure I could have survived."

"Yes, you would have, Al," the General told him. "You don't want to know how, but I have their service jackets, including prints, on my desk."

Smith continued. "Three days later, I had certified copies of their enlistment contracts, fingerprint cards, and separation records delivered by a Marine officer. General Walt will hold the originals in his safe until no longer needed."

The Oakland Police denied Becker's request for fingerprints. OPD and the Alameda County Sheriff's Office created a countywide booking system with an ensuing turf war that blocked all such requests.

Becker reminded Collins, "We have the copies at Mountain View PD."

Collins said, "Those copies should be enough for a search warrant."

"I have to call Smith anyway. I'll ask him to send you what he has, including the Marine Corps fingerprints."

"I appreciate it, Noah. I'm swamped. Please ask him to send by Registered Mail to preserve the chain of custody."

A few days later, Collins paid a visit to Joe Doll with the property records and copies of the Marine Corps documents in hand. "I have the prints, records, and known exemplars ready for the lab."

The captain was pleased. "Have you looked at them?"

"Oh, yes. The handwriting is a match."

Her captain agreed. "The 'James' on the military documents looks identical to the 'James' on the property records. Do you need anything from me?"

"The lab has been told to expect me and to give the case top priority."

"Yes." With a cock of his head, Captain Doll leaned forward. "Is there a problem?"

"No, no, sir, but if you could give them a call and tell them I'm on my way, it might make it go smoother."

Captain Doll picked up his phone. "Good morning. This is Captain Doll. May I speak with the director?" After ending a short conversation, he turned back to Detective Collins. "There won't be a problem. Before you leave, I'd like you to come with me and show these to the boss."

The two went to the Assistant Superintendent's office. Carter said he was pleased with the progress and then excused himself. "I have another useless, waste of time budget meeting."

Collins had a problem at the lab, which she overcame. The technician said, "These military documents are not originals. We need the originals to make an identification."

Collins was ready. "The military documents have been certified by the Marine Corps Assistant Commandant as true copies of the documents in their official records. You make the comparisons, and if you want to qualify your findings, include that fact in your report. If you need further clarification, I'm sure your director or Captain Doll would be happy to address the issue in person." The lab tech agreed and accepted the documents.

"When can I expect the results?"

The tech promised to have a verbal description to Collins in three days and an official report three business days later.

26

TRUE TO HIS WORD, the lab tech provided a verbal report to Detective Collins in the time promised. "Our handwriting analyst compared the known handwriting exemplars of James Tucker and Benjamin Tucker on the Marine Corps documents where they used the names James Dean and Benjamin Alexander. There was no handwriting on the questioned documents belonging to Benjamin Alexander."

"What about James Tucker?"

"We were successful with James Tucker. The signature on the deed of trust was identified as being written by him."

"Were you able to develop any latent prints on the questioned documents?"

"Yes, we developed twenty prints with enough points for comparison on the deed of trust."

"Any luck with those?"

"Yes, two were identified as belonging to the right thumb and index finger of James Tucker."

"How many points of comparison?"

"The thumb provided ten points of comparison. Adequate for an ID, but not enough for court."

"Damn."

"Hold on, Detective. We got eighteen positive points of comparison on the right index finger, more than enough for court."

Collins called Captain Doll with the news, who in turn made two phone calls. Things began to happen. The following day, she received the official report, hand-delivered, at 9:00 a.m.

At 10:00 a.m., Captain Doll and Detective Collins were seated in Assistant Superintendent Carter's office, who said, "Thank you for taking time from your busy schedules to meet with me. The California detectives should be calling any minute now. Any questions before they come online? Joe?"

"No, sir."

When Al Smith and Noah Becker's call came, Assistant Superintendent Carter summarized what his investigators had accomplished. Smith and Noah heaped praise on their friends in Oregon.

Assistant Superintendent Carter said, "It's not all here in OSP. Without Noah's suggestion about the documents, ninhydrin, and comparison, we'd still be scratching our collective heads."

"Thanks, Assistant Superintendent."

"It was a good use of your knowledge, Noah. The next step is for Jennifer to assemble all the materials we have and prepare the search warrant."

"Yes, sir," said Detective Collins.

"How long will you need?"

"Can you give me two days?"

"Done! Now I have to get back to playing Assistant Superintendent."

Collins put the packet of information and declarations together as attachments to the affidavit supporting the search warrant she wrote. To be on the safe side, she had Joe Doll read and give it his assessment. "It looks good to go." She next visited the prosecuting attorney in Coos County, who signed off and walked her across the street to the courthouse. The duty judge had no questions and signed the search warrant.

"Now that we have the warrant, we shouldn't wait more than a day or so before serving it. What about Al and Noah?" Captain Doll said before asking, "Jennifer, your thoughts?"

"They're an important part of the investigation, but I agree with the captain.

With all the activity, the risk of a leak worries me."

"Anyone on the team or at OSP that concerns you? If so, I need you to tell me right now."

"No, sir, but the chances of an accidental leak increase as time goes on."

"Agreed. Experience has proven your concerns to be valid. Today's Tuesday, and I want the warrant served on Thursday. Joe, is that doable?"

"It is. Once you give the go-ahead, I'll call Bill Whitmer's area commander and arrange to have Whitmer and Kilpatrick detached to assist. We'll rendezvous in Coquille tomorrow afternoon and hit the cabin Thursday morning."

"Do you plan on being there?" Before Doll could reply, Carter said, "Joe, Whitmer, and Kilpatrick are part of the investigation. I don't want them standing guard. You have my authorization for overtime to fill the uniformed slots. Understood?"

"Aye, aye, sir. Overtime pay it is."

The phone rang. They recognized the gruff voice of Detective Al Smith. "Hi, Assistant Superintendent. I'm here with Detective Becker. We're at his office. His supervisor, Sergeant Murphy, is with us."

"Glad you could join us, Sergeant Murphy." Assistant Superintendent Carter made a shrug and a gesture signifying, *Why is he here?* Doll, the only one in the room who knew about the sergeant, grimaced.

"I'm here to help Detective Becker," came from Murphy.

"Sergeant, Detective Becker has been a great help to us." Carter introduced the others in the room. The introductions complete, he turned to Collins. "For the benefit of Sergeant Murphy, please give us an overview of the investigation and then update our friends from California as far as obtaining a search warrant."

"Yes, sir."

After Collins completed the briefing, Smith was the first to speak. "Nice work by Detective Collins and all you folks. What's the next step?"

Assistant Superintendent Carter told them the plans for service of the search warrant and extended an invitation for them to participate. Murphy joined the conversation. "I'm not sure if Detective Becker or I will be able to join you. I don't think the chief will allow the time away from the department or travel."

"I get it. Would it help if I called the chief?"

"I can't be sure, but if you do, he might let me go," Murphy said.

The officers had similar thoughts about

Murphy from Carter on down—*What an asshole.*

Carter cut off further discussion. "Sergeant, please tell your chief I'll call him within the hour." It wasn't so much a request as an order. "Al, will you be able to make it?"

"I'll have to check. I'm sure my sergeant and the chief will allow it. Plan on me being in Coquille tomorrow."

Carter called his friend, Tom Rogers, the San Leandro Police Chief. "Hi, Tom. How goes the easy life in Sparkle City?" Rogers did not like it when people referred to San Leandro by that name as if it were crime-free in a sea of criminal activity. Rogers and Carter enjoyed a long history, back to when Rogers was with the Oakland Police Department. Theirs was more than a professional relationship, one built on mutual trust.

"It goes well here in civilization. How're things up in the wilderness?"

"I'm doing fine, but this isn't a social call."

"I figured. Murphy gave me a heads up. What do you need?"

After explaining the situation, and the potential of clearing an old San Leandro robbery, Carter asked, "Any chance of you sending the detective up here? I promise he'll be back by Monday."

"I find it odd that you wouldn't invite

Sergeant Murphy, but Becker will be there tomorrow in time for your briefing. Take good care of him. I want him back in one piece."

27

IT WAS AFTER 6:00 p.m. when the officers gathered at the Oregon State Police Barracks in Coquille. Captain Doll was the senior OSP officer present. Besides the investigators, the OSP area commander and two of his uniformed troopers sat in on the briefing.

After introducing themselves, Al Smith asked, "Where's the Assistant Superintendent?"

Doll explained. "Paul wanted to be here, but after briefing the super, he put the kibosh on it. He wouldn't risk his Assistant Superintendent of Investigations. Maybe it was Carter's age. I can tell you Paul's not happy."

Whitmer chimed in. "I bet the old man's fit to be tied."

"Like I've never seen." Captain Doll opened the briefing. He explained the Tuckers' history for the benefit of the area commander and the uniformed troopers.

Captain Doll continued with the assignments. "This is an OSP case. Detectives Smith and Becker will observe and provide backup. Detective Collins and Trooper Kilpatrick will take the front, accompanied by one of the uniformed troopers. I'll take the rear with Sergeant Whitmer and the other uniformed trooper. Detectives Smith and Becker will observe from the sides of the cabin. Any questions?"

The area commander spoke up. "What time will this kick off, and what do you want from me?"

"The judge didn't authorize night service, so we go at 7:00 a.m. Please have a trooper parked near the place in an unmarked car by 5:00 a.m. I would appreciate it if you could be available here at the barracks."

"We'll be there. How close to the property should my guy park?"

"As far away as possible. But close enough to see if a vehicle goes in or out of the driveway."

"What about the sheriff's office? Do we notify them or not?" Whitmer asked.

Doll looked to the area commander. "This is your district. You make the call."

"I would prefer we didn't notify them, but we have to. I don't want to set things back. The sheriff and I have our differences, but he's a good man. Unless you say otherwise, I'll give him a call."

"You're right. Besides, the sheriff needs to be ready if things go sideways."

28

JIM TUCKER WOKE WITH a start. *What is it?* He pulled a Colt .45 from beneath his pillow. Lying still, alert for any sound, there was only the silence he had become accustomed to in the years of living alone in his remote cabin. *What woke me?* Slipping from bed, he made his way to the rear door. Peering through a slit in the curtain, Tucker remained motionless but on full alert for ten minutes before repeating the process at the front window. *I don't know if anything's wrong, but I gotta check it out.* He built a fire in the stove. *If anyone is watching, the smoke should convince them I'm inside and off guard.* Once the fire was going, Tucker slipped out the back and melted into the silent forest.

Twenty minutes later, Tucker was at the main road. Not completely surprised, an unmarked police car was parked on the shoulder. He checked his watch, 4:55 a.m., before turning to head back. The low rumble of an approaching vehicle broke the silence. Concealed, he kept the cop car in sight. A marked sheriff's car approached and stopped alongside the other police car. They rolled down their windows to talk. Within three or four minutes, the sheriff's car drove away.

Back at the cabin, Tucker turned on the police scanner. It was usually silent this time of the morning. Putting on a pot of coffee, he thought, I've gotta get out of here. I should have time to eat and prepare to run.

The scanner came to life; not the sheriff's main channel, but the second one deputies used for personal conversations, usually to arrange a meeting for coffee. Tucker recognized the voice of Deputy Wilson. *He works the day shift. Why's he here now?* Tucker's question was answered as Deputy Wilson's chatter continued over the scanner. "Pete, I'm in early, on overtime. OSP is serving a search warrant on some big-time bank robber on Old Creek Road. I talked with a trooper parked there who claims he doesn't know anything. I doubt it."

A new voice came over the radio, "Wilson, your instructions were to maintain radio silence till after seven unless notified otherwise. Acknowledge."

It was too late. Wilson had already done the damage. His presence confirmed what

Tucker had surmised. *They'll be here by seven.*

Jim Tucker always knew this day would come—he was prepared. *The old OSP detective, Carter, that was it, Carter. Thanks to him, Ben and I spent time at San Quentin. I bet he's involved in this.* Finished with his preparations, Tucker decided to give Detective Carter a little jab. He tacked a note to the front door and put on a fresh pot of coffee.

Shortly after 7:00 a.m., Jim allowed himself five minutes rest when more than a mile from his cabin. Then it hit him. *I've only thought of myself. Damn. How do I warn Ben? They could be knocking down his door right now. It'll be days, a week before I can warn him. Good luck, Ben. You'll need it.*

The detectives and troopers met at the Coquille OSP Barracks on Thursday morning at five. After coffee and bathroom breaks, they loaded up in three marked OSP Suburbans equipped with four-wheel drive.

At 6:30 a.m., the trooper watching Tucker's driveway saw the OSP vehicles arrive. A glimmer of dawn's light shone between the Douglas fir and sugar pine trees lining the roadway as the officers made U-turns and pulled in behind him. Captain Doll and the team gathered around. "Good morning, Trooper. Anything to report?"

"There's been no activity around the driveway. But we had some unwanted traffic, sir."

"What do you mean?" Doll demanded, his face contorted.

"This is my regular beat. Normally I see a sheriff's unit once a night when I pass the diner at the crossroads. When I was coming in, one passed me headed out."

"Is that all?"

"No, sir. Deputy Wilson came by twice in the last hour. The first time he stopped and asked me about the search warrant. I told him I was watching a private drive for anyone coming or going. I didn't call dispatch. I had no idea who might be listening."

"Let's hope that's all he did. You did right, Trooper. Stay here until we call for you." Changing the subject, Doll continued, "We'll cut the lock on the gate when we go in. Jennifer, you take the point from here."

"Yes, sir. It's a mile up to the cabin. Once past the gate, we'll drive three-quarters of a mile and then walk the rest of the way. Are we ready?" A chorus of positive responses followed.

"Okay, let's go. Keep the noise down, and don't forget these guys are dangerous— killers. They will be armed."

They drove to the gate and met their first obstacle, a casehardened steel lock. Steve Kilpatrick, the youngest and, without question, the strongest, volunteered. "Let me give it a try." The bolt cutters did not scratch the lock's shackle.

Smith stepped up. "Give me the damn cutters." Taking hold of the tool, he bypassed the lock and cut the chain. With an expression of dissatisfaction directed toward Kilpatrick followed by a good-natured shake of his head, he said, "I thought you were a Marine. Oh well, brains over brawn." Beyond the gate, the narrow track was covered in old frozen snow. The evergreens were tight against the roadway. Smith asked Kilpatrick, "How do you get around in this stuff. It's so dark I can't see a hundred feet."

Kilpatrick answered, "Sometimes roads like this never see the sun. The snow and ice don't melt until fall. The good thing is it's like being in a cocoon. Sound doesn't carry much further than you can see."

They ran into their second obstacle about four hundred yards up the road. In the tree-shaded area, the snow was a foot deep and frozen. It would be noisy and hard to cross. It was time to walk. Smith had another question for Kilpatrick. "If the sunlight can't get in here, how does the snow?"

"It gets so cold the snow is like dry water.

It seeps and falls from one branch to another until it finds an opening and drops to the ground."

The California detectives would have suffered wet and freezing feet within five minutes if the Oregon troopers hadn't loaned them waterproof boots.

The delays brought them within sight of the cabin ten minutes after the hour. Until then, they did not know if anyone was inside. They were rewarded with two observations that allayed their fear the cabin would be empty. The chimney spewed a steady stream of smoke, and an old white Ford F-100 pickup was parked in front of the place. Certain at least one of the Tuckers was inside generated a refreshing sense of anticipation and heightened tension.

Many officers would have been intimidated by the presence of Captain Doll. Even though Detective Collins had a great deal of respect for the captain, she wasn't overwhelmed by him. An experienced professional used to directing operations. "Captain, please take your team and skirt the clearing. Take Detective Becker with you and station him on the right side of the clearing. Detective Smith, you work your way around to the left. At seven-twenty, we'll hit the front door. I'll do the knock and announce. Any questions?" There were none.

The anticipation Detective Collins and her group felt increased the tension more than the others experienced. While the others would remain concealed, her group would have to cross seventy-five feet of open space to reach the front door. If the Tuckers were inside and ready, the officers could be wounded or dead within minutes. Collins nodded to the two troopers at seven-twenty and stepped out into the clearing. Not knowing it, she mimicked Ben Tucker, "Let's go." Collins reminded herself, *I've got to follow the law. I'll have to knock and announce. Will it give Tucker time to arm himself and fire at us?*

Nearing the cabin, Collins saw what looked like a note pinned to the door. She stepped up onto the small porch to the left of the door. Kilpatrick and the uniformed trooper stepped to the right. Printed on the paper, "It's unlocked. No need to knock it down. Coffee's ready."

The three looked at each other in bewilderment. The paper was fresh, as if recently posted. Collins pounded on the door and announced, "Police. I have a search warrant and demand entry." No response. After repeating her announcement, she shouted loud enough for the other officers to hear, "Going in."

Collins' chest constricted. She could

almost hear her heart pounding with apprehension and fear. Bile rose in her throat; this was the moment every cop lives for and dreads. Trying the doorknob, she found it unlocked. She tapped it in a few inches, waited a few seconds, and then pushed it open. Met with silence, she shouted, "Police." Still no response, the three entered and, within seconds, confirmed no one was inside. Finally able to breathe, she went to the back door and shouted. "Captain, it's all clear. I'm opening the door."

They found a fresh pot of coffee on the wood-burning stove and another note. "Detective Carter, are you still chasing me after all these years? Please lock up when you leave." The note didn't puzzle Doll and Smith. They knew the history that Assistant Superintendent Carter and the Tuckers shared. Doll looked at Smith with a bemused expression. "Boy, will Carter be pissed."

Collins' portable radio worked sporadically at best. All she got was static, a hiss, and the occasional crackle. "Sergeant Whitmer, would you mind going back to the vehicles and radio in a status report to the Assistant Superintendent and the area commander? Take one of the uniformed officers with you and drive back to Coquille."

"Anything else?"

"Yes. Please release the trooper down

below and then see about getting up here with a Suburban."

"You got it. What about the other uniformed trooper?"

"I want him to remain for outside security. I doubt Tucker will come back, but he's a killer and well-armed. I'd rather play it safe."

Captain Doll offered an alternative. "Jennifer, I'll go. Bill is more capable of supporting you here. Remember, I've been out of the field for years. Besides, I can reach Assistant Superintendent Carter at home."

"Okay, Captain. Bill, please go with him and bring up one of the vehicles."

When the three started back down the road, the remaining officers helped themselves to the coffee and sat down to plan the cabin's search. "This isn't bad," said Detective Becker.

Smith expressed what he thought they might all be thinking. "No, it's not, but it sure leaves a bitter taste in my mouth. We almost had one of them. What went wrong?"

It was a small cabin containing a tiny bedroom and bathroom and a large room serving as a kitchen, dining room, and great room. Collins assigned the California detectives to search the bedroom and Kilpatrick the bathroom with the admonishment, "Leave anything you find in place. I'll be the official finder for the report and will recover all the evidence."

After thirty minutes, the officers completed their initial search. All they had to show for it was evidence that a man lived a solitary life in a cabin kept immaculately clean. Whitmer returned in time to help in a second search. "You find anything?"

Collins answered his question. "Nothing except the coffee. The note looks like Jim Tucker's handwriting. At least we've placed him in the cabin."

"There is a room that looked like a storeroom but felt like a closet," said Bill Whitmer.

"Whadda you mean?" Asked Becker.

"Come and look." The other officers came to the doorway and looked in. There was no hanger rack, and shelving covered the walls.

"Now look," Whitmer said. "There are shelves with old wooden fruit crates."

"So, that's not unusual in a storeroom."

"Look at how neat and clean everything is. Each crate is labeled as a clothing item. On the left side, we have socks, undershorts, and undershirts in that order. On the right side are the other garments."

"That is a bit strange," said Collins.

"In the main room, coats and foul weather gear are hung on hooks. Two hooks are empty, probably for the gear Tucker is wearing." Whitmer said, "Let's get back to work."

Changing rooms, they completed another search. This time Smith thumbed through each of the dozen or so books over the fireplace. Inside the third book, Zane Grey's *Robbers Roost*, he found a small slip of paper with a notation—B-493-4327. Showing it to the others, Smith said, "This has to be a telephone number for his brother, but where?"

Whitmer piped up, "Al, my in-laws live in Fremont, where 493 is the beginning of their number. It's a long shot. When we get back to Coquille, we'll check with Ma Bell for the listing. We might have our guy if it's in area code 415."

The officer outside asked if he could use the bathroom and have a cup of coffee. "It's okay by me. I'll take the security watch while you take a quick break."

Whitmer poured a half cup and said, "It's empty. We'll need to make another pot. I doubt Tucker will mind." Putting on the pot, Whitmer said, "We need to think this over. The warrant's for possession of firearms by a felon, but so far, we have nothing. Sure, we know it's Jim Tucker's place, but that's no crime."

Waiting for the coffee to finish perking, they sat around the table. Smith said, "What do we know for sure? Jim and Ben Tucker are bank robbers, convicted felons."

Kilpatrick added, "James Tucker bought this place using the name James Dean and bought ammo in both forty-five and thirty-aught-six caliber."

"And don't forget the Garands," Collins said.

Whitmer added, "We have a witness who knows his weaponry, as well as anyone in this room, saying he heard forty-five and aught-six firing from this area."

Kilpatrick said, "Detective Collins and I have the gun shop owner selling thousands of rounds of both to a man we know is Jim Tucker."

Turning to Smith, Whitmer said, "Steve's right. Al, you're an old Marine. What does that tell you?"

"Let's hold the old comments, old-timer. Here's what I can't figure out. We assume Tucker took a Garand and at least one forty-five and a supply of ammunition. He can't carry more than a few hundred rounds. Has anyone seen an ammo case, let alone a single cartridge?" There was a collective murmur of noes. "That's right. Now, where does Tucker keep his ammunition? He's a Marine who qualified as an expert with both weapons. He keeps those weapons spotless and ready for immediate use. Where are his cleaning supplies?"

Collins suggested, "Let's check for anything in the trees surrounding the cabin."

Forming a wheel with the cabin as the hub, they searched an area two hundred yards in circumference. They found a building ten yards into the trees. The small square structure had a quarter moon opening carved into the door. The wood was old and rotting; the image was of an outhouse not used for years, if not decades.

Back inside the cabin, Becker spoke first. "Did anyone check with the building department for blueprints for this place?"

Kilpatrick said, "I did, but it was a waste of time."

"Why?"

"You big city boys have records all the way back to the Civil War, but out here, we didn't have a building department until the forties. Like this cabin, many places were built long before building permits existed in these parts. Suffice it to say nothing's on file."

Collins asked, "Do any of us think there's nothing here?" No one answered. After a long silence, the detective said, "Right. Something's here, even if it's a single cartridge. So, let's think. What have we seen, and what haven't we seen?"

Combined, the officers had more than fifty years of experience. What were they missing? First, one got to his feet and moved about the cabin while looking at the place. Soon all five were examining every visible nook and cranny. Similar thoughts haunted Collins. *Something's here—I'm not going to let it beat me.*

Becker offered, "Growing up, my parents owned a cabin at Lake Tahoe. We used it year-round. In the winter, it was as cold as a well-digger's ass. Sorry, Jennifer."

"No offense. I know how cold that is."

"Anyway, the floors were wood, and they got damn cold. We had rugs in front of the fireplace, the couch, and under the kitchen table. Is there one in any of those places? Where's the one rug in this place? Yup, right under our feet. Remember the old western movies where the homesteaders hid from the Indians?"

Without a word, the five moved the table and pulled the rug aside, revealing a trap door with a recessed handle. Collins spoke, "It was your idea, Noah. You want the honors?"

"Thanks, Jennifer, but this is your case. Besides, I doubt my boss will let me come back to testify to opening a trapdoor."

As Collins reached for the handle, Whitmer took her by the shoulder and pulled her back. Irritated, she asked, "What?"

Whitmer looked at the group and signaled them to step away from the trapdoor.

With questioning looks from the other four, "Look, what if Tucker figured we would find it sooner or later and has a booby trap for whoever opens the door?"

"Thanks, Bill. I owe you one," Collins whispered. They tied a line to the handle. Backing out the front door, Collins pulled until the trapdoor was lying open.

Collins inched down the steps shouting as she went. "Tucker, I'm a police officer. If you're down there, speak up. Don't shoot!" A frightening and potentially fatal situation made all the more awkward as she took the stairs one at a time, holding her revolver in her right hand and a flashlight in her left.

Even with her police flashlight, it was dark. Shining it back and forth, she reported, "It looks about ten feet deep with a wood plank floor and the same for the walls. I can't see much else." After a brief pause, she spoke, "I found a light." A single bulb lit up the basement when Collins pulled a string, allowing her to see most of the area. Satisfied no one was in the room, she hurried on down. The rest followed.

In her written report, she describes the room as twelve by twelve with an eight-foot ceiling. One wall consisted of shelving stacked with cases of .45 caliber and 30-06 ammunition. Based on a count of the cases and boxes, she estimated five thousand rounds of forty-five and another four thousand aught-six. The wall behind the stairs was bare except for a safe. The safe stood open, empty except for the deed to the property.

A workbench for reloading ammunition occupied the third side. On shelves above were cans of gunpowder, empty brass cartridge cases, and several hundred bullets. The bullets were Sierra hunting for the 30-06. The fourth side held bookcases with dozens of how-to books for reloading enthusiasts.

Even before the search was complete, Kilpatrick went back out and retrieved his tech kit and began recovering latent fingerprints from the three rooms.

"Jennifer, I'm through up here. Are you ready for me?"

"Come on down and make sure you bring plenty of film."

With his kit in hand, Kilpatrick joined her. "I'll photograph everything. Anything special you want?"

"Get a close-up of the reloading equipment and ammunition. We don't have a firearm, but we can make a good case of possession by a felon."

Kilpatrick took over thirty photographs before dusting for latent prints. It was a slow process. Each time the trooper located useable latent prints, he took a photo from a distance allowing one to see where the latent prints were recovered. Then, he took a close-up that could be used if the latent was lost or damaged.

"Steve, we've been here almost twelve hours. How much longer will you be? It'll be dark in another hour," asked Whitmer.

"I know, Sarge, with a little luck, I'll finish in another twenty minutes. Would you mind packing up while I finish my photo and print logs?"

Ninety minutes later, the search team pulled into the parking lot at the Coquille Barracks.

A call came in for Sergeant Whitmer almost immediately, "Bill, Paul here. How'd it go?"

"Detective Collins handled herself as the professional we all knew her to be."

29

BEN WAS WORRIED ABOUT his brother. *It's been three weeks since I've heard from Jim.* That alone wasn't alarming—sometimes, as long as a month passed between Jim's calls—but today was Ben's birthday. *Jim always calls on my birthday. Maybe he's snowed in and can't get to town.*

Ben checked the weather for the Coos Bay area. Although unseasonably cold, it hadn't snowed since the last time Jim called. *Something's wrong. I'll give him until the end of the week. If he doesn't call, I'll take a ride up there. If I leave Friday morning, I'll spend the night in Myrtle Creek and get an early start checking the cabin.* Ben called the foreman of his landscaping business. "Miguel, I need a favor."

"*Si, Jefe.* What you need?"

"I got a gal I want to take to Lake Tahoe for a few days." *I hate lying to Miguel, but I don't have a choice.* "I'm leaving Friday. I'll be back sometime next week."

"Sounds good, Jefe. Things are a little slow with this cold weather."

"Tell me about it. I'd like you to swing by the office and make sure we have all the jobs covered. I'll leave a couple hundred bucks for you under my cigar box. You okay with that?"

"Si, Jefe. Get lucky with the tables and the lady."

"I hope so, but I doubt it. I'll be back sometime next week."

Working in his garage, Ben loaded his old model 400 HP Dodge pickup truck. *Nobody will recognize this for what it is.* Besides the hidden horsepower, he had installed a concealed storage compartment behind the bench seat. He placed an M1 Garand and eighty rounds of aught-six ammunition loaded in eight-round clips into this, along with two boxes and four loaded magazines of forty-five rounds. *I'll keep the forty-five handy.*

Ben finished packing enough food, clothing, and equipment to last five days in the wildness. *I gotta be ready if the weather turns bad.* Ben hoped that he would find his brother snowed in or otherwise safe and unable to get his old truck out to the county road. As much as Ben tried to be positive, he couldn't shake a dreadful premonition.

Ben kept an Oregon license plate under the seat and put it on the truck after gassing up in Yreka.

Jim worked his way cross-country over the mountains to the village of Allegany. In good weather, it would take three days. The weather wasn't good, with the temperature dipping below zero every night and failing to rise above 40° during the day. The cold close, oppressive, created a wet and dreary world. Jim's strength was sapped, leaving him freezing and depressed. The chill bored into his very soul. *Death waits around the next corner.*

With a bit of luck, I'll make it in four days, five at the most. Since buying the cabin, Jim loved hiking through these coastal mountains and fishing in the local rivers and streams. This time, the urgency and terrible weather conditions made for a hazardous trek. With three feet of snow, it was risky. Dangerous even for an outdoorsman with his experience. *I have to take it easy.*

The morning of the third day, working his way up the side of a steep incline on a narrow animal trail, Jim stumbled and dropped his rifle. It clattered over the wet embankment and came to rest ten feet below. *Damn. It's halfway between here and the lower trail. I'll have to walk down and climb up to it.* After he removed his pack, fatigue played a role in Tucker making a risky, ill-advised decision. *It'll take too long to go down the trail and climb up. I'll get down from here and come back on the trail.*

Jim had gone but six feet when he slipped on the icy slope and fell about a hundred feet down the steep mountainside before regaining his footing at the edge of a rushing creek. Bruised and dazed, it was an hour before Jim got back to his gear. His pistol had dropped from its holster when he fell. Finding it took another half hour. Collecting his rifle and getting back to the trail took a good part of the day. Falling snow and ice found their way down the back of his coat and into his boots. His thermal underwear and socks were soaked. With sunset looming, he was forced to set a hasty camp with little time to build a roaring fire, dry his wet clothing and eat some food. His body temperature rose, reducing the risk of hypothermia. The Garand was in bad shape, and it took him an hour to clean and repair the rifle.

Cold produces distinctive personalities. Whether in the alps in the dead of winter, traversing a lonely desert trail, or negotiating the coastal mountains of Oregon, cold has unique features. On a clear and quiet

January morning in the high inland mountains, one can almost touch the clear, clean, crisp air as it smothers you in an invisible coat of exhilaration. One feels alive; not so for Jim. The moist cold of the coastal mountain had always been the most debilitating.

The following morning, Jim waited for daylight before assessing his situation. He considered abandoning his kit, but survival depended on his food and supplies. He hadn't broken anything in the fall but bruised his hip. *The pain's going to slow me down.*

At noon, the fifth day, Jim was on the verge of exhaustion when the village came into sight. Allegany had a permanent population of less than three hundred. A stranger hiking into town during the summer wasn't uncommon. In the middle of winter, a stranger would draw the attention of all, including the resident deputy. Finding a flat area at the top of a bluff overlooking the short main street, he watched and waited an hour for any unusual activity. All was quiet. Not one car entered or left the village. *They found the gun room; by now, every cop in Oregon is looking for me. I have to lay low until nightfall, find a payphone, and call Ben. Then I'll steal a car.* Familiar with the area, Tucker eased down a few hundred yards to a picnic area closed in the winter. Crawling under one of the tables, he brushed away the snow, put down a ground cloth, unrolled his mummy bag, and slept undisturbed until nightfall.

Waking, Jim figured it would be six or seven hours before whatever he stole in the village was missed. *I have to get to a city and take another car. After I get another car, what then?* Near midnight, Jim found a closed gas station with an outside payphone and called Ben. The phone rang and rang. He returned to the park and waited an hour before trying again, but still no answer. His mind ran wild. *Did they get Ben? Damn it, Ben, where are you?* Jim waited until dawn and tried for one last time. Still no answer. *I can't wait any longer. I have to get a car and get out of here. Ben, where are you?*

Ben had the same question—two brothers, one shared fear—*Is my brother safe?* He left Myrtle Creek at four in the morning. Still dark, he parked deep in the woods off a seldom-used forest service road. As the crow flies, it would be five miles of rough terrain and snow, making it difficult to hike to Jim's cabin. Ben reckoned on being there between nine and ten. It was nearer to noon when he caught sight of his brother's hideout.

Ben watched the cabin, moving closer

after leaving everything except the rifle and pistol. It looked peaceful but much too quiet. For one thing, no smoke was coming from the chimney. *Something's wrong. Jim's the pioneer type, but he'd have a fire burning at the very least.* His brother's old truck was parked where he always left it. Still, something was amiss. Remaining far back in the trees, Ben took a tortuous ninety minutes to circle the place. The silence was deafening.

Satisfied no danger lurked within the cabin, Ben stepped behind a tree at the edge of the clearing and shouted. "Jim, Jim, are you in there?" getting no response. Waiting another ten minutes, Ben weighed his options either remain or leave. *That's not happening.* The remaining option was to approach and enter the cabin, so he took a first tentative step out of the trees. Ben had been ambushed and wounded on patrol on Corregidor before the island fell to the Japanese. *I don't like walking into the open— not one bit.*

Ben moved forward, fighting off the urge to retreat, and upon reaching the tiny porch, called out, "Jim. It's me, Ben. You in there?" Receiving no answer, he stood to the right side of the door before reaching over and trying the knob. It was locked. Ben found the key Jim always kept hidden. Unlocking the door, Ben flung it open and backed up against the thick outside wall—nothing. After stepping through the doorway—*the police have been here*. The cabin was a mess, and fingerprint powder was evident even with the bit of light coming through the opening. The table was moved, and the trapdoor stood open.

Ben saw no sign of a struggle nor any bloodstains. *Did they get Jim? How long ago were they here? Today, days, or weeks ago? It had to have been recently, or Jim would have contacted me. Is he in jail or out?* Ben didn't know why but he had an overwhelming sense that couldn't be ignored; he was sure that his brother hadn't been arrested—*Jim's way too clever by half to get caught unawares.*

Having discussed Jim's escape plan in the past, Ben knew his brother would hike over the mountains to Allegany. *God willing, my brother got away and hiked out.* Ben knew if his brother managed to escape, he would find a way to warn him. The two places Jim could call Ben were at his home or the landscaping business. *I'll call the office as a last resort. I have to get home, even if the cops are waiting.*

Ben was back in Fremont the following afternoon. After checking the business, he went to his neighborhood, found a good vantage point, and watched his house until well past midnight. Convinced no one waited inside, Ben walked down the alley and in through the back door. Easing from room to room, he saw that no one had been inside in his absence. *Stay or run? If I run, I'll never find Jim. If I stay, I'll get arrested. If I don't hear from him—I run. I'll give it three days.*

30

WHEN THE DETECTIVES RETURNED to Coquille, Becker got on the phone with the security manager at Pacific Bell in Oakland, California. He gave the number found in Jim Tucker's cabin, B-493-4327, to the retired San Francisco police officer, explaining it was part of an ongoing robbery investigation. Giving the man Detective Collins' phone number, he asked him to provide the information to her. The security manager confirmed that 493 was an exchange number used in Southern Alameda County. It would take him an hour or two to get the subscriber information and call back. By then, Becker would be on his way back to San Leandro.

Before Becker and Smith headed back to California, Captain Doll came by to discuss the day's events. Something had to be done about the deputy who leaked the information used by Jim Tucker to make good his escape.

The Coquille Barracks area commander told them, "I've already given the sheriff a heads up. We're meeting in the morning to make it official. I doubt the deputy will get fired unless he has a history of screw-ups." Doll wasn't satisfied but left the matter in the commander's hands.

Collins told the California detectives she had enough to support the charge of a felon in possession of firearms. "It ought to be enough for a conviction, but even then, the judge has the option to sentence him to a maximum of five years or as little as one year."

Becker said, "We'll have to get them charged with robbery in California. It's too bad we didn't find anything to tie them to our robberies."

Sergeant Murphy spoiled Becker's return to the office. Murphy complained Becker's long absence had created a drain on staffing resulting in extra work for Murphy and the entire investigations unit. Murphy was angry at the young detective—jealous would have been a more accurate choice of words.

Becker knew better. The police chief had permitted the young detective to make the trip to Oregon. Becker had missed only three days' work, returning on the weekend. No other detective was away from the office, nor had there been a rash of crimes. Murphy being the asshole he was, heaped low-priority tasks upon the investigator after a bombastic tirade about loyalty to the police department.

It was Tuesday afternoon before Becker could call Jennifer Collins. The call made up for all the bullshit Murphy had heaped upon him.

"Hi, Jennifer. Noah Becker here. How goes the battle?"

"Thanks to you, the battle goes a little better. The prosecuting attorney has issued a complaint against Jim Tucker for possession of a firearm by a felon."

"That's great. Let me know once the warrant's signed. Smith will be happy to hear the news. Did PacBell get back to you with the information on the phone number?"

"Yes. You and Al will be happy. The number is, without a doubt, Ben Tucker's. The listing is for 666 Cumberland Way, Fremont. It gets better."

"Alright, Jennifer, gimme."

"The subscriber is Benjamin Alexander. You remember that name?"

"You bet. It's the name Ben Tucker used to enlist in the Marine Corps. As soon as my sergeant lightens up, I'll head over to the Tax Assessor's office to check ownership and documents so we can compare his handwriting."

Sergeant Murphy continued to punish Becker. Becker called Smith. "Hey, Al, I've got good news." After filling Smith in on what he had learned from the OSP detective, "Murphy won't let me leave the office. Saturday, I'll swing by and take a look at the place. You want to come along?" Smith agreed to join him on Saturday at Prings Restaurant in San Leandro for an early breakfast. They wanted to be watching the place before dawn.

"About the property," Smith said. "I have time. I'll get certified copies of the records and bring them on Saturday. A buddy of mine is working intelligence at Fremont PD. He'll keep his mouth shut. I'll call him today and see if they have anything on Cumberland Way. Okay with you?"

"Sounds good. I'll meet you at 4:00 a.m. on Saturday. My wife'll be pissed—again. What about Bert? She will be on your case too?" Becker said.

"Boy, howdy. I'll blame it on you. Bert is sure you walk on water."

Saturday morning Smith and Becker were at Prings long before sunrise.

"Peggy, this is my friend, Detective Al Smith."

"Nice to meet any friend of Noah's."

Once the two detectives were huddled over pancakes and eggs, Becker told Smith the midnight waitress had worked at Prings

Restaurant since he had been in diapers. "She knows every cop in the department, all the Alameda County Sheriff's deputies, and Highway Patrol officers from three counties. She calls us her boys."

Smith put his information on the table. "Here are the certified copies of the records I got for the Cumberland property trans-actions. I'm sure this is our guy. Ben Tucker was paroled from Leavenworth in sixty-six. This house was built in sixty-seven. Benjamin Alexander, a single man, made a large cash down payment on the place. He listed his occupation as a landscaper."

Looking at the records, Becker examined the deed, the signatures on the Marine Corps records, and the copies of the old fingerprint cards. The more he looked, the bigger his smile. Glancing at Smith, "They're the same. This is Ben Tucker."

"I know, kid. We got him."

"Hey, old-timer, I'll let the kid comment slide this time. We did it. We got him. Now, all we have to do is get enough for an arrest warrant."

When the checks came, Smith said, "This is less than half what it should be. I can't accept a gratuity."

"Don't even try arguing with her. She'll throw your money back at you. Pay what she charges and leave a good tip. Now, let's get finished before we need to leave."

Becker smiled. "I checked DMV, and Benjamin Alexander uses the same birthdate for his driver's license that Ben Tucker used to enlist in the Marine Corps. If nothing else, we get him for perjury for falsifying his driver's license application. I requested a certified copy of his California driver's record, photo, and application. We won't have a problem identifying him."

"You're right, Noah. Who knows what we'll find on the driving record? We'll get even more charges if we get certified copies for any vehicles Ben Tucker has registered to him or his landscaping company. Perjury on those documents is still a felony. Now let's get out to Fremont before sunrise."

Because it was Saturday, Becker wasn't on duty, so he drove his personal vehicle, a ten-year-old Chevrolet station wagon. Smith had his Dodge Polaris, which looked like an undercover cop car.

"Your car looks like a cop car. Let's take mine," Becker said.

"Old and battered might blend, but the paint's shot, and it looks more like something from the ghetto, no offense. And, I bet it has a six-cylinder."

"It is a six and even has a three-speed column shift. It'll work fine. After all, we won't be chasing anyone."

Leaving the Polaris parked at the restaurant, they took the old Chevrolet, hoping it would blend into the Fremont neighborhood. Arriving on Cumberland a half hour before sunrise, they figured they could make two passes by Tucker's place without drawing attention.

Smith slumped in the back seat. He told Becker, "One person passing through the neighborhood looks more natural. I'll sit up in the passenger seat on the way out. Anyone looking will think you picked up a buddy, maybe for golf."

The house was dark, with no cars in the driveway. There were few cars on the street. Finding a place to park and observe the house unnoticed proved difficult. They settled on a spot on the next block. They couldn't see Tucker's house, but they could see if any vehicles came or went from the driveway.

Smith commented, "We don't have to be at Fremont PD until nine, so we have a couple of hours. What do you suggest we do if he comes or goes?"

"Nothing. We don't have enough for a probable cause arrest."

"I agree. Even if we do see Tucker, we shouldn't follow him. The risk of him spotting us and going into hiding is too great."

They were detected at 8:00 a.m. when a

man, a few doors behind them, came out for his newspaper. Seeing a strange car with two men in it was suspicious. Five minutes later, a pair of Fremont police cars, one with lights flashing, pulled in behind the detectives.

Becker saw them first. "Shit."

Startled, Smith said, "What? What is it?"

"Fremont PD," Becker said, getting out of the car, holding his badge above his head. The lights on the first car continued to flash. An officious-looking officer strutted forward. The second, older cop shook his head, hurried over to the first car, reached through the open window, turned off the lights, straightened up, and walked to where the younger officer was demanding Becker's driver's license.

"Don't you see his badge and I.D.?" he asked the younger man.

"That doesn't tell me if he has a driver's license. I want proper identification."

The older officer's nametag identified him as T. Warren. Ignoring the younger one, "Officer Warren, I'm Detective Noah Becker from San Leandro Police Department, and this is Detective Al Smith from Mountain View P.D. We have a meeting at your department at 9:00 a.m. In the meantime, we thought we would take a run by a house that's come up in our investigation."

"It's Tom. Tom Warren. I hope we haven't

blown your cover." He didn't mention the obvious—the other officer was fresh out of the academy.

Smith said, "We're okay. What say we take this away from here?"

Warren turned to the younger officer, "Does that work for you?"

"Sure, Tom. If the detectives want to head for the station, I'll get back to what I was doing before the call."

Officer Warren said, "Do me a favor. In the future, call dispatch and let them know you'll be in the area. It'll save trouble all the way around."

A sheepish Becker said, "You're right. It won't happen again."

Arriving early for their meeting at Fremont PD, they were escorted to the break room. Officers and civilian employees were chatting over coffee. The detectives sat at a table in the corner after helping themselves to coffee.

One of the Fremont officers inquired, "You the ones we heated up over on Cumberland?"

An already embarrassed Becker said, "Yup."

Smith's friend rescued them before it could get any more embarrassing. "Hey, Al. Grab a cup, and let's head up to my office."

Ensconced in the intelligence officer's

cubicle, Smith gave the Reader's Digest condensed version of the ongoing investigation. "We're hoping you can give us something on Ben Tucker, AKA Ben Alexander."

"I've checked back to sixty-seven when the name Benjamin Alexander was used to buy the property. We've had no contact with him. No arrests, no reports, not even a ticket." Turning his hands out with an apologetic expression, the detective went on. "I went over to city hall and checked with Finance and the Building Department. He does not have a license to run a landscaping business in Fremont. According to the building inspector, there are no applications on file for any building permits."

Becker said, "You've been pretty thorough. We appreciate you trying. We should have an arrest warrant and a search warrant for Tucker in a week. Can we get some help taking him down?"

"Absolutely. I imagine you want to keep this quiet until then?"

Smith answered. "Yes. We don't want to get the place heated up. His brother's on the run and may try hiding out with Ben."

"You met two of our patrolmen earlier today, right?"

Smith and Becker looked at each other. Then, finally, Smith said, "Jeez, does everyone at FPD gotta remind us?"

"No, Al. Remember the older officer, Tom Warren? Tom's been around a while. He served as an investigator and has worked in the area around Cumberland for years. Tom can be trusted." After a gulp of coffee, "He might have something not in the records. I'll have him come in and talk to you. I'm sure he'll be of help. Besides, when you serve your warrants, I'll have him assigned to cover you."

"If you trust him, bring him in. We need all the help you can give us," Smith said.

Tom Warren knew many people on his beat, including Ben Alexander, and where the man lived. "I've seen him mowing his lawn a few times. I try to meet everyone on my beat and talk with them at least once. I stopped and talked to him twice in the last couple of years."

Becker, all ears, said, "What can you tell us about him? Maybe identify him from an old photo?"

"He was polite and didn't volunteer anything other than owning a landscaping business in case I wanted a deal. I didn't. If I had to guess, I say he's fifty to sixty. I should be able to identify him. Show me what you got."

Smith handed him copies of the photographs taken when the Tuckers were granted paroled in 1966. Warren pointed to the picture of Ben Tucker and said, "This one's a younger version of the guy who lives on Cumberland. I don't know the other." Warren agreed to keep the investigation to himself and to keep an eye on Tucker's place. If he saw anything, he would call.

Becker said, "Thanks, Tom. We're headed back to San Leandro."

Smith was hungry and suggested grabbing lunch at Prings. Becker recommended that they stop at the best hamburger place in the Bay Area. "You gotta try Val's. They've been around a while. You won't be disappointed."

Looking over the wall menu, Smith said, "I'm going for a Papa Burger with cheese, French fries, and a strawberry milkshake."

"You sure? That's a lot more than you think."

"Yup."

Becker settled on a Mama Burger and a glass of water. Much to his surprise, Smith cleaned his plate and added a dish of ice cream.

While eating, they discussed the case between bites. They agreed they lacked enough for an arrest warrant but might have enough for a search warrant.

"Noah, where do we stand the best chance of getting the warrant signed?"

"You have a stronger case in San Mateo

County, but we need to get an Alameda County judge to sign it. George Nichols is an aggressive Deputy District Attorney who knows search and seizure as well as anyone. I'll set a meeting with him next week. That work for you?" Smith agreed they should get the search warrant signed in Alameda County, where the place to be searched was located.

"Okay, Noah. You set the meeting with Nichols for next week. After that, I'll meet with my DA and try to convince him to give me an arrest warrant for Ben Tucker. I don't have enough for his brother."

Becker said, "Sounds good. If you get an arrest warrant, it'll make our chances of getting a search warrant even better."

31

JIM TUCKER FINALLY REACHED his brother by telephone. "Ben, the cops searched my place. By now, they must have a warrant for my arrest. Are you okay?"

"I'm fine. When you didn't call me on my birthday, I got worried. So after a couple of days went by, I made a trip up to your place. The cops left the place covered with fingerprint powder, and they found your gun room. How'd you get away?"

"My scanner. A dumbassed deputy was blabbing on the radio. It got me an hour to pack up. I hiked to Allegany, but it took longer than I had planned. I called the first chance I had, but no answer."

"I figured they had you, and I would be next. So when nothing happened, I got into your place during the night. After I got back here, I watched for the cops. No one has been in the house. Why don't you come down here for a few days?"

"Just because they haven't been there yet, doesn't mean you're safe. It's time to run."

"I should be safe for now. Nothing links me to you or your cabin." The brothers talked until Jim ran out of coins. Ben insisted on staying put. Finally, Jim agreed to come to Fremont, but not until the following week.

George Nichols, a career prosecutor, loved nothing better than an opportunity to put bad guys in jail, and the Tuckers were bad guys. So after Becker introduced Al Smith, Nichols said, "You got thirty minutes. Who's giving me the story?" Two hours later, Nichols told the detectives, "You have more than enough for a search warrant for the Fremont house. We have enough to charge Benjamin Tucker with perjury. It's not much, but it'll get him arrested if the search comes up empty."

"Thanks, George. I'm sure we'll come up with something when we serve the warrant," Becker said.

"I have to get to court. When can you be back here? Becker should be the affiant." Both detectives would work on it together. They promised to have a draft for Nichols to review the following morning. "Okay, meet me at the San Leandro Courthouse at 8:00 a.m. Make sure you bring me a crime report for the DMV perjury."

Back at SLPD, Becker met with Murphy. "Sarge, we met with George Nichols. He says we have more than enough for a search warrant for Ben Tucker's place."

"Do you have enough for an arrest?"

"Not enough for an arrest on our robbery cases, but Nichols will issue a complaint charging perjury for the falsified driver's license application. It'll be enough to get Tucker arrested. We have to be back at Nichols' office first thing in the morning with the affidavit ready to go and a crime report for the DMV perjury."

"It's weak on probable cause. When you finish the search warrant affidavit and crime report, I want to review what you wrote before returning to Nichols. Have them ready for me to review at 9:00 a.m. tomorrow."

"But Sarge, we're supposed to be at Nichols' office at eight."

"You heard me Becker, nine, at my office. These guys have been out for years. Another hour to make sure nothing's missing can't hurt."

Becker started to object when Smith quieted him with a discreet nod. "Yes, sir. We'll be here at nine."

The detectives went to work. With fifteen

years of experience writing search warrants, Smith took the lead. "I'm not saying you couldn't do this on your own, but working together, we'll get it done much sooner."

Becker said, "Murphy wants the credit if it goes well, and you're patronizing me. You're the expert, and I'm new at this. You lead—I'll follow."

After assembling all the evidence on the Tuckers, they started writing. By the time the detectives finished the document, it was past midnight.

Smith and Becker met with Nichols at eight, as promised. Becker gave him copies of the affidavit and crime report and explained his problem with Murphy. Nichols would keep their counsel. "I understand, don't worry, go ahead and meet with your sergeant at nine. Then, once Murphy finishes pontificating, come to the Hayward Court-house. I have a hearing at ten, but I'll devote the rest of the day to you."

Sergeant Murphy spent more than an hour reading over the documents Becker and Smith gave him. He used a red ink pen to mark throughout the documents. There wasn't much for him to say about the perjury crime report. Finished, "Okay, make the changes I've directed. Then you go see the district attorney."

On the way to Hayward, Becker drove

while Smith read Murphy's comments. "The asshole doesn't have a clue. If we make these changes, no judge will ever sign it."

"Don't worry, Al, he'll never remember what he wrote. But, when we get the warrant signed, he'll tell us that without his help, no judge would have signed it."

Nichols made a few suggestions. Both investigators agreed his ideas strengthened the probable cause. While his clerk retyped the affidavit and warrant, Nichols issued a felony complaint for perjury. Once the documents were completed to his satisfaction, he took the detectives to Judge Robert Delucchi. He was the best search and seizure judge in the San Leandro-Hayward Municipal Court. Nichols told them, "If Judge Delucchi approves the warrant, you can count on it holding up to appellate review." The judge's clerk expected the trio and escorted them to his chambers. Nichols made the introductions. "Judge, you know Detective Becker, and this is Detective Al Smith from Mountain View P.D. They have a search warrant request and a complaint I would like to file. The affidavit is extensive. I've read it and believe it provides sufficient probable cause for you to issue a search warrant."

The judge came from behind his desk and shook hands with all three. "Detective

Smith, it's a pleasure to meet you." Then, glancing at the affidavit, the judge said, "This is pretty long."

Becker said, "Yes, sir. It's twenty-eight pages."

"I've got an in-custody arraignment in a few minutes. Would you mind coming back after three? It will give me time to study this and prepare any questions I have for you."

Nichols answered for them, "No problem, Judge, we'll be back."

When the trio returned at three, the judge asked a few questions, which they answered. Next, he made notations on several pages. Before continuing, he asked Becker to read it over, paying close attention to his notes. "Please initial each of my comments." When Becker finished, the judge initialed each of the notations. Once the search warrant was signed, the judge turned to Nichols. "George, I'm a little curious. Why are you requesting an arrest warrant for perjury instead of robbery?"

"The detectives don't believe they have enough for a robbery conviction. I agree with them. We hope to get enough evidence to charge robbery when they serve the warrant and have Tucker in custody."

"I'm sure you have enough, but you and the detectives know best. I'll issue the arrest warrant for the DMV perjury charge."

Nichols asked the judge to set bail at $100,000. Judge Delucchi consented and signed the arrest warrant. "I hope you have more before Mr. Tucker's bail hearing."

32

THE DAY STARTED PLEASANT enough for Ben
Tucker. With the rebirth of his flower garden,
he knew spring was around the corner. The
weather was clear and warm. A high of
seventy was expected. *I'll weed the
flowerbeds and then mow the lawn.*

A week had passed with no sign of cops
or surveillance. Ben wanted to believe the
Oregon State Police raid on Jim's cabin was
an Oregon thing. As far as Ben could tell,
each day had been free of danger. Lulled into
a false sense of security, Ben failed to notice
a pickup truck with a camper shell parked a
half-block away. He was finishing the front
yard flowerbed when they came. Down on his
knees, weeding dandelions in silence, car
doors closing, Ben was alert to the danger
even before a firm voice commanded,
"Benjamin Tucker, don't move, police." Ben
didn't.

After being handcuffed, Ben saw seven of

them, three uniformed cops and four in plainclothes. The youngest spoke first. "Mr. Tucker, I'm Detective Becker of the San Leandro Police Department. We have a warrant for your arrest and a search warrant for your home. Do you understand?" Tucker stared at him, not saying a word. "Is there anyone else in the house?" Tucker remained silent.

"Please confirm you're Benjamin Tucker."

"My name is Ben Alexander. Who's Benjamin Tucker?"

The oldest-looking detective spoke. "Becker, he isn't going to tell you anything. Stick him in a car and have him transported. I want this over with so I can get back to the office."

The tallest detective addressed the older guy. "Sergeant Murphy, I have a suggestion."

"Go ahead." At the direction of Smith, the three detectives moved behind a marked police car.

"Becker and I will handle the search with the Fremont guys. If you want, you could go back to SLPD and update the chief before you hold a press conference."

"Detective Smith, that sounds reasonable. Now that we have Tucker, we should hold a press conference. I'll handle that while you and Becker finish up here. Call and let me know what you find. Are you sure you'll be able to get along without me?"

Smith said, "If we run into a problem, we'll call you for direction." Without another word, Murphy turned and walked to a car.

Smith turned to Becker. "That work for you?"

"Hell, yes. Let's get Tucker settled and start the search."

Two of the uniformed cops placed Tucker in the back of a police car while the others talked. The Fremont detective suggested, "Why not have Tom Warren transport Tucker back to the police department? The other two will provide security while we search. Tom will make sure no one talks to him until you're ready."

They agreed that it would be the best course of action. Becker added, "Make sure he doesn't make any calls until we get there."

The Fremont detective said, "Even though it's my jurisdiction, it's you guys' case. I'll help as much as possible, but let's agree on who will do what." Because Becker was the affiant on the search warrant, it was his job to collect the evidence. Smith would take photographs and prepare the diagram. After complying with the requirement to knock and announce, they went in through the unlocked front door. The officers found a clean and tidy home. The walls were painted in fresh and bright shades, no pictures or paintings adorned the walls, and all the furniture was new and immaculate. Becker found a small library of classics, dozens of the pulp westerns popular in the early part of the century, an entire collection of Zane Grey, and a first edition of Owen Wister's *The Virginian.*

A police scanner set to the Fremont frequency squawked from the fireplace mantel. A few minutes after they entered the house, the radio squawked with Officer Warren's announcement of his arrival at the jail with one in custody.

The carpeting was new in appearance but an older style with vacuum cleaner lines throughout the home. The kitchen was sparse. The breakfast dishes had been washed and put away if there had been any. The cupboards contained two place settings, not three or four. A three-bedroom house, two were spic and span with bedspreads as tight as those on a Marine's bunk. A dresser contained a man's underwear and socks, all neatly rolled. The clothes in the closet were starched and ironed. The third bedroom had been converted into an office complete with an IBM electric typewriter. Next to it, on the desk, was an old Precisa adding machine. Tucker was modern enough to use an electric typewriter but seemingly didn't trust an electrical device for his numbers.

The officers experienced an eerie aware-
ness as they began their search. Discussing
it later, Becker said it reminded him of a
prison cell. Smith agreed, "It does and also
like a Marine barracks."

One item seemed out of place in the
otherwise austere house. In the living room
sat an oblong table that appeared to have
been made from a sixty by a twenty-inch
piece of roughhewn redwood and then
finished to a high gloss. Centered on the top
was a Marantz 2270 Receiver, a Technics SL-
1200 turntable atop it, and high-end
speakers on either side.

Becker said, "I wish I could afford a
system like this. It and his record collection
would cost me a half year's salary."

One of the uniformed officers commented
on the LP albums. "Simon and Garfunkel,
Neil Diamond, Nina Simone, Carole King—
looks like this guy has good taste."

Before they began to search in earnest,
Smith photographed the house inside and
out. The Fremont detective started in the
master bedroom. "Hey guys, take a look at
this."

Becker and Smith entered the room and
saw the pillows were pulled back, exposing a
large pistol. Smith announced, "Colt .45
military issue." Smith smiled at Becker.
"These guys wouldn't own anything else.

Now, where's the Garand?" They tossed the house twice but came up with no other weapons. Nor did they find anything to identify the suspect as Ben Tucker or tie him to his brother Jim.

Finished with the house, Becker said, "Time for the garage. I hope we do better out there."

"Amen," Smith responded.

Becker went through the knock and announce requirement before entering the locked garage with a key ring taken from a hook near the back door. The structure had been a three-car garage with a single and double door. An older model Dodge pickup was parked next to a late model Chevrolet station wagon. In violation of the city's building code, the single-car bay had been walled in. The Fremont detective said, "He didn't get a building permit for this."

Gaining entry with two more of Tucker's keys, they found a room similar in design to the one beneath Jim Tucker's cabin floor. The walls were stout, two-by-four reinforced. Security included a heavy door with two sets of deadbolts. Inside, above the door, was a Colt .45 pistol. Smith checked it. "Full magazine with one in the chamber. It's ready for action."

Unlike Jim's, Ben Tucker's gun rack held three Garands. Smith, the Marine veteran, examined the weapons. Once finished, he said, "All three are immaculate. They've been field stripped and cleaned—loaded now."

Like Jim, Ben had a small safe. But, contrasting Jim, his was locked and attached to the cement floor. The Fremont detective offered to call a locksmith. Instead, Smith suggested asking Ben Tucker. "After all, we don't have anything to lose," Smith called the jail and asked for Tom Warren. "Tom, how's Tucker behaving?"

"He's a perfect gentleman. Insists, he's Benjamin Alexander, has never heard of Ben Tucker."

"Okay. Do me a favor?"

"Sure. Whatta you need?"

"Take him into an interview room—one with a telephone—just you two. When you're set, I'll call you."

"Okay, Detective, give me ten minutes. I'll raise you on the radio once we're ready."

Warren picked it up when the phone rang. "Warren here."

"Hey Tom, Smith here. Please put Tucker on."

"Hi, Ben. I'm Al Smith, one of the detectives at your house."

"You the tall one?"

"That would be me. I got a favor to ask. How about you give me the combination to your safe?"

"Now, why would I wanna do that?"

"You don't, but it would save me some time and effort. Besides, this way, I won't have to damage your safe."

Tucker started laughing. It took him a second to settle down and answer Smith. "Look, Detective, you got me, and we both know I ain't going anywhere for a long time. And I'll never see my safe again. So, like I said, why would I help you? Ain't nuthin' in it for me."

"You're right. Nothing in it for you. You're a Marine, right?"

"Yeah, W-W-Two. Why?"

"First Marines, Chosin Reservoir, November fifty."

"Semper Fi. I still don't see any reason to help you."

"Ben, I know. I figured us old Purple Heart Marines could work something out. All I have to offer is protective custody if you want it."

"Okay, Detective, let's pretend we're two old Marines shooting the breeze. May I call you Al?"

"Fine by me."

"Look, Al, nothing in the safe will give you anything of use. No guns, nothing to tie me to anything. The only stuff is an old picture of my mother and father on their wedding day, a couple of books, and the papers about my house and car. I don't need protective custody, but I'd take it kindly if you bring me some books to read."

"Happy to. Any books in particular you want?"

"Yeah, a couple of the Zane Greys. There are three autographed copies in the safe, including a first edition of *Riders of the Purple Sage*. Please make sure they're not damaged. Did you see the first edition of *The Virginian* in the house?"

"I did. Nice."

"Do me a favor, lock it and the signed Zane Grey's in the safe when you finish up. You got a pencil?" Tucker gave Smith the combination to the safe.

"I'll be careful."

"Thanks."

Smith and Becker, the combination in hand, went back into the garage. Smith tried the numbers but had trouble. "Damn it."

"Here, let me try. Your fingers are as big as bananas," Becker said.

"Give me a break," the bigger man said as he rose.

Becker made a few quick spins of the dial, rotated through the numbers, and the safe came open. "There you go. The honors are all yours."

Smith went through the contents. "It's as Tucker said. Nothing we need."

Once finished with the search warrant, the detectives returned to Fremont PD, bringing two Zane Grey books from the house. Their attempts to interview Tucker met with a polite refusal. While transporting Tucker to San Leandro, Ben and Smith talked about their time in the Marine Corps. Both cop and criminal agreed they loved the Corps but could have passed on the experience.

33

WANTING TO FIND HIS brother and knowing the police were looking for him, Jim could not go through Coos Bay. Instead, he headed north and east to central Oregon before heading south to California, stealing a third car in Grants Pass and heading south on the new Interstate 5. Traffic on I-5 was heavy during the daylight hours but less so during late-night hours. It was dark when Tucker got to Redding. He decided to spend the night and get an early start the next day.

Jim was minutes away from Ben's place when a marked Fremont Police car, lights flashing, sped past him at well over the speed limit. He slowed, stopped, and waited. Soon another police car sped by in the direction of Ben's. After waiting another five minutes, Jim drove to Ben's street and passed the house and two marked police cars parked across the front. A pickup with a camper shell stood in the driveway with the doors open. Uniformed cops and four in plain-clothes stood in front.

Ben was cuffed and face down on the front lawn. *I can't get into a shoot-out with all those cops.* Jim kept moving and didn't stop until he was back in Oregon.

Jim couldn't do anything for Ben until he discovered why his brother had been arrested. It had to be for a bank job. *I'll hire a lawyer for him and get the answers.* Jim called information for criminal lawyers in Fremont, California. He settled on Barry Chalmers, an attorney willing to take on a bank robbery case. Jim imagined it would be a simple matter. *I'll give Chalmers a few thousand dollars to talk with Ben.*

Jim knew his brother would give the lawyer a message and have him get back with everything about the charges. Chalmers, an ethical lawyer, refused to provide Jim with any information or even represent Ben, saying, "I have to ask him to sign a represen-tation agreement before we talk."

Three days later, Jim called Chalmers. Chalmers explained that Ben would have to agree to allow James Dean to pay for his defense. "My client will have to decide if he will let me discuss the case with anyone else." Jim had no qualms agreeing to what Chalmers said—Ben would want him to know everything. Jim sent Chalmers a cashier's check. As expected, Ben signed off on all the provisions. Besides the San Leandro cases, there was now enough evidence to charge Ben in San Mateo with armed robbery, a felon in possession of a firearm, and three prior felony convictions.

"Look, Mr. Tucker, an arrest warrant for robbery was issued for you, and the DA told me an arrest warrant for James Tucker, also known as James Dean, was issued in Oregon, alleging possession of a firearm by a felon. I'm guessing that's you."

"Yeah, I figured that was coming."

Chalmers talked with Deputy District Attorneys in both Alameda and San Mateo County. They intended to bring Ben to trial in both jurisdictions. If convicted in either county, Ben faced forty years to life. With Ben's record of arrests and convictions, he would die long before being eligible for parole. The cases looked good, with the DAs claiming to have fingerprints and eyewitness identification. It would be weeks, maybe months, before Chalmers was granted discovery and learned what the cops had on his client.

Jim knew it was a matter of time before he was caught and arrested. *I'll be lucky if I don't get shot by a gun-happy cop.*

34

DEPUTY DISTRICT ATTORNEY NICHOLS filed five counts of possession of a firearm by a convicted felon. Smith and Becker had a solid case based on Tucker's possession of the forty-fives and the Garands. Nichols told the detectives, "Ben Tucker'll die of old age in prison. But, without more proof, I don't have enough to charge him with robbery."

"With Ben Tucker in custody and his brother on the run, we'll have the time to work on the bank robberies here in San Leandro and Smith's holdups over in San Mateo," said Noah.

Noah Becker went back through the case file on the Crocker Bank robbery. He was not happy. The original investigator had not documented a thorough investigation, kissing it off with a minimal inquiry and a notation: "FBI has primary jurisdiction." A crime scene technician had been assigned, but no tech report was in the file. More out of desperation than anything else, Becker paid a visit to the officer in charge of the Evidence Room.

"Hey, what do you need, Noah?"

Becker explained the mention of a technician at the scene. "I can't find his report in the file. Any suggestions?"

The evidence technician said, "Let me dig around and see what I find. Give me a couple of days."

Al Smith showed photo lineups of both Tuckers and a photograph of the rental car to the witness who had seen them get into the getaway car. *I've got nothing to lose.*

"Mr. Brown, do you remember we talked outside the Bank of America after the robbery?"

"I do. What can I do for you?"

"Please tell me what you remember about that day and what you saw. Leave nothing out. Even the smallest detail could be important."

Mr. Brown was quiet, looked up to the sky, and seemed lost in a world of his own. His eyes seemed to glaze over, and he scratched his cheek.

"Mr. Brown."

"Sorry, detective, I was trying to relive what I saw that day. Give me a minute, please."

"No, sweat. Take your time."

Mr. Brown waited another moment or two before speaking. "I was looking in the direction of the bank, and I saw two men wearing ski masks running."

"Please go on."

"Even though they both wore masks, I'm sure they were older than me. One of the men carried a pistol in his left hand."

Surprised, Smith said, "Left hand? You didn't mention that before." *What the hell! What's next?*

"Sorry, I just remembered."

"Okay, go on."

"The guy with the gun got in on the passenger side. The other guy drove. The driver pulled his ski mask off."

"Did you get a look at him?"

"Yes. I did."

Smith had interviewed Brown right after the robbery, and the man had left out two important details. *What else has he left out?*

A frustrated, Smith asked, "Would you recognize the guy if you looked at photos?"

"Maybe."

Smith explained there were two sets of photographs with six in each group. He had placed James Tucker in one and Ben Tucker in the other. "I'll show you one group at a time. The person you saw may or may not be in either set. Here's the first set. Take your time. Don't feel like you have to identify anyone." Smith laid out a file folder with six pictures of men of similar appearance. Ben Tucker's photograph was in the sixth position.

Brown looked for a moment before asking, "May I pick up the folder?"

"Sure."

Brown studied the photographic lineup before setting it down with, "None of the guys in these pictures looks familiar."

"That's fine, sir." These photographs had Jim Tucker in the third position. "Please take a look at this set."

Without hesitation, Mr. Brown put his finger on the photograph of Jim Tucker. "That's him. I'm certain it's him."

"Are you positive?"

"Well, it's been a long time. But I'm sure that's the guy who drove the car away from the bank." Smith directed Mr. Brown to date and sign his name on the folder below Tucker's image. He then showed him a color photograph of the rental car. Mr. Brown wasn't so optimistic. "It could be the car. I can't be sure."

Becker got a call from the Evidence Room technician. "Detective, I may have something for you."

"I'll be right down."

What the tech told him about the missing report upset Becker. It was one more example of shoddy police work.

"You were right. There was a crime scene investigator's report. Who knows why the original detective didn't ask. He should have."

Becker asked, "Why? What happened to it?"

"While I can't tell you why the detective didn't ask for it. I can tell you what happened. The robbery is filed under Case Number 1113409."

"So?"

"Noah, don't be impatient. Let me finish. The evidence report is logged in under 1113409 but was filed with 1113408 three days later. That's why the detective never saw it. Case number 1113408 was an abandoned vehicle. The CSI report was misfiled.

"Crap. What was in the CSI report? Anything useful?"

"Here's the good news. The tech got prints from the counter where the suspect put his hand. I've looked at them. If the prints belong to your suspect, you should be able to get a positive match."

"I owe you big time. How soon can I get a comparison?"

"Get me something to compare, and I'll have it done in a day or two."

The next afternoon, Becker got the fingerprint evaluation. Ben Tucker's right index finger on the counter was a match with eighteen positive points of comparison. His right palm matched with twenty-four points. Deputy District Attorney Nichols amended the complaint to charge Benjamin Tucker with armed robbery.

35

WHEN DETECTIVE AL SMITH presented the witness identification of Jim Tucker and Ben Tucker's prints in the getaway car to the San Mateo County District Attorney, she issued complaints charging the brothers with armed robbery. Ben Tucker's bail hearing for Alameda County was scheduled in the San Leandro Municipal Court. Al Smith and Noah Becker attended. They served the robbery arrest warrants on Ben and met with attorney Chalmers.

"Mr. Chalmers, we want to talk to your client," Becker said. "We don't intend to interview him. We want to talk about his brother."

"I'll ask my client. I can't promise anything. Still, with these new charges, he may be amenable to a deal. But he'll never give up his brother."

"We know," Smith responded.

Chalmers and the two detectives were

sitting in a San Leandro jail interview room an hour later. The small, windowless room was painted a drab, white speckled yellow, covering the walls, door, and ceiling. The ceiling was dark from the smoke of countless cigarettes. Mental health experts touted the hue as a way of reducing anger and hostile behavior—it looked like vomit. The furniture consisted of a small rectangular table with one chair against the back wall and two more across the table in front of the heavy door. An ashtray was on the table. The detectives, both smoking, occupied the chairs in front of the door. Chalmers was uncomfortable being trapped in the chair against the back wall.

"I don't smoke. Would you mind putting out your cigarettes?"

Neither detective responded to Chalmers, who then asked a second time. The detectives glanced up and pointed to the door. Smith said, "Wait outside if it bothers you."

Chalmers declined. *Assholes.*

A marshal brought Tucker through the underground tunnel from the courthouse to the jail. He was directed to the chair occupied by Chalmers. With only three in the small interview room, the attorney had no choice but to stand in a corner next to his client. Once Tucker was seated, the marshal returned to the courthouse. "Call me when you're done."

Tucker greeted the detectives while directing a nod toward his attorney. "Well, Detective Smith, do you have more questions for me about this guy Ben Tucker?" followed by a laugh.

Chalmers spoke up. "Mr. Dean, I am recommending against talking with these detectives. We are here because you insisted on the meeting. So once again, I advise you not to answer any questions." Tucker looked at his attorney for an instant before turning to the detectives. Smith offered him a Lucky Strike. Ben took a long drag when the cigarette was lit and exhaled to his side, the smoke hitting Chalmers.

It was Becker's jurisdiction, so he led off. "Mr. Tucker."

Tucker interrupted, "Call me Ben. I don't know Mr. Tucker."

Al Smith shook his head. "Knock that shit off. We made you on prints. We know who you are, and you know we know."

Becker spoke. "Okay, Ben. We aren't here to interrogate you on the charges against you. We want to explain to you and your attorney what we have and what you can expect. Mr. Chalmers says you're interested in a deal. That's not happening—no deal—period—end of discussion."

Chalmers said, "What do you mean, no deal? Not even a plea bargain?"

Smith said, "I speak for San Mateo County. No deal. You plead as charged or go to trial. We'll seek the maximum sentence. You won't be eligible for parole for at least forty years."

Becker asked Tucker, "How old are you now, fifty, fifty-five?"

Tucker took a long slow drag on the cigarette, one eye squinting against the flair. Lowering it, he flicked the ash on the floor. Picked a flake of tobacco off his tongue, then flicked it before asking, "Does it matter?"

"Yes. San Mateo wants forty years, and my county wants another forty. We might even be able to get consecutive sentences, eighty years. You'll be over a hundred before you can even think about parole," Smith said.

Looking Smith in the eye, Ben asked, "Why's he telling me this?"

"He wants you to know this is the end of the road. It'll be the same for Jim—we'll get him. Besides what we have, Oregon is also after him."

"Since you've made it clear that there's nothing in it for me if I cooperate, I ask again, why tell me?"

"Every cop and FBI agent in the country is looking for your brother. They all know Jim's shot people—he's armed and dangerous. You want some hotshot cop to shoot first and ask questions later?"

Tucker put his cigarette out in the ashtray, laid his hands, palm up on the table, and said, "Even if I wanted to help you, I can't do anything sitting in jail."

Becker pointed to the attorney, "I bet he has a way to get a message to Jim."

Chalmers broke his silence. "We're done here. Call the marshal and get my client out of here."

Ignoring the attorney, Ben spoke. "I'll think about it. How about fronting me the rest of your pack?"

"Do even better," Smith said, pulling two fresh packs of Luckys from a jacket pocket and sliding them over to Ben.

"Thanks."

After the marshal took Tucker away and Chalmers was gone, Smith pointed at the walls and said, "Let's go. This place makes me sick."

36

A MONTH AFTER MEETING with Ben Tucker and his attorney, Detective Smith had put Jim Tucker to the back of his mind. With his job and pending marriage to Bert Jordan, Smith didn't have time to worry about the Tuckers. Bert was anxious to get the deal done and move on to the next phase—a home and children. Although now committed to marriage, he still suffered doubts. *Can I buy a house? Do I want kids*? Smith was finding it difficult to concentrate on police work.

Another job was a possibility. Smith was old enough and had enough time on the job to qualify for retirement—though he couldn't get by on that—alimony alone made retirement impossible. He needed another job. *If I find one with decent pay, I'll take it.* They could make it with Bert's salary as a Registered Nurse, his small disability retirement from the Marine Corps, the police pension, and another job. *But if we have kids, what then?*

The phone on his desk rang. "Smith here."

"Hi, honey." Al smiled, relaxing at the sound of Bert's voice.

"What's up?"

"Let's go away. I've got vacation days; we can relax and plan the wedding. How about your buddy's houseboat? We haven't been on it since our first date. Remember how you got cut up climbing over the gate, and I had to nurse you back to health?"

"Very funny. The Secret Service Agent who owned it transferred to Reno and sold it."

"That's too bad. Friends at work told me about a great place for houseboats on Lake Shasta. We could rent one. What do you say?"

"I'd have to take a week. What's this place anyway?"

"Packer's Bay."

The sergeant interrupted their conversation.

"What is it, Sarge?"

"A guy on the phone insists on talking to you."

"I'm busy, get a number, and I'll call him back."

"Al, the guy says he's an old Marine, and you'll want to talk to him."

"I love you, honey, but I gotta take this." Al broke the connection. Within seconds, his line rang. "Smith here."

"You the Marine who arrested my brother?"

"I'm Detective Al Smith. If you mean Ben Tucker, yes, I arrested him."

"Okay, I hear you have a warrant for my arrest. What can you tell me?"

"Why don't you turn yourself in, and we'll talk?" Smith knew he'd have to keep Tucker on the line for at least a half-hour for a trace. So he didn't even try. Tucker was shrewd and knew it would be impossible for Smith to trace the call.

"When and where did you serve, Detective Smith?"

"Chosin Reservoir, winter of fifty."

"Medals?"

"A few. Why?"

"Before I make you an offer, I wanna make sure I trust you. You ready to tell me what you have on Ben and me?"

"I'd rather talk face to face."

"Well, that ain't gonna happen. Are you going to level with me or not?"

I have a better chance of getting him arrested if I play it straight. "I'll tell you what I can, but nothing confidential or still under investigation."

"One Marine to another?" Tucker was

wary, and it showed in his voice.

"Yes, one Marine to another."

"I'll trust you not to lie. So, what now?"

Smith went into detail explaining the warrants, but did not give Tucker any specifics about the Oregon case. It wasn't his to divulge, but the warrant was public information. By now, Ben Tucker's attorney would have gotten copies of the Affidavit in Support of the Search Warrant for Tucker's house and all the documents related to his arrest. Smith assumed Jim Tucker had either seen the documents or had been told about them by Chalmers.

"By the way, thanks for the coffee at your cabin. How did you know we were coming?"

"Scanner. Some dumbass deputy couldn't keep his mouth shut. So, I hiked out over the mountains and froze my ass off. The whole time laughing and worried that Detective Carter was waiting for me."

"Assistant Superintendent Carter is now head of the OSP Detectives. He wasn't with us, but boy was he pissed. He took the coffee stunt as a personal insult."

"He's been after us for thirty-odd years—might get us both this time." Tucker chuckled.

"All this chitchat's nice, Tucker. Why'd you call me?"

"I got your message—about some rookie

hotshot shooting first—I don't want to get shot. I've never had a problem with cops, not even Carter. You got enough to put us away for a long time. Ben's never getting out, and I'm too old to run for long. I don't want to do time in Oregon. That would make Carter way too happy."

"What do you want?"

"What I don't want is Oregon, federal prison, or to be separated from my brother. You understand?"

"Yes, but I can't make you any promises. I know Ben will surely die in prison, and that's the same situation you'll face once you're in custody. And trust me, it's only a matter of time before that happens."

"I know. That's why I want you to speak with the prosecutors, locals, and the Feds. The Feds will charge in and grab the case if they think they'll get an easy conviction and send us back to federal prison. I will not go back to federal prison. I'll go out fighting. Trust me, I will, and believe me when I say I don't want to take any of you cops with me."

"What do you propose?"

"Talk to the prosecutors and see if they'll talk a deal before I come in. Will you do that?"

"I can't promise anything other than I'll try. How do I get back in touch with you?"

"Nice try, detective. I have another favor to ask."

"What do you want?"

"Ben's a cribbage player, always has been. Back when we were doing time in Georgia, he carved a cribbage board from a barrel stave, carried it to Corregidor, and then to Japan. It's at his house. Do me a favor and make sure Ben gets it."

"I will," Smith promised. The call cut off.

It was going to be a long and arduous meeting. Deputy District Attorney George Nichols knew even before the arrogant Assistant US Attorney Robert Strauss said, "Why would we agree to forego prosecution? We have more than enough to take the cases and file in federal court."

FBI Special Agent Steve Jones represented the US Department of Justice, with Joe Doll and Detective Collins there on behalf of Oregon. In deference to the Feds, they held the meeting at the US Attorney's office in San Francisco.

A day before the meeting, Smith and the DA talked. "George, we need all the pressure you can bring to bear on Strauss."

"I'll do what I can."

The egotistical Assistant US Attorney Strauss stated more than asked, "As I said earlier, why would I agree to forego prosecution?"

Agent Jones joined in. "We have the resources to bring in Tucker and send him back to McNeil Island and his brother to Leavenworth."

Accustomed to dealing with large egos, George Nichols knew where to go with these two. "We know you could find Tucker and get the two convicted."

Strauss said, "That's a given." Everyone watched as Strauss sat back in his chair, crossed his arms, and leaned back. As if his posture did not convey the message, the negative shake of his head confirmed his disdain.

Nichols said, "As I already pointed out, we're aware of what you have the power to do. Where I was headed was the cost of that prosecution."

"Cost? What do I care about cost? My office has unlimited resources."

To bring Strauss down a peg or two, Nichols called him by name. "Bob, we all want the same thing. You were a local prosecutor once. But that doesn't mean we can't help each other."

Becker, Smith, and Doll shared a look of contempt for the pompous federal prosecutor. It wasn't missed by the FBI agent who shared their opinion of the political appointee. Jones, a former New York Police Department detective, now the Special

Agent-in-Charge of the FBI's San Francisco Office, was nobody's fool. "Mr. Strauss, we could find out what Tucker wants before we come to a decision. For my part, I would like to hear what Detective Smith has to say."

Strauss had to agree that Special Agent Jones might have a point. "Detective Smith, do us the honor." Then, almost as an afterthought, he added, "Please."

As Smith began to speak, Strauss interrupted. "I don't have all day."

Nichols was sure that the thought shared around the table about Strauss was *What an asshole.*

"The Tuckers have a forty-year history of robbery. We're sure they committed at least two or three murders but can't prove it. Nobody can. They served time in Georgia, California, and federal prison."

"I know," Strauss interrupted.

"Yes, sir. We believe they have committed around fifty armed robberies, and at least twenty were bank jobs."

Yet again, Strauss broke in. "Agent Jones, with all these bank jobs, why haven't you guys made a case?"

"We put these guys in prison for twenty years," Jones retorted.

Nichols came to the rescue. "Before we get into questions, please let Detective Smith finish."

Smith continued, "The folks in Oregon gave us information suggesting the Tuckers were responsible for robberies in San Mateo and San Leandro. Our combined efforts resulted in search warrants in Coos County, Oregon, and Fremont. Joe here from the Oregon State Patrol has an arrest warrant for James Tucker for a variety of gun charges. Captain Doll, do you want to add anything?"

"Not yet. We need to know what James Tucker wants before deciding what we'll do. I have the authorization to speak for Oregon."

Smith continued, "We arrested Benjamin Tucker on perjury and weapons charges and then made him on two bank robberies."

Strauss once again interrupted, "I still don't see any reason for me, my office, to take a pass on these guys. Jones will have your reports summarized, bring me the file, and I'll issue indictments. It's that easy."

"If you hear me out, I'll answer your questions. Ben Tucker isn't going anywhere. His brother is another matter. Jim Tucker has nothing to lose by running. The man is dangerous. He's a Marine with combat experience, an expert marksman with rifle and pistol. We know Tucker had access to a large quantity of ammo when he fled Oregon. Likely, he's still got it."

"I'm still waiting for a reason to step back."

"The FBI will track him down. Whoever tries to take him faces the prospect of a serious firefight. The possibility of an officer being killed exists. Tucker is as proficient with firearms as any law enforcement officer, more so than most. None of us wants to see anyone hurt."

"Go on, Detective."

"Tucker called me and said he wants a deal in exchange for his surrender." Smith paused long enough to reach for a pitcher of water and pour a glass full and down it in one gulp before adding, "It's as simple as that. Jim Tucker surrenders or dies. He seems to be open to either option."

"What does he want?" Strauss asked.

"If we guarantee the brothers that they will serve their time together in a California prison, Jim Tucker will surrender. They'll plead guilty, and we avoid a costly trial. Both men are in their fifties. This deal will, in effect, be a life sentence."

Strauss turned to the FBI Agent. "Steve, can we live with it?" *I'll blame the FBI if things don't go right.*

"Yes, sir. I want to interview them and see if they'll clear any other cases. Al, do you think the Tuckers will talk to us?"

"I'll have to talk with Jim Tucker and work out the details. We all want to interview both brothers and, with any luck, get a few unsolved cases cleared. If I tell them they won't be charged with any new cases, they won't have anything to lose."

"George, I still don't see much benefit to my office. What do you or these other good folk have to add?"

Changing tact, Nichols played to Strauss' ego. "If we agree and Tucker surrenders, we avoid the cost of several trials. Trials that could take years to prosecute. We would have to face the possibility of an acquittal, whether in state or federal court."

"I doubt that, but go on," Strauss said.

"If you chose to prosecute in federal court, I may still take the Alameda County cases to trial in state court. This is a team effort. We all benefit if Tucker surrenders. Not to mention the danger to law enforcement officers and any innocent bystanders caught in the crossfire."

Agent Jones knew the key to Strauss's ego. "I have a suggestion."

"What's that, Steve?"

"Well, sir, after both men are in custody and we've interviewed them, we'll hold a press conference with all the involved agency representatives standing behind you."

"Go on. I'm listening."

"Your office could arrange it. Bring representatives from San Mateo, San Leandro, the Oregon State Police, and these detectives. You could describe how a joint federal and local task force under your direction led to the arrest of two career criminals who have been charged and convicted of multiple robberies."

"I'm still here."

"You could mention how many robberies were solved by these arrests. You thank the local police agencies for their help and support in bringing the Tuckers to justice."

"We could," Strauss said while thinking, my office and I will come off as responsible. "George, what obstacles do you envision if we go ahead?"

"We'll have to get buy-in from the California Department of Corrections. They don't like being told where to house their inmates. We'll have our work cut out for us, but I'm sure, with your help, we'll overcome any objections they have."

"Detective Smith, what are the next steps?"

"We wait for Tucker to call."

"How long will that take?"

"Soon." Neither Smith nor Becker mentioned a call to Ben Tucker's attorney would ensure a quick response. No one trusted Strauss. They all knew he would call Chalmers if he thought he could get away with it.

"As I said earlier, I'm a busy man. Don't

let this drag out." Strauss left without another word.

Agent Jones said, "I hope I didn't overstep myself with the press conference suggestion. Strauss loves to get in front of the TV cameras. He would never pass up the opportunity."

The rest of the men and Detective Collins assured Jones they understood, and it was a good move on his part. The conversation turned to Captain Doll and what his boss would expect. "My boss is a pragmatist and a team player. He will be more than happy to give up prosecution in Oregon if Tucker surrenders. None of us wants a confrontation with the chance of an officer or innocent bystander getting killed. I'll confirm with Assistant Superintendent Carter and give Smith a call."

Nichols said, "We all agree that we don't want anyone killed. Jim Tucker called Al, so he remains the point of contact."

37

DETECTIVE SMITH UPDATED HIS sergeant and lieutenant. Both listened without interrupting. When Smith finished, his do-nothing lieutenant, Josiah Cooper, leaned back in his oversized office chair and asked one question. "What happened with the Department of Corrections?"

"That went easier than anticipated. As soon as I told the director how dangerous it might be arresting Jim Tucker, he gave the okay to house them together."

"Well, Detective, it sounds like you have it handled." Cooper continued, "If you think of anything I can do to help, let me know."

"Thanks, Lieutenant. I appreciate it." After Smith and his sergeant left Cooper's office, Smith expressed surprise. "What was that?"

"If I had to guess, I'd say the chief told him to stay out of your way. Now go call Tucker's lawyer."

Back at his desk, Detective Smith reviewed his notes and jotted down a few questions he wanted to be answered. Before dialing Tucker's attorney, he called Noah Becker and discussed what he intended to ask Chalmers. Becker agreed and told him to go ahead.

"Mr. Chalmers, this is Al Smith. You got a minute?"

"I've been expecting your call. What have you got for me?"

Smith explained they had a tentative agreement but needed to get some answers from the Tuckers.

"I'll speak to my client and get back to you, and I'll let you know if Mr. Tucker has any questions."

"Make it quick. I don't know how long I'll be able to keep the Feds in line. We all want Jim Tucker off the street."

"I understand."

A few days later, Smith got a call on his private line. "Smith here."

"Tucker here. You got some questions for me?"

"I do when you surrender."

"You mean if I surrender."

"Look, Jim, let's not play games. Be straight with me, and we'll get this worked out."

Both men knew it was only a matter of

time before the Feds or some local cop stumbled on the bank robber. Following a few minutes of back and forth, the two came to an understanding. The Oregon case would be dropped if the Tuckers pled guilty to the California charges. Jim Tucker would have to talk with his brother before agreeing to cooperate with other law enforcement agencies about any other robberies they had committed. "I'm sure Ben will agree with me. We'll talk to the FBI and cops here in California and clear up any jobs we did as long as they guarantee they won't file new charges."

"What about Oregon?"

"We never pulled a job in Oregon."

"OSP Assistant Superintendent Carter thinks you did."

"He's wrong. Well, we did boost a few cars over the years."

"What about Ed, the snitch up in Oregon. Carter is sure you killed him."

"Let him think what he wants. The only things we'll talk about are robberies. We want to do our time sharing a cell at Folsom. Can you arrange that?"

"Folsom? Why Folsom?"

"If it was good enough for Johnny Cash to visit, it should be good enough for us."

Smith said, "Seriously?"

"We've done time in San Quentin. It's a

pigsty run by Black, White, and Mexican gangs. Folsom's still full of old-time cons, and they treat each other with respect. We'll die in prison and want it to be from old age, not shanked by some gangbanger."

"Anything else?"

"Yes. Did you get Ben's cribbage board to him?"

"Not yet. Can't have it in county jail. Your brother will get it back at Folsom."

"I was afraid of that."

Puzzled, Smith asked, "What do you mean?"

"Ben loves cribbage, and we'll play every day as long as we're alive."

"I still don't get it."

"I hate cribbage."

It took the agencies involved another week to reach a formal agreement. James Tucker would surrender to Al Smith at a mutually agreed upon location. The Tuckers would plead guilty to the Mountain View and San Leandro robberies. No other charges would be filed for any other crimes they had committed, except murder, should one be found. George Nichols wrote up the agreement.

Smith, Becker, and Deputy DA Nichols met with Chalmers. "Detectives, this addresses all my client's concerns. I'll go straight from here to the county jail and meet with Ben. If he agrees, I'll sign acceptance for my client. You should hear from me by late afternoon."

Ben Tucker agreed to the deal. Chalmers delivered the agreement to Smith and Becker the same day. All that remained was for James Tucker to surrender. The following morning, Detective Smith got a call from the desk sergeant. "Al, a guy at the front counter wants to talk about a cribbage board."

EPILOGUE

IT WAS A BEAUTIFUL spring day. The weather couldn't be more conducive to Detective Al Smith's feelings of happiness as he joined the commute traffic. He didn't honk or swear at the beat-up old Caddy that interrupted his merge onto Highway 101. *It might be cliché, but everything's coming up roses.*

The previous week the Tuckers' pleas had been accepted. Sentenced to two consecutive terms of forty years to life, they would share a cell in Folsom for however much time remained for them. *Score one for the good guys.* Smith was happy.

Monday, Al Smith would start a new career. George Nichols' boss, Lowell Jensen, the Alameda County District Attorney, had called Al and set up a meeting with his Inspector's Bureau captain. The discussion had been unbelievable. He offered Al an inspector's position and said he could start on Monday. Today was his last day with the Mountain View Police Department. Tonight, he'd attend a retirement dinner in his honor. *Now I can afford to marry Bert.*

Al Smith would have three incomes; a few hundred bucks from the Marine Corps, the Mountain View retirement, and inspector's pay from Alameda County. He and Bert could marry and buy a home. *Hell, I might even go all the way and have a kid. Life's looking good for Al Smith.*

CPSIA information can be obtained
at www.ICGtesting.com
Printed in the USA
BVHW040526261022
650289BV00001B/1

9 781737 824664